SANTA
CRUISE

FERN MICHAELS

SANTA CRUISE

KENSINGTON
PUBLISHING CORP.

www.kensingtonbooks.com

SANTA
CRUISE

Chapter One

June
Ridgewood, New Jersey

The big banner read WELCOME RIDGEWOOD HIGH CLASS-MATES! For some, it was a frightening experience. For others, it was an opportunity to show off how far they had come in the fifteen years since leaving high school.

Francesca (Frankie) Cappella was on the fence. She had built an excellent reputation in the publishing industry, marketing books for authors and publishers, but her love of music and the desire to perform had never left her. After graduating from a top music school, she had spent six years in New York City, auditioning for every part for which she thought she was suited. She had a "big voice" with a lot of nuance, but the producers were looking for a big *nasal* voice, something that made her cringe. Sure, she could sing that way if she had to, but she hated it. Why would she want to do something she hates? It took all the pleasure out of singing for her. Eventually, every singer sounded the same. She had spent too many years working on her own sound. Taking matters into her own hands, she found a producer and cut a few tracks. She got some radio airplay, but without the backing of a big record company, she could only go so far. During the years she had spent following her dream, to pay the rent she had worked as a temp for a number of large corporations, eventually taking a full-time job with a publisher of comic books. Her parents knew that working in corporate America wasn't in her heart, but it was a living, and living in New York was challenging enough.

She eventually worked her way up to the top at a major publishing house, but she never felt as if she was a success, especially after the incident at the last reunion, when Drew Aikens said something right to her face. "Gee, Frankie, you were such a good singer. Too bad you never made it." Those crushing words almost kept her from coming to this reunion, which included several classes besides hers. Still feeling the sting of those hurtful words, she thought to herself, *Maybe that creep won't show up.*

Frankie knew that some would be envious of her position as a vice president of a successful publisher. Her life was interesting and filled with a lot of professional events, but she still felt that a piece was missing. A lover, a partner, a friend. Sure, she could have three different men, but what she really wanted was a man who was all three. *Yeah. Good luck with that.*

She took one more glance at her reflection in the glass of the hotel artwork. *Hair?* Jet black, slicked, and pulled into a long ponytail. *Dress?* Figure-flattering little black dress that showed off her well-toned calves. *Lipstick?* Bright. She then had the horrifying thought she might have lipstick on her teeth. Next came the angst of her eyeliner running. But before she had the chance to pull out a small mirror, the squeals of Nina Hunter were heard across the lobby.

"Frankie! Oh baby." Nina Hunter pushed through the crowd and gave her friend a huge, crushing hug.

Nina was five feet eight inches tall, towering over Frankie's five-foot-four-inch frame. In high school, Nina had been in every school play, community-theater production, and summer-camp program. That's where she and Frankie had bonded. Frankie was the singer; Nina was the actress. Nina's love was acting, and she was particularly good at it, so much so that she had landed a part on a television sitcom after attending the University of Southern California. She wasn't the star of the show but had enough screen time to make her a fan favorite. Her long brown curly hair, big brown eyes, and long legs were hard to miss.

"Nee-Na," Frankie howled back, making sure her makeup didn't smudge on Nina's silk dress. "I wasn't expecting to see you here!" Frankie was surprised but also tickled pink.

"I have an audition in the city in a few days, so I thought I'd return to our old haunts."

"You mean Shut Up and Eat?" Frankie joked, referring to the local diner where they would hang out after football games or other school events. Only the coolest kids would go there.

"Is it still there?" Nina asked.

"It is. Butch Anderson organizes breakfasts there several times a year," Frankie replied. "I've been to a few; but to be honest, I don't feel I have anything in common with them anymore."

"I think I know what you mean." Nina put her arm around her friend. "It's married couples talking about either their latest renovation or bragging about their kids." Nina made a snoring sound, causing Frankie to burst out laughing.

"Oh my goodness. You are *so* right." Frankie nodded in agreement. "I feel like the only thing I talk about is work or some function I've attended. They look at me as if I'm some kind of snob. Or weirdo."

"I totally get it. If I'm not surrounded by Mr. and Mrs.

Whoever, it's someone in the biz blowing smoke about their latest script, treatment, and who *might* be reading it next. I mean, it *is* Hollywood, but it can be so superficial."

"I can only imagine," Frankie said. "I had a small taste of it when I was trying out for musicals. Funny thing, though, publishing isn't all that different. It's a sliver of show business. Besides, most of the publishing companies are owned by big conglomerates. But enough of that. Tell me about you. Besides your acting success, what else keeps you out of trouble?" Frankie chuckled.

"My dog." Nina smiled. "He's a big Bernese mountain dog named Winston. We go for hikes in the hills. He makes me feel safe on the trails even though he's really a mush."

"I assume you live in a house?" Frankie asked.

"Oh yeah. I cannot imagine Winston in an apartment. It would be like a bull in a china shop!" Nina chuckled. "I rent a small house in Topanga Canyon. It's just far enough from the hustle that I can drain my brain after long days of shooting."

Glancing at the posters covered in student photos, Frankie said, "You're probably the most successful graduate."

"Oh, I don't know about that. Yes, I am incredibly lucky to have landed this part, and I mean *incredibly lucky*. It's really about being in the right place at the right time."

"Speaking of being in the right place, I think I may need to go to the bar and get a little something to soothe my nerves." Frankie linked her arm through Nina's.

"Nervous? You?" Nina was surprised. "You were the ringleader, party thrower, class president, lead singer in a band, *and* captain of the gymnastics team."

"That was *before* I knew anything about life." Frankie laughed. "Back then, I thought if you went for something and gave it your all, you'd be rewarded. And if you tried really hard but made a mistake, all would be forgiven, and you would get another chance. Nope. You make one mistake, and it goes into your permanent record." Frankie used air quotes for "permanent record." "This grown-up stuff isn't easy."

Nina burst out laughing. "Kinda like you make one creepy low-budget film to try to get exposure, and you're pegged as 'Oh yeah, that Nina Hunter. Didn't she play a disembodied creature in that hack movie?' "

The women howled and continued making their way toward the bar. As they waited in line to be served, Frankie whispered to Nina, "Who *are* these people?"

Nina let out a guffaw, then whispered in return, "I think we went to high school with most of them." She ordered a gin and tonic for herself. "Frankie? What are you having?"

"Hemlock?" Frankie chortled.

"Ha! Wine? Or a stronger adult beverage?"

"I'll have what you're having," Frankie replied, and Nina held up two fingers to the bartender.

Frankie lowered her voice further. "They all look so frumpy! Sure, you would expect that of the people who graduated a few years before us, but even our own classmates! Most of them look like they gave up caring years ago." She nodded to a woman wearing clogs. Nina almost spit out her drink.

"Oh my gosh. That's Amy Blanchard. She hasn't changed a bit." Before either of them had an opportunity to say hello to Amy, a loud cry came from the throng.

"Ladies!" It was Rachael Newmark, one of their old pals, doing a little rumba dance in their direction.

"Honey!" Nina gave her a one-arm hug, trying not to spill her drink. "You look great! Still dancing, I see?"

Rachael Newmark was the shortest and most petite of the three, with a brown pixie haircut, turned-up nose, and green eyes. "*Chicas!* So good to see you. You both look fabulous."

They immediately huddled and joked that they were not old enough to be at the reunion.

Amy caught a glimpse of the three women and started in their direction. "Well, if it isn't the unholy trinity," Amy teased.

Frankie bit her lip, Nina was taken aback, and Rachael couldn't help but blurt out, "I see the fashion police haven't been here yet."

Amy blinked. "Oh these?" She pointed to her feet. "I broke my toe and, quite frankly, I don't give a darn."

"When did you ever?" Rachael said, with a touch of sarcasm.

"Good point," Amy agreed. "But I'll have you know that it's quite the geek fashion statement now." She took a bow.

All four women laughed. Amy had been the geek, dweeb, nerd of the group. She was president of the science club in school but had a lot of team spirit and would always sign up to be the stage manager for the plays. She would often get teased because she was much more the intellect than most of her classmates, but Nina, Rachael, and Frankie always included her. They would refer to Amy as "the brains of the operation." She still wore the same big black-rimmed glasses. Her ash-blond hair was adorned with a pink headband that matched her maxi dress. She had a pretty, round face with a milky complexion and rosy cheeks. There was a spunk and youthfulness about her that belied her age of thirty-three.

Nina took the lead. "Well, ladies, perhaps we should grab a table before we're forced to sit with some creep from biology class." They all laughed, recalling Billy Gwyer chasing the girls around with a garden snake.

"Do you think he might be here?" Frankie surveyed the room.

"The big question is, is he as cute as he used to be?" Rachael snickered.

"You were always boy-crazy." Amy poked at her.

"And look where I am now," Rachael replied. "I got married because my parents didn't want me running all over the world chasing men. And how did that turn out? Well, now I'm divorced."

"But are you still chasing men?" Nina joked.

"I've given up." Rachael sighed.

"*You?*" they mocked in unison.

"It's slim pickings out there, girls. Even old Slim Pickens himself is no longer available."

The women hooted. "I hear you loud and clear." Frankie joined in. "I haven't had a date—I mean a *real* date—in probably three years."

"You can't be serious." Nina crowed. "Look at you. You're stunning and successful."

"Thanks, but that doesn't seem to make for a great date, let alone girlfriend. My friend Ken once told me that I'm very intimidating." Frankie shook her head. "I don't get it. I'm so charming." She smiled wryly.

"Honey, I'm in the same single boat," Nina confessed.

"But you're in the land of glamour and excitement," Amy protested.

"It's a lot of smoke and mirrors. Trust me," Nina replied. "If I were a high-powered producer or an agent, I'd have a new date every night. But unless you can do something for someone, you're not dating material."

"I don't believe it," Amy objected. "You, famous actress, can't get a date?"

"I'm not that famous," Nina said.

"Well, you are to us," Amy insisted.

"Yes, you are," Frankie added, and Rachael agreed.

All eyes were on Amy. "So? What about you? Have you found geek love?" Nina asked.

"Nah. Most of the guys I meet are asexual or indifferent."

"Funny how things change. When we were in high school, we had to beat the boys away with a stick." Frankie laughed.

"That's because *you* weren't so intimidating back then." Rachael poked fun at her friend.

They leaned conspiratorially toward each other, ignoring everything that was going on around them, and caught up on the past fifteen years.

After high school, Rachael Newmark had attended NYU. After she graduated, she had traveled to South America, where she met a suave but unemployed Paulo. With her trust-fund maturity on the near horizon, her parents clamped down on her escapades, forcing her father to hire a private jet to bring her back home. Following weeks of pouting, Rachael realized that if she ever wanted the money left to her by her grandmother, she needed to think about settling down. The thought sent chills up her spine, but reality had set in. She took a job at a bank, working in their international department, and began dating one of the accountants. She wasn't madly, passionately in love with Greg, but he was steady and would be a good provider. Love was not her parents' main concern. Stability was. A year later, they got married.

Two years after getting married, they had a son, but being a stay-at-home mom just wasn't *her* thing. She was restless and needed a purpose, something Greg couldn't understand. Greg left the bank and went to work for an independent accounting firm. Rachael's parents thought it would "look better" for Greg in their social circle if he worked at a high-powered company. If she wanted, Rachael could be a local socialite, join the garden club or the Junior League. But Rachael's personality was not compatible with women who were prim, proper, and phony. Especially phony.

Before Ryan started school, Rachael would arrange playdates with other moms and kids, but after a period of time, she would get bored with the vacuous conversations and move on to another group.

By the time Ryan entered kindergarten, Rachael was ready to climb the walls, so she took a part-time job at the local dance studio. She had always been an excellent dancer and had taken lessons in jazz, ballroom, and a variety of other disciplines. By the time she was eight, her parents had her schedule completely filled. Dancing lessons, piano lessons, tennis lessons, and water skiing were planned. Tutoring in foreign languages was also on her calendar. It was no surprise that she had rebelled after graduating.

Of all the extracurricular activities, it was the dancing that made her feel alive. She could lose herself in the music and the moves. Plus, it was important to know how to dance, especially when you had to attend galas and fundraisers. It wasn't surprising that she was everyone's favorite dance partner.

Within two years of working at Salon de la Danse, her classes became so popular that there was a six-month waiting list if you wanted to learn to salsa, rumba, or swing. People of all ages were clamoring for Rachael's dancing excitement.

But when Rachael was home with Greg, the only excitement was the argument du jour. It became obvious that their marriage wasn't going to last, at least not without a lot of door slamming, yelling, and sulking.

Finally, after an uncomfortable dust-up at the country club, Rachael's family intervened and encouraged her to get a divorce. They could see the pain in their daughter's eyes whenever she and Greg would meet them at a social event or dinner. Her father took her aside and said, "Sweetheart, your mother and I have been talking." That sentence was always a warning signal, but this time it worked to her favor. "We can see how unhappy you are, Rachael. I know your mother and I pressured you into getting married and having a family. But we never expected it to make you this miserable. It's the last thing we want. We will help you with whatever resources you need, particularly a good lawyer."

Rachael was shocked and elated. Never in a million years did she think her parents would approve of a divorce. *You made your miserable bed and now you have to lie in it* was a much better summation of their take on life. But getting married hadn't really been her choice. She *had* been pressured into it. Yes, her parents wanted stability for her, but they hadn't counted on the misery that went with it.

Aaron Newmark was a man of his word and provided Rachael the counsel of the best divorce attorney in the state, Lloyd Luttrell.

She and Greg tried to keep the divorce civilized, although Rachael was always seething when it came to Greg. Over the course of their marriage, Greg had spent a good chunk of Rachael's trust fund buying luxury cars and expensive designer clothes. That, too, caused a great deal of contention. He said it was important to look rich. No one was going to trust a poor-looking accountant. He had a point, but he had carried it much too far. He was supposed to be the breadwinner and she the dutiful wife, whose half-million-dollar bank account was at his disposal. As soon as the smell of divorce was in the air, Rachael's father and her lawyer tied up all of her assets so Greg could no longer treat them as his personal piggy bank. They sold the elaborate McMansion they had bought with part of Rachael's trust fund and put some of the money away for Ryan's college education. Greg was lucky to get out of the marriage with the fancy designer shirt on his back.

To that day, Rachael had never had a total grasp on how much of her money he had milked. She knew she was complicit by not paying attention. But still. It was not *his* money to spend.

Once the divorce was final, Rachael used the rest of the money from the sale of the house to buy the dance studio from its owner. She renovated the space and hired more instructors, and the studio doubled its clientele in less than a year. It helped that she was located near a senior-citizen community with most residents only in their midfifties. Part of the studio's service was planning dance parties for organizations. Rachael had finally hit her stride.

The women stared at Rachael. Nina was the first to speak. "Wow, he really took advantage of your family's money."

"Oh, that's not all." Rachael tossed her head back. "He was cheating on me the whole time."

Screams of "What?" "Are you kidding?" "You can't be serious!" went around the table.

Rachael crossed her arms across her chest. "No, I'm not kidding, and yes, I am serious."

"Holy smokes!" Amy broke in. "How did you find out?"

"It all came out after the divorce. A few people knew about it, but no one had ever told me. And frankly, I do not care. I had no physical interest in him at all." She paused. "Probably ever." She burst out laughing. "Talk about stupid choices."

Frankie chimed in and lifted her glass. "What doesn't kill you makes you stronger!" The rest followed suit, uttering words of cheer.

It was now Frankie's turn to catch the women up on her escapades. She had moved to New York after graduating from the University of Miami. She auditioned for musicals and got a few small parts in Off-Broadway shows, but that and temp work paid very little, forcing her to live with a variety of roommates, two to three people at a time. One summer, Frankie rented a bedroom in a large two-bedroom apartment on the Upper West Side. They had divided it up so that Dave and Laura would have the living room as their space, Marilyn would have the other bedroom, and they shared a ridiculously small kitchenette. It wasn't ideal, but it was doable for the few months she was there.

Finding a suitable place to live was a full-time job. She eventually moved into a duplex with a work associate and stayed for several years until she was able to afford a modest studio apartment in Gramercy Park.

Frankie and Rachael had stayed in touch and met for lunch a couple of times a year, so they were familiar with each other's horror stories. Rachael was getting impatient and urged Frankie, "Cut to the chase. We want to hear your stories. I *know* you have a few lulus."

Frankie took a deep breath. "Are you sure you want to hear the gory details?" Nina and Amy urged her on. Frankie confessed that she had been through a boatload of relationships, affairs, heartbreaks, and deceptions. New York. Lots of men. It was easy to meet someone at a bar, club, event, or concert. Learning about someone was another story, especially with most New Yorkers her age coming from all parts of the country and the rest of the world. She often thought it was ironic that someone could be in the biggest city in the country and still feel lonely and isolated. That's probably why she was eager to have something meaningful with someone. Too bad she had made a lot of lousy choices in her pursuits. Frankie continued, "Then there was the medical intern who had not one but two other girlfriends."

"Two?" Amy gasped.

"Yes, two." Frankie took a sip of her drink.

"How did you find out?" Amy was curious.

"I had spent the night at his apartment. The next morning, he left before me. I opened the door to the linen closet to get a towel."

"Oh sure. You were spying." Rachael poked her.

"No. Honestly," Frankie continued. "I was getting a towel and noticed a small container on one of the shelves." She took a sip of her drink. "It was a diaphragm." Another sip, waiting for a reaction from her friends.

"A what?" Amy blurted.

Nina patted her hand. "Oh, honey. It's one of those contraceptive contraptions that women use so they don't get pregnant."

"I know what a diaphragm is. Duh," Amy shot back. "I was kidding."

Nina patted her hand again and turned to Frankie. "So what did you do?"

"I did what any other red-blooded woman would do. I took it with me and threw it in a dumpster several blocks away."

The women were doubled over in hysterics. Frankie continued, "I never said a word to him. I figured he would be squirming enough when she went looking for it."

Nina was laughing so hard, tears were streaming down her face.

"Did he call you?" Rachael tilted her head.

"Yes, he did." Frankie played with the small straw in her glass.

"Spill, girl!" Amy was almost shouting. "What happened?"

"I didn't answer the phone but he left me a voice mail saying how immature it was of me to take someone else's property."

Amy's mouth was agape. "He said what?"

"You heard me. But, I must say, I got a lot of satisfaction out of that call. He was so pissed. Too bad, too sad. Such a jerk."

"So how did you know he had been seeing two other women?" Amy asked curiously.

"A friend of mine. One could say it was a coincidence, but think about this. New York City has a population of eight million people, and over ten thousand doctors."

Nina pushed, "Get to the good part!"

"As I was saying, a friend of mine was introduced to him at a hospital function. He was with a woman named Victoria. Well, while they were chitchatting, a woman named Michelle walked up to him and slapped him in the face." Frankie sat back in her chair with a wry smile.

"Wow." Nina gasped. "Well, at least he got the slap he deserved."

"Yeah, too bad it wasn't from me." Frankie chuckled. "I felt vindicated without having to do anything except dispose of something gross. It's funny. Odd, I mean. I wasn't angry. I was stunned. But when I tossed that thing in the garbage, I felt elated just thinking about how he was going to talk his way out of its absence."

"He sounds like a real piece of work," Nina observed.

"Yes, indeed. I pity his patients. Now he's a psychiatrist."

The women almost spit out their drinks. "Seriously?" Amy barked.

"Yep." Frankie nodded. "I feel like I dodged a bullet with that one. And several others, I suppose."

Silence fell across the table.

Frankie's eyes twinkled. "I have an idea."

"Uh-oh," Amy said.

"I know we all hate Internet dating . . ."

Nina held up her hand. "I am going to stop you right there, girl. There is a NO DIVING sign at the dating pool." The women laughed.

"Seriously. Listen," Frankie went on. "Let's make a pact. I know this is probably something we swore we would never do. But"—she took a deep breath—"if none of us have dates for New Year's Eve by this Thanksgiving, we'll go on a singles cruise together."

"What?" Nina's eyes almost bugged out.

"Huh?" came from Amy.

"Count me in," Rachael said, jumping at the idea.

"Really. What's the worst that can happen? We'll have fun, get a tan, and come home with some duty-free perfume," Frankie assured them.

"That could be fun," Nina agreed. "It's only June now, so we have plenty of time to either ruin our lives again with a man or get ourselves into bathing-suit shape."

A groan went around the table. "OK. So we'll wear sarongs," Nina added.

"And cover-ups," Amy said.

"And big hats," Frankie suggested.

"Let's not forget the dark sunglasses." Rachael put her two cents in.

"Caribbean?" Frankie asked. "We can meet up in Miami and take one of those four-or-five-day singles cruises. Come on! Like I said, the worst that can happen is we get a tan."

"Or tossed in the drink for being too rowdy." Nina chuckled.

Rachael clapped. "I love it!"

"Don't get too excited there, missy. We'll keep you on a tight leash," Nina said.

"Ha. Isn't the whole point to have some fun?" Rachael protested.

"Absolutely!" Frankie was pleased with her idea, and her friends were enthusiastic about it, too. "It will be like *The Love Boat* with eggnog."

The women reached across the table and grabbed each other's hands. "Pinky swear!" They locked fingers the same way they had in high school when they set out to accomplish something.

Frankie surveyed the room. "I think our work here is done. Are any of you staying here at this hotel?"

"I'm at my folks'," Amy replied.

"I'm at a B and B off Henshaw Drive," Rachael said.

"I'm at the Courtyard," Nina put in.

"Oh good. So am I. I couldn't get a room here, which is

fine. I don't know if I want to keep running into people I don't remember," Frankie said almost apologetically. "Let's go over to the Courtyard and hang out. I don't see anyone or anything worth pursuing here." She giggled.

"Splendid idea," Nina agreed.

"Pajama party?" Amy almost begged.

"I have two beds in my room. You can join me, but won't your mother be upset?" Frankie asked.

"You mean my mother and Mister Charm? Nah. They're at the club. I'll send her a text so she won't worry."

Rachael frowned for a moment. "Can I come and play, too?"

Nina put her arm around Rachael. "Sure thing, babe. I also have an extra bed."

In unison, they high-fived each other, grabbed their purses, and headed toward the door when a loud voice came over the speaker. "Let's all say hello to the famous Nina Hunter!"

Hoots and applause filled the room.

"Uh-oh. I thought we could make a quick getaway," Nina said with clenched teeth, feigning a smile. "Hello, everyone!" She made her way up to the podium while the three other women waited near the exit.

"It's so nice to see all these familiar faces," Nina lied, with a big, bright smile. Frankie was stifling a laugh. Then Nina said, "Let's have a round of applause for the reunion committee. Didn't they do a great job?" Lots of clapping, whistling, and cheers filled the room. Once the noise subsided, Nina ended her impromptu appearance with, "I trust everyone tunes in on Thursday night for a half hour of laughs and crazy family fun! See you on the boob tube! Enjoy the evening! Be safe!" She gave a wave and stepped away from the microphone as the group gave her the appropriate applause. She hustled toward her friends to make a quick getaway in case other people wanted to talk to her. In spite of her big personality and her love for theater and acting, Nina was basically shy. She said it was her acting skills that helped her deal with people.

As the four women exited the hotel, Frankie pulled up her Uber app and ordered a car to pick them up. When they got to the Courtyard, they raided the minibars in their rooms, settled in, and made plans for their seafaring adventure.

Chapter Two

August
Santa Clara, California

The women kept in close touch over the summer. Rachael had already gone through two boyfriends in two months, so odds were she might ditch the cruise for boyfriend number seven. Nina was still flying solo, and there were no prospects on the horizon for Frankie. Nina was waiting to hear about a part for which she had auditioned, but Frankie and Amy decided that even if the other women bailed, they would still be going on the cruise. The opportunity to get a suntan, lounge on deck chairs while being served pretty drinks with tiny umbrellas, and bring home duty-free perfume was all the encouragement they needed.

Since Amy's parents' divorce, the holidays were stressful, what with trying to balance out how much time she would spend with each one. She wasn't fond of her mother's new boyfriend, and her father was always traveling on business, which was what had led to their divorce. At least that's what her mother used as an excuse. For the past few years, their marriage had been hit-or-miss, mostly miss, but that was fine with Amy.

Normally, she would be spending the holidays with friends or helping out at the local animal shelter so the staff could spend time with their families. She felt a little guilty that she would not be there this year, but she offered to work during Thanksgiving weekend to make up for it. She enjoyed preparing a special meal for the pooches and purrs. It was a tradition at the shelter. In spite of the dogs' yapping, it was still a serene place to spend a holiday, especially since Amy had no other place to be.

After the animals were fed and the dishes removed, she would sit in the cattery and visit with the cats. The cattery was a large, twenty-by-twenty-four-foot sun-filled room with perches, scratching posts, and toys. There were always at least two dozen cats and kittens lounging about. Amy would sit in the middle of the floor and play with the cats, using a small fishing rod with a funny-looking toy attached. The cats would jump and somersault and chase their tails.

Amy felt great comfort knowing that these kitties were safe from harm, even if they were never adopted. It was a no-kill shelter, one of the largest in the country. The good news was that they had an 85 percent adoption rate, which meant most would get a forever home. The rest would live out their lives at the shelter. It was hard to resist taking a dozen of them home, but Amy stopped herself and picked two: Blinky, who was blind in one eye, and Hop-Along, who had a club-foot. Amy knew they had little chance of getting adopted, so she adopted them. Now she had to figure out who was going to take care of them when she was on the boyfriend-hunting voyage. When she brought Blinky and Hop-Along to the vet for their annual check-up, she asked Molly, one of the veterinary assistants, if she could recommend a kitty sitter. Much to her delight, Molly was available and would be able to check on them twice a day. Having that taken care of, Amy moved on to her next challenge: a new wardrobe. She laughed to herself. Rachael was right. *The fashion police would get her sooner or later.*

Chapter Three

August
New York

Frankie was on a mission. She was gathering information for the singles cruise. She printed out pages from cruise-ship websites and requested brochures from travel agents. She was surprised at the number of options. So many more than she had expected. There were several to the Bahamas for three nights, as well as more exotic trips to Belize City, Cozumel, and Grand Cayman for a total of seven nights. The ship for the seven-night luxury cruise could accommodate eight hundred passengers with almost four hundred crew members. She typed out a quick e-mail to the women:

Exotic for 7 nights? Or routine Bahamas for 4?

Within minutes, everyone responded. Nina chimed in with:

Exotic! Why pack for only 4 nights?

Amy sent back:

I'm in!

And Rachael replied:

I'm not sure yet. Jimmy said he wanted to take me to New England but he didn't say when.

Amy countered her with:

Jimmy who?

Frankie typed:

It's cold in New England!

And Nina added:

You'll be on to someone else by then! LOL.

Nina wasn't far from wrong. At this rate, Rachael would certainly be on boyfriend number seven by the holidays. Rachael, always hoping for Mr. Right, responded:

He's different. He's warm and sincere.

Whatever you say.

Nina clicked away at her keyboard, knowing she had heard that story before.
Frankie typed back:

Can we have a Zoom call? It will make things much easier.

Everyone agreed, and Frankie sent out the invitation for the women to dial in.

Within seconds, all four faces appeared on each other's computer screens. Lots of "hello"s and blown kisses went around.

"Hey, girls!" Frankie was the first to speak. "I have to make the reservations soon. Apparently we're not the only people looking for love." She chuckled. "I'll book four state-rooms and get cancellation insurance. We said we each had a two-thousand-dollar budget, not including airfare."

Murmurs of agreement came through. Frankie continued and held up a handful of brochures. "It's a new ship. Launched two years ago. We'll have luxury staterooms with balconies. First stop is Key West, on to Cozumel, Belize City, then Grand Cayman." She paused as she watched her friends' faces light up in delight.

"Sounds pretty fab to me," Nina hooted.

"I'm in," Amy added.

Rachael was silent for a moment. "It sure sounds like a lot more fun than shivering on the side of a ski mountain."

The women shouted words of delight. "Finally coming to your senses, eh?" Nina teased.

"If things work out with Jimmy, I'll have him take me somewhere after New Year's."

Amy snickered. "If you don't meet someone on the cruise."

Frankie howled. "More than one, I'm sure."

Rachael rolled her eyes. "OK. OK. I know. I know." Then she put on a mischievous grin. "Jimmy who?"

A roar of laughter came through everyone's computer. Rachael knew she couldn't fool her friends, even after all these years.

"OK. We have a plan." Frankie was pleased she could get the ball rolling. Things at work were busy, what with the

Christmas season in front of her and the release of the big books for the holidays. After a quiet summer, pandemonium was upon the publishing community. Thankfully, this year it was more about cookbooks, pets, and do-it-yourself books instead of the flood of books about political shenanigans. "I'll put the deposit on my credit card and you guys can send me a check. When I make the reservation, I'll have the cruise line put the staterooms in each of your names, and you can pay the balance on your own."

"Perfect," Amy said.

"Sounds good," Nina added.

"*Maravillosa*." Rachael was already brushing up on her Spanish.

"Oh right," Amy remarked. "You speak fluent *espagñol*."

"*Sí, señorita*." Rachael laughed.

Rachael checked her watch. She and Frankie were on Eastern time while Nina and Amy were in the Pacific time zone. "I've gotta run and pick up Ryan from camp. *Hasta la vista, chicas!*"

"Bye, babe. See you soon," Nina replied.

"*Ciao* for now!" Frankie added.

"See ya later," Amy chimed in.

As Rachael's face disappeared from the screen, the three other women said their good-byes and planned another Zoom call in two weeks.

Frankie gazed around her studio apartment and sighed. She didn't know how long she wanted to be a prisoner to her rent. The studio was spacious for a New York flat. At $2,500 a month, the 480-square-foot space seemed like a bargain, especially in her Gramercy Park neighborhood. It was a pre-war building with high ceilings. The entrance area had a large closet and two three-foot-high half walls that separated it from the living room. It was large enough for a desk and a bookshelf. A small but separate galley kitchen was situated on the right of the living room, and a dressing-room area was adjacent to the bathroom on the left. Beyond the living room was a platform with two wrought-iron railings that served as her bedroom area. A large lead-glass casement window filled the back wall above the bed.

The bad thing was the view. There wasn't one, except for the huge exhaust fan from the building behind hers. Making the most of it, Frankie kept the window shades down and put plants on the windowsill. Fake plants because nothing would be able to grow. She had carefully placed can lights in the corners and behind the sofa to give the space enough ambient light to compensate for the lack of real sunlight. It was a comfortable place, but after several years, she felt as if the walls were closing in. Finding something bigger would cost a fortune, and rentals were at a premium, even after Covid-19. The mass exodus hadn't lasted long, and things had started to return to normal. Whatever the new normal was.

The city seemed to have gotten out of control, with home-lessness at a fifteen-year high, crime on the rise, and the streets looking rather filthy to her. Maybe it was her age, but the thrill of living in the city was waning. Many of her friends were married with kids and had moved to Long Island or Jersey. Sitting around her coffee table with her friends, drinking wine and pooling money for pizza, was a thing of the past. Everyone seemed to have moved on except her. Her career was her consolation. But her weekends were empty.

She looked over at her cat, Bandit. "Wouldn't you like to have a window where you can watch birds?" He stretched and yawned. "I guess you don't know what you're missing." She reached down and pulled him up on her lap and scratched him under his chin. She pushed the pile of brochures to the side of the coffee table and reached for the folder of take-out menus. "So, what shall it be tonight? Chinese, Italian, Indian?" Bandit gave her another indifferent yawn. "Did you say you were in the mood for some manicotti? With a side of broccoli rabe?" Bandit stretched again, inviting more chin scratching. "Or do you want something a little more exotic?" Frankie smiled down at her companion. "No? Italian? OK. Italian it is then!" Bandit rolled over in agreement. Frankie hit the speed dial for her favorite local Italian café.

"Marco? *Buonasera!* Frankie here." She paused. "I'm well, thank you. How is Anita doing?" Frankie listened as Marco brought her up to date on Anita's pregnancy. "A girl? How wonderful. Have you decided on a name yet?" Frankie was happy for the couple. They were the first people she had met when she moved into the neighborhood. They had an upscale but cozy place around the corner from the Flatiron Building. The aroma of garlic in the air reminded Frankie of her uncle's place, Ilvento's, in West End at the Jersey Shore. Just like her aunt and uncle, Marco and Anita lived in one of the apartments above the restaurant. Frankie recalled the history of the family and Marco's Ristorante, the place she called her "second home."

Marco's granduncle Marco, for whom he was named, had purchased the building in 1962 when the neighborhood was on the brink of either collapse or revival.

The original intention was for the elder Marco's two brothers to follow him to America, but only one had. Marco's grandfather had an excellent job working as the sous chef in the kitchen of a five-star hotel, and his wife had just given birth to Marco's father. The plan was for him to eventually join his two brothers in America. But as his family grew, he chose to stay in Italy.

When Marco's surviving granduncle passed in 2000, Marco's father had to decide what to do with the family's real estate in America. He hadn't been to the States since he was a child and remembered that it wasn't a particularly fancy neighborhood. But when he arrived in New York City, he was impressed with the way the neighborhood had flourished. Over several decades, it had become a center for designer shops, cosmetic boutiques, offices, and upscale restaurants that catered to the business clientele.

Marco's father decided this was where he was going to raise his family. He had a wife, Rosevita, and two sons—Marco, fifteen, and Giovanni, thirteen. When the family arrived from Italy, owning real estate in America was a dream.

Marco and his brother spent their teens living above the restaurant his father had inherited, and the young men spent the time they weren't in school helping at the restaurant. Both Marco and Giovanni went to school for restaurant management and continued the family tradition after their father retired and moved back to Italy.

Marco met Anita when she came into the restaurant for a business lunch. They were both in their late twenties at the time. Both were fiercely determined to have a career. They fell in love and married, but both maintained their goals. Anita was a special-education teacher. She felt the city needed people like her more than ever. Marco and Anita were around Frankie's age, in their midthirties. They were on their second child, with their first about to turn three. They had been married for several years but had postponed having children until they were comfortable that the restaurant was a financial success. And indeed it was.

Normally, one had to make a reservation, but when it came to Frankie, they always had a table for her, so it wasn't surprising she was a regular customer. Not only did she feel safe and at home, it brought back many wonderful memories of her childhood, especially of Sunday mornings, as her mother, grandmother, and Aunt Millie were beginning the Sunday-dinner ritual. While most kids would wake up to the smell of bacon frying in the kitchen, Frankie woke up to the smell of meatballs. She would hurry downstairs to nab a few before they were put into the gravy. She smiled to herself, thinking about gravy versus sauce. Gravy had a combination of meat such as sausage, braciola, and meatballs in the tomato sauce. Sauce was tomatoes with seasoning and herbs. Some would argue that it depended on what part of Italy you came from. Unless you were talking about brown gravy, as far as Frankie was concerned, gravy was gravy. Sauce was sauce.

Frankie loved to cook, but most New York apartment kitchens were minuscule, including the refrigerators. She joked that it was a conspiracy between apartment owners and restaurants. If there was no room to cook, you had no choice but to go out or take in. Every once in a while, if Marco's wasn't busy, he would bring her in the kitchen and show her a new recipe. She would frown at her thoughts about not having someone to share it with.

She spotted the brochure for their cruise and smiled. Maybe, just maybe, she would have someone who would appreciate a good home-cooked meal. Frankie knew that the only person responsible for her happiness was herself. And she *was* a happy person. But some human companionship would be fine with her. Provided it was someone she liked. She smirked at the thought.

Marco snapped her out of her daydream. He had been prattling on about the nursery and picking out the paint, and she had drifted off thinking about families and how much she missed the days of growing up with so many people around.

"Frankie? You still there?" Marco barked into the phone.

"Yes, Marco. Sorry, we had a bad connection for a minute. You know how these cell phones are in the city."

"So how about I fix you our special tonight? Eggplant Milanese. A little fresh mozzarella and basil."

"Sounds divine. And a *tricolore* salad, too, please."

"*Molto bene!*" Marco exclaimed. "You wanna pick up or delivery?"

"Can you deliver, please? I've had a long day, and I just finished working on a project."

"A project? Frankie? It's past dinnertime! You work too hard."

"Oh no, Marco. This is a fun project. Three of my friends and I are going on a cruise for New Year's Eve."

"A cruise? You no gonna stay in the city? Watch-a the ball drop?" Marco's Italian accent was always bright and cheerful. In reality, he should have lost the accent by now. He had been in America since he was fifteen, but it seemed to work in his favor. It gave him more authenticity.

"Nah. So far, none of us have dates, so we decided to get a tan and some duty-free perfume." Frankie laughed lightly.

"I don-a understand. Such a pretty girl like you. And so smart. I tell Anita all the time. I worry you're alone."

"Aw, thanks, Marco, but I'm OK. Really. I may be alone, but I'm not usually lonely." She stroked Bandit's belly.

"OK, Frankie. But you know if you ever get lonely, you come to me and Anita. *Capisce?*"

"*Capisce!*" Frankie smiled at the phone.

"I'll send Giovanni over with your dinner in about half an hour, forty-five *minutos.*"

"*Molto bene! Grazie!*" Frankie used what little Italian she knew. Neither she nor her cousins had been taught to speak Italian. Their parents wanted them all to be as American as possible. The only time her grandparents would speak in their native language was when they didn't want the kids to know what they were talking about. Consequently, they learned the basic greetings and all the curse words.

"*Prego!*" Marco replied "*Ciao*, Frankie!"

"*Ciao*, Marco!" Frankie put down the phone and went into the kitchen to pour a glass of Chianti and grab plates, silverware, and napkins. She found herself singing "Che la Luna," and burst out laughing. She looked down at Bandit. "Your mamma is *pazza*," she told him, using the Italian word for "crazy." Speaking to her gal pals about the trip and her conversation with Marco had made her feel light on her feet. She felt a sense of renewal. A new adventure awaited.

Chapter Four

August
Topanga Canyon, California

Nina wanted to get one good walk in for Winston before she called it a night. She had to be on set at five the next morning. As much as she hated to admit it, she was getting excited about the cruise. Her only concern was the possibility of work. She hadn't gotten the part for which she had auditioned in June. It went to some other actress who had connections among more of the power players. The business was starting to get to her. She knew she was good, but it was more about whom you knew and how well you knew them. The Me Too movement was important, but it hadn't trickled down below the A-list of Hollywood. She had thought about moving to New York, where acting was still considered an art, but she wasn't sure about how much work there would be for her. She could try getting on a soap opera, or doing commercials, but her agent dissuaded her. Said it would tarnish her credibility. But it seemed as if her agent wasn't working terribly hard on her behalf. Nancy, her agent, was always looking for package deals that would include an actress, writer, director, or producer she also represented. It was no wonder you kept seeing the same faces all the time. It didn't seem fair to Nina.

Perhaps she should move to London? They didn't seem to have a celebrity-centric approach to acting. Maybe that was because the royal family were the celebs in the UK, leaving no room for or interest in other people. She was going to be thirty-four in two months, no longer an ingénue in the land of film. And if she hadn't made it to the big time by now, her chances were getting slim. Sure, there were dozens of actresses over forty, fifty, and sixty who were making films, but they had been around for years. Granted, her role in *Family Blessings* was keeping her bank account afloat, but who knew how long it would last? Shows get canceled, and characters get written out of scripts. The years ahead would be a crapshoot.

Winston was making noises and pacing about. "OK, big guy. Let's go." She laced up her hiking boots, wrapped her curly hair in a bandana, pulled on a denim shirt, and clicked his leash into place. Winston was getting so excited, he almost knocked her over with his tail. "Easy does it, pal."

As they made their way to the trail, Nina decided she was going to focus on the upcoming trip. It was something to get excited about. She had few expectations of making a love connection. But the idea of getting far away from the pressure of auditions, spending time with friends, and having some fun put a spring in her step. "Come on, boy! Race you to the fence." With that, Winston trotted briskly ahead while Nina clung to his leash.

After their usual forty-five-minute romp on the trails, stopping to say hello to passersby, they headed back to the small ranch-style house Nina rented. It was built in the early 1950s, when the movie business was really starting to blossom. A cameraman from Warner Bros. Studios had it built on a piece of land that backed up against Topanga State Park. The property was lush with incredible vegetation, with different plants flourishing at different times of the year. There was the big-leaf maple, maidenhair ferns, spike moss, and giant mountain dandelions. When she had first moved there, Nina thought she would start a journal identifying the foliage. But then she realized she was spending too much time challenging herself instead of simply enjoying the beauty.

The house was modest in size, but the cameraman had had the keen eye to install giant windows and sliding glass doors along the wall facing the lush greenery and mountainside. The view was an organic work of art, with changing colors and patterns as the seasons changed. Nina thought it was only logical that someone who made his living looking at the world through a camera lens might look at the world differently. Or at least with a different perspective and appreciation.

The interior of the house was mostly wood paneling that had darkened over the years. It added to the atmosphere. It had a U-shaped kitchen with a peninsula that served as a counter for eating, with stools on the side of the large living room. Today they call it an open floor plan. There were two bedrooms, one on each side of the house. A deck flanked the entire back of the house and was accessible from the living room and both bedrooms. No matter where you sat, Mother Nature was the canvas.

Nina looked around. She loved her place and hoped she could continue to afford to live there. It was a slice of heaven in a sometimes very treacherous business. Careers in show business were tenuous at best. Until she could count on a certain amount of money each year, it was always going to be an uneasy way of life. But for now, she shrugged off her doubts about the future of her career. Instead of spending precious time worrying, she would enjoy the position she was in.

She rummaged through the refrigerator, trying to decide what she should fix for dinner, as Winston patiently waited for his. He nuzzled the arm holding the refrigerator door open.

"Oh what?" She looked lovingly at her big pooch. "Is there something I can get you, sir?" He nudged her arm again. "OK. OK. Gee, I wonder if all pet owners have conversations with their pets? What do you think, Winston?" He gave a woof of agreement. "I thought so." Coming up empty-handed, she closed the fridge and pulled out a can of dog food. "Oh, don't be ridiculous," she addressed Winston. "I have no intention of eating your dinner. I just need to figure out what I should fix for myself." She spooned out his wet, grain-free chicken-and-beef medley and placed it in his bowl. "You're welcome, mister."

She scratched his head and looked in the pantry cabinet. Pasta. "That's a start," she mumbled. There were still some fresh herbs in her kitchen window. She knew she had olive oil, butter, and Romano cheese. "Remind me to thank Frankie's mom for her instant-dinner tricks." Winston barely acknowledged her statement as he lapped his bowl clean.

Chapter Five

October
Frankie's Apartment, New York City

The women were due for another Zoom call. Rachael had already dumped Jimmy and was on to Miles, but it didn't seem serious. Frankie couldn't wait to hear the latest. She sent out the Zoom online invitation for everyone to dial in.

Nina was the first to do so. "Hey, babe! What's shakin'?"

"Not much. Working like a maniac. We have a new cookbook to go with the latest diet trend. A mash-up of keto, Atkins, paleo, and South Beach. If you ask me, they're all alike anyway. No carbs. No sugar. No fun."

"Whatever happened to low-fat?" Nina asked absently.

"That was also a bit of a scam. If you look at the labels of some of the products, what they lack in fat they make up with in sugar, corn syrup, and a lot of other multisyllabic words you can't pronounce. I must say, I am glad the vegan craze has leveled off. Our editors bought a slew of vegan cookbooks last year. Trouble is, you can get so many of those recipes online. And how many vegan cookbooks does one need to own?"

"Sounds like a total snooze festival to me," Nina joked. "Some vegan things are OK, but I'm still a carnivore, thank you very much."

"I have a cookbook for that," Frankie retorted, laughing.

A chime came over the speakers indicating another person was logging in, and Amy's face appeared.

"Amy! What have you done to your hair?" Nina exclaimed.

"You like it?" Amy was sporting a new look. It was a drastic but stylish blunt cut to her chin, in a pale pink. Surprisingly, it was quite attractive on her. "Pink! Like the singer!"

"Fab-oo," Nina exclaimed.

"Looks terrific," Frankie added. "What made you do it?"

Amy perked up. "I was going through my closet and decided I needed a total makeover. My clothes were so blah. I went to a boutique in the Bay Area over the weekend and told the sales associate that I wanted something for a cruise, but definitely not cruise wear. She fitted me with some cute skirts and tops and a couple of maxi dresses from *this* century. Then I realized my hair didn't go with the new hip clothes. I asked her to recommend a hairstylist, and she did. She even brought me there and introduced me to Magill, the owner of Crowning Glory. She showed him the outfits I bought and he clapped his hands with glee. He said he knew exactly what I needed."

"Well, he was right," Nina exclaimed. "Loving the makeup, too!"

"Yeah. Can you believe it? Me? Makeup?"

"And I'm digging those new glasses," Frankie chimed in.

"They're still big and black but much more stylish." Amy was ecstatic about her new look.

The computers chimed, signaling that Rachael had joined the call, and her face appeared on their screens. "*Hola, chicas!*" she exclaimed. "Amy! Is that you?"

"Yes. You like-y?"

"¡*Mucho gusto!*"

"Oh cripes. Are we going to have to listen to you show off your language skills?" Nina wrinkled her brow.

"*Me rogarás cuando lleguemos a Cozumel*," Rachael replied.

"I think she said something to the effect that when we get to Cozumel," Frankie offered.

"*Sí, señorita*. You will be begging me when we get there." Rachael folded her arms smugly.

"I am sure we will," Frankie said. "So what's the latest in the boyfriend category?" Everyone knew her question was directed at Rachael.

"Danny and I had a great time the other night."

"Danny? What happened to Miles?" Amy asked.

"He was too clingy," Rachael replied.

"I swear, you have had more boyfriends in the past few months than I've had in the past four years." Frankie sighed.

"We'll fix that once we get on that ship, *chica*." Rachael's enthusiasm for meeting men never waned. She didn't seem to be able to keep them, nor did she choose wisely. It was always a crapshoot with her.

"Whatever you say," Frankie countered. She had lowered her expectations for a love connection. That way, she wouldn't be disappointed. But she was looking forward to a seafaring adventure with her gal pals and visiting places she hadn't been before.

At the end of the month, the women were back on Zoom for an update. Frankie gave them more details.

"OK, ladies. We are booked on the *Medallion of the Seas* cruise ship, scheduled to depart Miami on December 27. That means we should all plan on flying in the day before. I'll book two double rooms at Vie Vay, a small boutique hotel fifteen to twenty minutes from the port. There's a great Peruvian restaurant nearby where we can grab dinner. It's low-key. And, yes, Rachael, we'll expect you to order our food in Spanish."

"*¡Mucho gusto!*" Rachael exclaimed, and started singing "Vaya con Dios."

Nina rolled her eyes. Amy snickered. Frankie knew it would be just a matter of time before Nina would lose her patience with Rachael's penchant for theater, and not the kind Nina was accustomed to in her profession.

Frankie was about to say something to Rachael but thought better of it. No need to start a squabble two months before their trip. She decided at that moment she would bunk with Nina the night before they set sail. Amy had the patience of a saint and could tolerate any over-the-top behavior from Rachael.

Frankie continued, "Have you guys taken the virtual tour of the ship yet?"

Everyone answered in the affirmative. "And the list of activities is incredible. I think I might take one of those cooking classes they are offering at the culinary studio," Amy exclaimed.

"Certainly better than shuffleboard," Rachael squealed.

"Do they actually have shuffleboard?" Nina asked.

"Yep. Bocce, croquet, darts, pong, a pub crawl, wine tastings, and bingo," Amy added. "And that's just when we're on the ship. There are tons of things to do when we get to each destination." Amy's exuberance was contagious. They could each feel the other's excitement. "Snorkeling, visiting ruins, glass-bottom-boat rides."

"Let's not forget shopping." Nina chuckled.

"Ladies, I think this trip is going to be packed with fun, sun, and maybe a little romance." Frankie smiled.

"Oh, right. Romance," Nina said wryly. "I almost forgot."

Frankie snickered. "I know what you mean. I was so involved looking at all the activities on and off the ship that I lost track of the purpose of this cruise."

Frankie changed the subject. "Did you see the staterooms? One is almost the same size as my apartment. I may remain a stowaway." She raised her eyebrows in a mischievous way.

Amy chimed in. "Let me see if I have this straight. Nina is going shopping, and I'm going to learn how to cook. Frankie is going to figure out how to remain onboard, while Rachael runs away with the bosun. Splendid." The women were roaring with laughter.

Frankie was the first to speak. "I'm glad we're doing this. If nothing else, we'll have a glorious adventure, eat great food—"

Nina interrupted with, "And duty-free perfume." That phrase had become their running joke.

Frankie started again. "I'll send you guys an e-mail, but there are a few things to do beforehand. There's online check-in two weeks before. You need your passport and another form of ID. You'll print your luggage tags ahead of time as well." Frankie tried to keep a straight face when she added, "Remember, no firearms, sharp objects, candles, incense, or pepper spray."

"I guess that means no whips either, Rachael," Nina teased.

Rachael immediately defended herself. "I am not that kind of girl."

"Oh, I've seen you crack the whip when you were with Greg," Frankie said, waiting for a response.

"Yes, in a cowboy kind of way." Rachael laughed. "Believe me, if I could have beaten him with one, I would have."

"That's probably why your father opted for getting you a divorce lawyer. It was cheaper than bailing you out of jail."

At that point, Amy was laughing so hard she was clutching

her stomach. Nina tossed her head back and guffawed. Frankie snorted. Not appreciating the joke, Rachael put her hands on her hips in defiance.

If one were to describe the four women, it would go something like this: Nina was strong, likable, but often serious. Amy was sweet, smart, but a little naïve. Frankie was outgoing, quick-witted, and compassionate. Rachael was a bit of a drama queen. She could be kind but was often oblivious to other people's feelings. It was an odd combination, but they appreciated the camaraderie they had fostered in high school. Each had an appreciation for the other.

"Take it easy, Rach," Nina advised. "We're just kidding. Jeez, girl, chill."

"You're always picking on me," Rachael blurted.

Frankie knew that this was going to happen sooner or later. Better now before they set sail. "Oh, Rachael. We love you. You just make it so easy for us." Frankie smiled into the camera.

"That's right. You're an easy target," Nina added. "That simply means you are a very interesting individual."

Nice save, Frankie said to herself, and changed the subject back to the cruise. "We should plan on getting to the pier around eleven. We'll drop our bags at the curb, then go inside to register and get our keycards and go through a security check, like we do at the airport. Depending on the readiness of the ship, we may be able to board right away. Pack a small carry-on, like a tote bag, with whatever you think you'll need before we get our luggage. It may be a couple of hours before they bring it to the staterooms. We can tour the ship or get lunch at one of the restaurants. There's a deli, Italian, Asian, burger joint, steak house."

Amy put up her hand. "Stop! You're making me hungry."

"Deli?" Nina asked. "I could go for a really good lox and bagel. They don't seem to be able to make a good bagel out here. They blame the water," she joked.

Frankie smiled. "I don't know what kind of water they use on a cruise ship, so don't get too excited."

"I remember when you used to ship H&H bagels to me when I was in grad school at MIT." Amy grinned. "I could swear they were still warm when I got them. My roommates would go crazy."

"I would pick up two dozen and take them to FedEx. The guy who worked there always got a kick out of it. He could smell them through the box. Now H&H delivers all over the country."

"They do?" Nina's eyes widened.

"Yep. Didn't you know that?"

"I do now. Wow. This could change my life," Nina joked.

"OK, ladies. Are we all set? Any questions?" Frankie asked.

"I'm good, I think," Amy answered. "Thanks so much for doing this. I am really excited. Finally, a holiday I am not going to dread."

"It will be a nice change of scenery," Nina added. "I'll miss Winston, but he'll have company. One of the assistants from the show is going to stay here with her dog. She has a black Lab, and he loves to play with Winston."

"That's great. I have someone from the animal hospital coming by twice a day for Blinky and Hop-Along."

"Marco's brother, Giovanni, is going to take care of Bandit," Frankie said.

"Rachael, do you have any pets?" Amy asked.

"Not likely. I have a kid and an ex. That's more than enough to deal with. Ryan is going to stay with his father the entire week. I'm sure there will be some calamity before, during, or after. Greg's new wife isn't one of Ryan's favorites."

"And my mom's new boyfriend isn't one of mine." Amy laughed.

"Isn't that always the case?" Rachael mused.

"I'm still in touch with Tina, Dennis's daughter. She's ten

now. And she hates her father." Frankie smirked. "I guess that makes two of us."

"How long did you guys date?" Nina asked, remembering that Frankie and Dennis had dated in high school and again after Dennis's divorce.

"Too long." Frankie snickered. "Let's see, it was between the crazy psychiatrist and the audio engineer. Hmm. Maybe two years. Tina was only five when I first met her, but we bonded over his being a jackass. She said he always smelled funny, as in beer. Even at five years old, she could tell he was a loser." Frankie smirked. "Boy, I wish I had that kind of radar."

"You and me both, kiddo." Nina chortled.

"That makes three of us," Amy added.

They all looked at Rachael. "What? I think I have good radar."

Her comment sent everyone over the top in hysterics. "Yeah, you sure know how to pick 'em. You go through men like I go through a pair of underwear. A fresh one every day."

Amy had tears rolling down her face as her rosy cheeks got redder and redder.

Rachael put her hands on her hips again. "I catch them, then release them once I discover they're not right for me."

"Well, you'll have an entire ocean to fish from. There will be approximately five hundred fish in the singles cruise dating pool," Nina joked.

"We just have to watch out for sharks." Amy giggled.

The women chuckled, then said their good-byes, each clicking the END MEETING button.

Frankie leaned back in her chair, stretched, and yawned. She hadn't realized how much research went into planning a trip for four people, but everyone seemed genuinely excited. Bandit rubbed up against her leg indicating it was time for his dinner. She picked up the big kitty and snuggled him against her neck. "You gonna miss your mommy? Don't worry. Giovanni is going to look after you." He purred in satisfaction. "Now, the big decision for me tonight is what should *I* have for dinner?" She nuzzled him again. "Oh, I am sure you would like me to order sushi, now wouldn't you?"

She set him down on the floor, and he followed her into the small galley kitchen. Frankie pulled out two cans of cat food. "Tuna or salmon?" He made a cooing sound, but Frankie still could not understand cat talk. "Tuna it is." She laughed to herself. After setting the food down on the floor, Frankie pulled out her folder of menus. "Sushi does sound like a good idea." She picked up her phone from the coffee table, dialed Kyoto Sushi, and ordered a vegetable spring roll, a Philadelphia roll, and a tuna roll. She looked down at her cat. "Might as well have what you're having."

Frankie padded her way back to her laptop, which was sitting on her desk. She thought about doing a marketing plan for the spring titles but remembered what Marco had said to her weeks before. "You work-a too hard!" Maybe it was the timing and pace of publishing. You're always working on books almost a year ahead of their publication date. Even though it was late October, she was planning the strategy for books coming out the following summer, with the anticipation that the lead titles would be huge successes. *Where is my crystal ball when I need it?* She snickered to herself. She closed her laptop, plugged in the charger, and addressed the inanimate techno object. "*¡Hasta mañana!*" Then she stopped short. "Jeez, Rachael is rubbing off on me!" Bandit meowed in agreement.

"Oh, you just shut up, Mr. Puss." Frankie reached down to give him a long pet from head to tail. Within a half hour, her buzzer sounded. "Hello?"

"Delivery!"

Frankie pressed the button that would allow him into the

foyer of the building. A few minutes later, the knock on the door signaled that her dinner had arrived.

"Hello, Hiroshi!" Frankie knew all the local deliverymen by name. He gave her a courteous and respectful bow. Frankie took the delivery tag from him and handed him the cash for her food. "*Arigato!*" Hiroshi answered "Thank you" in Japanese, and gave another polite bow.

Frankie answered in kind and also bowed. "*Arigato!*" Before she could close the door, Bandit was at her heels, eyeing the bag of sushi.

"Oh no you don't, mister. This is mine. All mine. Now scoot." She stepped over the tenacious kitty and began to pull the small trays of sushi and chopsticks from the bag. She knew that if she sat on the floor in front of the coffee table, she would be battling with Bandit for her own tuna, so she opted for the fold-down table against the wall. The table had two leaves so that when opened, it could accommodate six people, but tonight it was just Frankie. She knew it would be almost impossible to keep her cat off the table, so she decided to put another bowl of his food in the kitchen. He eyed her suspiciously. "Aw, come on, kitty. Let me have my dinner in peace." He gave her an annoyed look and begrudgingly sniffed at his dish. "Yeah, yeah. I know. It's from a can. Get over it." She gave him another long pet from head to tail and scurried back to the table, where her raw fish was waiting. The Philadelphia roll had smoked salmon and cream cheese. She always thought that combination was strange for Japanese cuisine, but apparently it was introduced in the 1980s, when sushi became popular in America. No matter whose idea it was, it was one of Frankie's favorites. Like a bagel with cream cheese, but instead of the bagel, it had rice.

Frankie was finishing up her dinner when her phone rang. It was Nina.

"Hey, girl! What's up?" Frankie answered.

"I just found out they're canceling the show. This is the last season." Nina sounded concerned but not crushed.

"Oh no. That's terrible." Frankie tossed the empty trays in the trash and went over to her sofa. She figured it was going to be a long conversation. She could hear Nina huffing a bit.

"Are you OK?"

"I hope so."

"You sound out of breath," Frankie said.

"I'm walking with Winston. I figured some fresh air would clear my head. I just needed a friendly voice. Winston isn't the best conversationalist." Nina grunted.

"How many more episodes are they going to shoot?" Frankie asked.

"Three more, then we're done. Looks like I'll be totally free by the holidays," Nina said halfheartedly.

"What are you going to do?"

"I have a meeting the day after tomorrow with my agent. I don't know what she has in mind. Probably nothing. Did I ever tell you that I had an opportunity to get a secondary role in *Happy Times*?"

"No, you didn't. What happened there?" Frankie asked.

"Apparently she and her partner had 'bigger ideas,' and I'm using air quotes. They thought it wasn't a large enough part for me." Nina let out a big sigh. "What irritates me is that they never even told me about it."

"How did you find out?"

"The actress who got the part told me. I ran into her at the studio. She said she was thrilled that I had turned it down. She couldn't thank me enough. Imagine my surprise."

"What did you say to her?" Frankie was aghast.

"I kept my cool and told her that my agent had other things lined up." Nina took another deep breath. "I was furious and called my agent right away, and she gave me the 'bigger picture,' no pun intended, speech. Meanwhile, she hasn't sent me on an audition since June, when I came to the reunion."

"Wow. That really stinks." Frankie knew how frustrating and disappointing show business could be.

"And it's almost impossible to change agents when you don't have a gig." Nina sounded exasperated. "Thankfully, I have some money stashed away, so I can make my overhead for the next couple of months."

"That's good." Frankie thought for a moment. She wondered if that was going to put a damper on the travel plans. "Do you still want to go on the cruise?"

"Oh, babycakes, now more than ever. If anyone needs a change of scenery, it's me. I am so fed up with this town."

Frankie laughed softly. "I know what you mean. These four walls have been closing in on me, and the corporate world is getting less and less attractive by the day."

"Well, maybe this trip will be the beginning of new adventures for us," Nina said, her tone more optimistic.

"You bet. We'll make sure of it." Frankie was glad her friend wasn't a hot mess over this latest news.

"I've been reevaluating my life and what other opportunities I might have, and where. So far, I haven't been able to come up with much." Nina scoffed.

"Then the timing couldn't be better for this cruise," Frankie offered. "Fresh air, water, food, culture, music, and a few spa treatments will do us both a world of good." Frankie's enthusiasm was always contagious.

"You're my Pollyanna pal, Francesca Cappella."

"Indeed I am," Frankie replied with gusto.

"So tell me, how many outfits are you packing?" Nina was on to the subject of fun times with friends.

"I'm thinking we'll need two per day. Of course, we can rotate them or do some mixing and matching."

"We're definitely on the same page, my friend."

"And, of course, accessories can change the look of any outfit," Frankie said with assurance. She had enough hand-bags, hats, costume jewelry, and scarves to turn anything into something else.

"You were always the accessory queen," Nina noted.

Frankie laughed. "I think my apartment is getting smaller. Or my scarves and hats are multiplying behind my back."

Nina chuckled in response. "Uh-huh. It has nothing to do with your going to all those thrift shops in the Village, now does it?"

"Mea culpa!" Frankie confessed. "But the thrift shops help subsidize a lot of charities."

"Good answer," Nina teased.

"Very funny."

"Winston is pulling me in the direction of home. Thanks for the chat, sweetie. I know things will work out. Somehow."

"Keep me posted," Frankie urged.

"Will do. Love ya."

"Love you, too." Frankie ended the call and looked around her studio apartment. "Maybe it's time for a change for all of us." Bandit jumped on the sofa and sat next to her. "And what about you, mister? You ready for a little brother or sister?" Bandit eyed her curiously. "I know you get lonely, too." He stretched and put his paw on her lap. The cat had an un-canny way of sensing Frankie's moods. She grabbed his cheeks and kissed him on the head.

Chapter Six

Thanksgiving Week
Santa Clara, CA

Amy was relieved when her father told her he wasn't flying out to visit for Thanksgiving. She had already promised to work at the animal shelter, and trying to entertain her father at the same time would be stressful. Amy loved her dad, but he always wanted to fill his schedule from morning until night, including a good part of the night. It was exhausting. He also told her he was planning a vacation between Christmas and New Year's Eve since the family unit was no longer intact, and he hoped she didn't mind. They would plan to visit after New Year's. Now all she had to do was come up with a really good excuse to avoid her mother and Mr. Charm. She could fly to New Jersey for Christmas, then to Miami, but it didn't seem worth the trip. Her mother and new boyfriend would be busy with their phony friends at the country club. She'd roll two visits into one big trip back East after her getaway with the others. When? She didn't know, nor did she really care. She had to admit that she missed her father. Actually, she had missed him most of her life. He would be gone on business trips for up to three weeks at a time. But he always brought her presents from his trips and would scoop her up in his arms and spin her around. Those were some of the happiest times of her life. She began to ponder if his absence was the reason she didn't have a relationship. Fear of being abandoned, perhaps? She shrugged. "Could be," she said aloud.

Amy opened her new suitcase and carry-on. She felt like she was on the verge of a new beginning. It reminded her of getting ready for the new school year. She felt her excitement building, and she had the luggage, clothes, glasses, and hairstyle to meet it head-on.

She thought about Benji, one of the guys she worked with. He was sweet and supersmart, but there was no chemistry between them. *Chemistry*. She had majored in the subject in college. Then she had gone to graduate school and incorporated her chemistry background with technology and became a much-sought-after technician in the field of biotechnology. She earned a salary well over six figures and had a generous expense account. On the one hand, she appreciated the financial rewards, but on the other, she felt that many of the ways the company spent its money were lavish and extravagant. She didn't need a fifteen-hundred-dollar monthly car allowance. Sure, it was a great perk, but even $500 could get her a nice Audi or Lincoln. Multiply that by the dozens of coworkers on the same track, and the company could invest the money in more research, or, God forbid, lower their prices to pharmaceutical companies. Oh, yeah. Those guys.

She was wondering if she had gotten into the wrong profession. She enjoyed academia but had been encouraged to work in the private sector. That way, she could pay off her student loans in no time. Not that she had all that many. She had received a full scholarship to Stanford University as an undergraduate and was a teaching assistant while working on her master's degree. She had gotten a small grant while she was working on her PhD, but it didn't pay for housing, meals, or transportation. If she could do what she really wanted, she would teach at a college or university. It was much more stimulating being around people who had new ideas and the willingness and opportunity to pursue them. Where she currently worked, she had to turn whatever theories were given to her into a consumer end product. Sure, it was challenging to turn an idea into something sellable, but what she had to work with were mostly someone else's ideas. Not particularly challenging for her creative mind. Working at the animal shelter seemed to give her more satisfaction than her job these days.

Amy ruminated over the fact that one had to decide on a life plan before turning twenty. Who knows anything at that age? Now she was thirty-three and felt restless. Perhaps the cruise would give her some perspective, and she could plan the next thirty-three years in a more enlightened way.

She jumped when her phone rang. Hardly anyone ever called. It was mostly text messages. The caller ID indicated it was her mother. She always got the heebie-jeebies when she had to speak to her. Dorothy could be demanding and was often unreasonable. That was another reason why Amy had decided to stay on the West Coast. She wouldn't have to play the dutiful daughter when her mother was being a socialite. But as Amy matured, it occurred to her that perhaps her mother was insecure. Not having your husband around for most of the time could make a woman feel unloved. Amy always felt the love from her father, but having an absentee husband is a different ball of wax. She almost felt sorry for her mother. She knew that her mother wasn't in love with Rusty, but he made her feel important. Still, Amy wasn't keen on the guy. At times, she wished she could be closer to her mother. If not geographically, at least emotionally. Maybe that would come in time.

Amy hit the ANSWER button on the phone. "Hello, Mother." Amy put feigned pleasure in her voice.

"Amy, dear. How are you?"

"Fine, Mother. And you?" Amy sat down on the futon next to the open suitcase. If she were as small as her cats, she would have crawled into it, too. She wrapped her fingers around Hop-Along's clubfoot. Hop-Along never seemed to mind. In fact, he seemed to enjoy it, as he gently stretched his paws in return.

Dorothy let out a small dramatic sigh. "I got a blazing headache at the club this afternoon."

"How are you feeling now, Mother?"

"Better. Thank you. But I would feel even better if you would consider coming home for the holidays. Rusty and I have an announcement to make this coming weekend, and I was hoping we'd have some family time before the year is over."

Amy cringed at the thought of her mother marrying the smarmy Rusty Jacobs. He claimed he was related to the wealthy Jacobs family, who owned the Adecco Group in Switzerland. And Switzerland being the tight-lipped country of secret bank accounts, there was no way anyone could verify his claim. Amy thought it odd that he lived in a modest cottage and, to her recollection, had never once picked up the check for dinner. Amy sensed he was a gigolo, but there was no talking to her mother when it came to Rusty. According to Dorothy, "He's attentive and always by my side." *Yeah, because he's attached to your purse strings.* Amy shivered.

"Oh, darling, can't you spare a few days for your dear mother?" Her mother was just short of begging.

Amy rolled her eyes. *And there it is. The guilt trip.* "Oh, Mother, as much as I would love to share the holidays with you, I have to be in Miami the next day, and I can't take off any more days at work," she lied. The offices were closed the week before and after Christmas. But Amy knew that it would require more than a seven-day cruise to recover from the stress of two days with her mother and smarmy Rusty. Amy had been away from home now for over a decade, and her relationship with her mother was basically cordial. Not all mushy like Frankie and her mom. She wished she could have a mother-daughter conversation about life, men, work, anything.

"I'm happy for you, Mother. Congratulations. I hope you have the marriage you always dreamed of." Amy's stomach was churning.

"I'm sure your father will be delighted. He won't have to pay alimony anymore," Dorothy huffed.

"Mother, you always had your own money from Grandpa."

"Yes, but it didn't belong to your father. I was entitled to spousal support." She paused. "According to the courts."

Amy thought to herself, then she asked, "What was the name of your divorce attorney? Was it Lloyd Luttrell?"

"Why on earth do you ask?" Dorothy asked.

"Rachael Newmark. Her dad fixed her up with someone he described as the best in the state. I thought it might have been the same one. You know, all coming from the same town and country club." Amy waited for a response.

"Yes, it was Lloyd Luttrell," Dorothy said, a rather snotty tone creeping into her voice. "But why does it matter?"

"Don't get all defensive on me, Mother. I was simply asking because my friends and I had a conversation about it. No biggie."

Her mother gave another huff. "So when will I see my brilliant daughter?"

Amy winced again. "I'll have to check my schedule when I'm in the office. There are a lot of new projects coming up in January."

Heaving an overly robust sigh, Dorothy broke the silence. "Well, I do hope you'll find time to make it to the wedding."

Amy thought she was going to puke. "When is it, Mother?"

"April. We're going to honeymoon in Paris." Dorothy sighed with delight.

"I'll be there." Amy cringed again.

Of course you are, and I am sure you're paying for it. Amy's thoughts veered toward her suspicions of Rusty being a gigolo. She couldn't help it. Something in her gut was letting her know. "That's nice, Mother. It will give me time to plan things. You know how the lab can get when we're under a deadline."

Dorothy sighed again. "I know you are doing important work. Well, dear, I hope you have a nice Thanksgiving. We'll be missing you."

Yeah right. Amy knew Rusty wasn't keen on her. She felt *he* knew that *she* knew what he was all about. "I'll be at the shelter fixing a special dinner for the purrs and pooches."

Amy didn't mind helping to keep the critters safe, clean, and fed. She thought she heard her mother groan. "OK, Mother, I've gotta run. Take care and have a lovely Thanksgiving." She ended the call before having to hear another word about the amazing Rusty.

Amy let out a big sigh. She needed to switch gears after speaking to her mother. She went into the spare bedroom to survey her wardrobe and accessories. Even though the cruise was a month away, Amy was delighted with her purchases and had laid out all her outfits on the futon in the spare bedroom. Blinky had already beaten her to the suitcase, which was lying open, and he was snoozing comfortably on top of a new pashmina.

"Hey, you. You don't have a passport. You can't go." He lifted his head, opened his one good eye, then rolled over. "You big goofball." Hop-Along hobbled into the room to see what the fuss was about. He looked around and saw something new to explore. Amy's suitcase. Even with one clubfoot, that rascal could jump, and he made himself comfortable on the far side of the open suitcase.

"Oh, come on, you guys. You're going to get kitty fur all over my new stuff. You have your own beds." Amy was almost whining. But after being around cats, she had discovered that no matter how many toys, beds, or scratching posts they have, they will choose a rock from a potted plant to slide on the floor at two o'clock in the morning, or pick the sweater you planned to wear, as their bed. There was no way around it unless you wanted to lock them in a separate room, but for Amy that made no sense and seemed cruel. *Why have a pet?* She thought about that question for a moment. Having worked at the shelter, she knew the answer. Some people had pets as an accessory, others had pets to torment. She was glad she was on the adoption committee. They would meet once a week and go over the applications, then do a home inspection. It was surprising how many people were turned down. She never approved an application where it indicated they wanted a "working animal." The stupidity of checking off that box was indication enough that the potential owner had a few dim bulbs in his personal chandelier.

Amy lifted Blinky out of the suitcase and put him on the floor. When she picked up Hop-Along, Blinky was right back in the suitcase. She knew she was fighting a losing battle. "OK. Fine. Stay there. But you guys are going to have a lot of ironing to do." She shook her finger at both of them. Neither seemed to care. They were too busy enjoying their new beds.

Amy was still having a hard time shaking off the disturbing conversation she had had with her mother. She wondered if Dorothy would have Rusty sign a prenuptial agreement. She looked at her watch. It was seven on the West Coast and ten back East. She sent a text to Rachael:

Can you talk?

A few minutes later, her phone pinged.

Sure. Call me.

Amy dialed Rachael's number.

"What's shakin', *chica*?" Rachael asked brightly.

"My mother is getting married," Amy responded glumly.

"To that creepy guy?"

"Yep."

"Is she happy?" Rachael asked.

"She sounds happy. But I'm concerned that Rusty is using her for her money."

"Well, that wouldn't be a first," Rachael said wryly.

"That's why I called you. Turns out her divorce lawyer was the same as yours. Lloyd Luttrell."

"It's a small community," Rachael noted.

"I need to find out if she is going to have Rusty sign a prenup."

"Why don't you ask her?"

"Have you met my mother?" Amy replied sardonically. "She would freak out if I asked her."

"So what are you going to do?"

"Do you think I should call Lloyd and give him a heads-up?"

"What do you mean?"

"I am sure he wouldn't want his fine work to go down the drain. Not that there's anything in it for him anymore, but maybe if he approached her?" Amy was thinking out loud.

"Wouldn't that be awkward?"

"Once they announce their wedding plans, Lloyd could reach out to her. After all, he did a splendid job in getting her pretty much everything she asked for. It would be a shame if all his hard work got left in the dust of the Rusty Highway."

"Good point," Rachael agreed. "Hang on. I have his phone number. Might be worth having a conversation with him. Tell him you're concerned for her financial well-being."

"Excellent idea." Amy felt a sense of relief. It wouldn't hurt to get in touch with him, even if he charged her $400 for a quick phone call. In all honesty, Amy loved her mother, but their relationship had been guarded ever since the divorce. Even so, she surely didn't want to see her mother get hurt or taken advantage of.

Rachael gave Amy the phone number. "Let me know how you make out."

"Thanks. You're a pal."

"No problem. You and I have a lot in common."

Amy and Rachael had bonded in high school. Coming from wealth, both had had to suffer through the bombardment of lessons, language classes, and pretentious parties. More often than not, Amy and Rachael would see each other at various social events. But once Amy discovered a microscope and a Bunsen burner, any interest in the trappings of upper-middle-class expectations went out the window.

Her mother was horrified that Amy would rather watch things mutate than perfect her tennis backhand. But Amy was a straight-A student. No one could argue with that.

"OK, *chica*. Let me know how it goes."

"Will do." Amy ended the call. She felt a sense of relief. Even though she hadn't spoken to Lloyd Luttrell yet, she knew he would have no problem sticking his lawyerly nose into Dorothy's business. She thought it was serendipitous that Rachael had mentioned her lawyer, giving Amy the opportunity to bring it into the conversation with her mother.

The next morning, she phoned Lloyd Luttrell. She hoped he hadn't left for the long weekend yet. She told his receptionist she was Dorothy Blanchard's daughter, and she had a question for him. In less than a minute, he took the call.

"Ms. Blanchard. What can I do for you?" He sounded very smooth.

"Hello, Mr. Luttrell. Thank you for taking my call. I know this is a little out of the ordinary, but I am hoping you can help me out. Especially my mother."

"I'll certainly try. What seems to be the problem?"

"My mother told me that she and Rusty are getting married."

"Oh?" Lloyd Luttrell's voice had an odd ring to it.

"Yes, and I'm concerned that she might not consider having him sign a prenup."

"What does this have to do with me?"

"I was wondering when they announce their wedding plans if you could take her aside and suggest it?" Amy grimaced, waiting for an eruption. But none came.

"That's really none of my business," Lloyd said softly.

"I know, but I'm worried. She is all gaga over this guy because he's all over her. If you know what I mean."

"I do indeed. I've seen him in action at the club." Lloyd cleared his throat.

"Could you do this for me? For her? I'll gladly pay you."

Amy was on the edge of begging.

"Pay me? That's not necessary. Your mother is, was, a client. I should have her best interests in mind. Wouldn't you agree?" Lloyd sounded kind and reasonable. *So un-lawyerly*, she thought.

"Oh, Mr. Luttrell, that would be fabulous. I'm on the other side of the country, so it's hard to keep an eye on her." Amy laughed nervously.

"I'd be happy to suggest it to her. Do you know when they're going to make the announcement?"

"This Saturday. At the country club."

"When is the wedding?" Lloyd asked.

"April. She wants to honeymoon in Paris," Amy answered glumly.

"That should give me more than enough time to work on this for you. And your mother," Lloyd said with an unusual amount of enthusiasm. "I plan on being at the club on Saturday. I'll ask her to have lunch with me the following week. That way, what I say won't put a damper on her euphoria."

"Mr. Luttrell, I cannot thank you enough." Amy appreciated the support.

"My pleasure. I've always been fond of your mother. I wouldn't want anyone to take advantage of her."

Amy noticed what seemed to be a protective tone in his voice.

Amy ticked off her phone number to him. "That's my cell, Mr. Luttrell. Please keep me apprised. And as I said, I would be glad to pay you for your time."

"And as *I* said, that is not necessary. I'll enjoy having lunch with Dorothy. Be well." Lloyd Luttrell ended the call.

Amy sprung from her chair. She felt as if a weight had been lifted. If Rusty turned out to be a dirtbag, at least her mother's financial future would be secure.

Chapter Seven

Thanksgiving Week
Frankie's Apartment

Frankie looked at the wall calendar she kept in her linen closet. She felt that it was always good to write things down and have a visual look at the week. It was the day before Thanksgiving. So far, none of the women had dates for New Year's Eve, although at this point it did not matter. They had all agreed to go, regardless of their relationship status. Rachael was the only one who had a potential date, but that wasn't unusual. *Rachael always had a potential date.* Frankie chuckled to herself.

She sent a text out to the other women asking for a Zoom call:

Thanksgiving, ladies! Are we ready for our seafaring adventure?

She received the following responses:

You bet!

Absolutely!

Can we leave now?

Frankie sent out the invitation for the call, and within a few minutes, everyone's face appeared on her laptop screen.

Lots of hellos, hey-theres, and blown kisses went around. Frankie started. "Is everyone ready?"

Amy was the first to speak. "Check it out!" She turned her laptop for everyone to see her bounty of clothes, and her two cats sleeping in the suitcase.

"They're not coming with us, are they?" Rachael asked in a horrified voice.

"Don't be silly. They just think it's their new bed. I figured I'd let them sleep in it until they find another spot. Don't panic, Rachael." Amy smiled. "I cannot imagine taking them on an airplane, then a cruise."

"Well, you know, some people have to take their animals with them," Rachael reminded everyone. "It seems like everywhere you go, someone has a 'support' animal with them." Rachael used air quotes.

"But I'm not that person." Amy almost sounded indignant. "Besides, I told you I have a kitty sitter."

Nina broke in. "Rachael. Are you OK? You seem a little tense."

"I had another argument with Ernie."

All three exclaimed at the same time. "Who is Ernie?"

"What happened to Tommy? Or was it Miles?" Nina joked.

"Ernie is someone I met at the dance studio."

Frankie was counting on her fingers how many boyfriends Rachael had had since the summer. "Remind me. Jimmy, Miles, Tommy, Ernie. Am I leaving anyone out?"

The women chuckled. "Very funny," Rachael squawked.

"Well, that's four in six months." Frankie was being pragmatic.

"OK. OK. So what if I went through a few in a few months? I'm making up for lost time." Rachael had a big grin on her face at that point.

Amy shook her head. "I don't know how you do it."

"When we get on that ship, you can watch and learn," Rachael said, a twinkle in her eye.

"Yeah, but I don't want to go through a new guy every six weeks. I want something stable."

"I agree," Frankie chimed in.

"Ditto here," Nina said.

"Well, so do I, girls. You know what they say, 'You have to kiss a lot of frogs before you meet a handsome prince.' "

Nina couldn't help herself. "You should be covered in warts by now!"

Frankie and Amy howled. Rachael stared blankly. "What are you, a bunch of comedians?"

The teasing continued for a few more minutes until Frankie directed the conversation back to the trip ahead.

"OK. So everyone is going to check in in two weeks. Print everything out. Ticket, copy of your passport, luggage tags, and customs declaration pages. We won't need them until we return, and the ship will provide them, but it's always good to have a spare set."

The women exchanged weekend plans with each other. Frankie was going to rent a car and drive to Ridgewood to spend time with her parents; Rachael was having dinner with Ernie, maybe; Amy was working at the shelter; and Nina was cooking for two of her friends who lived far away from their own families.

Amy informed them that her mother was announcing her engagement to Rusty on Saturday at the club. Suddenly, the screen went silent.

"Oh dear," was all Frankie could say. She knew how Amy felt about the man.

"Yikes!" was Nina's response.

"Well, I'll be there, so I can report back to you," Rachael indicated.

"Oooohhh . . . a spy! I like it!" Nina added.

Rachael wasn't sure if she should bring up the subject of Lloyd Luttrell, but Amy had no compunction about it.

"I spoke to Lloyd Luttrell, my mother and Rachael's divorce attorney, yesterday."

"Divorce attorney? Why?" Nina asked.

"Because I want my mother to ask Rusty to sign a prenup, but I'm too chicken to bring it up with her myself. I thought Lloyd would be a good go-between."

"What did he say?" Frankie was intrigued.

"I told him what was in the works and that I was concerned about her financial well-being. Of course I'm worried about her emotional well-being, too, but if Rusty turns out to be a creep and takes advantage of her and her money, she'd be devastated. With a prenup, at least she'd have some protection."

"Good thinking, girl," Nina said.

"Thanks. Lloyd said he was also planning on going to the club on Saturday and was going to invite my mother to lunch the following week."

"Brilliant!" Nina clapped her hands.

"Indeed," Frankie concurred.

"I'm kind of excited, actually," Amy continued. "If Rusty is a stand-up guy, he'll have no trouble signing it, especially if he really is related to the Jacobs family. The *rich* Jacobs family from Switzerland."

"That assumes that Lloyd can persuade your mother to have a prenup drawn," Amy observed.

"Lloyd Luttrell can be very convincing," Rachael quipped. "I can assure you of that."

"You must be relieved that someone has your back," Frankie added.

"I always thought my mother was overbearing, but now I think the problem is that she's been insecure," Amy mused.

"Huh. Interesting," Nina said.

"When they were going through their divorce, she told me that being a father is different than being a husband. Being a husband is different than being an employee. Not all roles are interchangeable. I think I'm finally figuring that out."

"That's an excellent observation," Nina remarked. "It's kind of like acting. All the roles are different. You play a part in one script, and a different one in another." Nina furrowed her brows. "That explains a lot."

Frankie inched closer to the screen. "Wow. It certainly does. Think about all the TV interviews reporters have with neighbors when someone goes off the rails. 'He was a quiet guy.' Meanwhile, he was actually a serial killer!"

"Freaky." Nina contemplated. "Looking back, I can see how that fits with so many relationships I've had. Not just with men. Friends, coworkers, family. A different face for different situations."

"OK, let's not get all Sigmund Freud, ladies," Rachael jumped in. The women chuckled. "Therapy time is over."

"Well, I'm glad you called Lloyd; and now you'll be able to let this dilemma go for a while," Frankie chimed in.

"I can't wait until Saturday," Rachael exclaimed. "I'll fill everyone in!"

"Good deal," Amy said.

"Can't wait to hear," Nina added.

Frankie jumped back in. "Listen, I have to go. Giovanni is coming by to pick up a key. He's going to look after Bandit tomorrow and Friday while I'm at my parents'. No sense in driving back after a big meal tomorrow." Frankie meant a big meal indeed.

There would always be at least a dozen or more people at the table. Frankie's father would bring in the four-by-eight-foot sheet of finished plywood and set it on top of the regular dining-room table. Frankie's job was to set the table. That had been her role every holiday since she was tall enough to reach it. They used her great-grandmother's lace tablecloth. The one she had smuggled out of Italy during World War II. The fine china and crystal came out of the hutch, as well as the sterling silver place settings. Ever since Frankie had moved into the city, she would place an order at the local Ridgewood florist to deliver the centerpiece. This year it was going to be a table runner of small gourds, pumpkins, berries, votive candles, and gilded leaves.

They would start with antipastos. Cold and hot. Cold would consist of prosciutto, mozzarella, and figs; soppressata, capicola, provolone, Genoa salami, black and Cerignola olives, and roasted peppers. The hot antipasto was clams oreganata, eggplant rollatini, mussels fra diavolo, and shrimp scampi.

Then came the pasta dish. Either lasagna or ravioli. Add a side of sausage, meatballs, braciola, and loaves of garlic bread. That took well over an hour. Once those dishes were cleared, out came the turkey and all the fixings. Frankie used to joke that her mother made lasagna in the shape of a turkey. The entire meal took several hours, with more than a few conversations happening all at the same time. Jokes from Uncle Ralph rounded off the festivities.

The women had signed off, and Frankie was pondering the feast ahead, when the buzzer rang. It startled her, but not as much as when she saw Giovanni at her front door. In the past he had always worn a polo shirt with the MARCO'S logo on the front left pocket, a baseball cap with the same logo, and khaki pants. She was taken aback seeing him now in a freshly pressed white button-down shirt, slacks, and loafers, his full head of thick black wavy hair stylishly groomed. She hardly recognized the fine-looking man standing before her. "Giovanni! You look very handsome tonight," Frankie exclaimed.

He blushed. "Grazie, Miss Frankie!"

"Please, just call me Frankie." She gazed into his deep blue eyes. She hadn't noticed them before. Probably because he was always wearing a cap, and they would briefly exchange greetings. She had never really had a long conversation with him. Not the kind she would have with Marco. She also realized that Giovanni was about her age. For some reason, she had thought he was much younger. Maybe that was because he did all the deliveries and she would see him cleaning up at night.

"Come in." Frankie opened the door wider for him.

He nodded respectfully and looked around. "You have a lovely place, Miss Frankie." Giovanni's accent was not as strong as Marco's. Also, it was a bit more refined.

"Please. Just Frankie." She smiled at him.

"*Scusi!*" He apologized in Italian, and Frankie stifled a giggle. She found him quite charming.

"Can I get you something to drink?" she offered.

"No, thank you. I'm meeting our mama tonight. I have to go to the airport. She was visiting her sister in Salerno."

"Doesn't she live in one of the apartments above the restaurant?"

"Sometimes. She spends most of the time in Italy, with my father, but now, with the new baby coming, she wanna help. It's good for Marco and Anita."

"And you? You live upstairs, too?"

"For now. My plan is to move to New Jersey and open my own restaurant. As soon as I finish culinary school." He was shuffling his feet.

"Where in New Jersey?" Frankie was hoping it wouldn't be too far away. Not that it mattered. At least she didn't think it mattered.

"There are a couple-a places we are looking at."

"We?" Frankie figured the other person was his girlfriend.

"Me and Marco. We will be partners. He will keep his place, and I will have mine. This way, it will be better for us to purchase from the vendors and purveyors."

"That's exciting," Frankie remarked.

"I think Marco may sell his place here once the babies start to go to school. The city is no place for children. Sophia is three, and the baby comes soon." Giovanni smiled.

"But then what would Marco do? Heck, what will *I* do?" Frankie exclaimed.

Giovanni laughed nervously. "You come and see us. We'll make the best-a dinner you ever had."

"Do you know what type of restaurant you want to open?" Frankie thought she might be prying a little too deeply. "Sorry. I don't mean to be so nosy."

"Not a problem, Miss—. I mean, Frankie." She could have sworn his eyes sparkled.

"It will depend on-a the space, but we think maybe two separate places. Also a liquor license. We have maybe one, two more years to plan."

"Wow. That's big news." Frankie was surprised.

"Please, no mention to Marco. He's a little superstitious. *Il malocchio!*" Giovanni made the sign of the cross as he referenced the expression for the evil eye.

"Oh no. Never." Frankie made the sign of the cross in response.

"I guess we are both a little-a superstitious, too?" Giovanni chuckled.

"Please. My mother has every good-luck piece from Italy *and* China! She said that the Chinese have been believing in certain things for thousands of years. They have to be right about something."

Giovanni flashed a beautiful smile. "Your mama, she's-a right."

By that time, Bandit had sauntered over to where the two of them were standing. "And this is my roommate and best friend, Bandit." Frankie picked him up and gave him a hug.

"He's beautiful. A black cat. You must be very, how do you say, spiritual?"

"I guess that's better than calling me a witch."

Giovanni laughed. "Oh no, *signorina*. You? Witch? Never."

"Whew. Thanks. I didn't want you to get the wrong idea about me." Frankie giggled nervously. Focusing on the task at hand instead of acting like a schoolgirl, she started to walk toward the kitchen. "Follow me."

"Anytime," Giovanni replied.

Frankie's legs were starting to feel like jelly. It had been a long time since a man was so disarming. Could he tell? She tried extremely hard to keep her composure.

"Here's his food. One can in the morning and one at night. A cup of dry food in the bowl and fresh water."

"*Capisce!*"

She set Bandit down in front of his dry food. "Here comes the not-so-fun part." Frankie directed Giovanni toward the bathroom, where she kept the litter box. She showed him her routine. She removed the soiled litter that was contained in a liner and tossed it into a small trash bag. She replaced the liner with a new one and put several large scoops of litter into the pan. "That's it. No scooping. It's a waste of money and litter."

"*Va bene!* OK. Easy. You change in the morning or night-time?"

"In the morning. I should be back Saturday around noon, so you don't have to change it on Saturday."

"Oh no, Frankie. You must-a come home to a clean house."

"It's fine, I . . ."

Giovanni interrupted. "This is gonna be-a my job, no?"

"*Sì!*"

"OK. So, I do it my way." Giovanni smiled that smile again.

Frankie reached for the envelope that contained one hundred dollars and handed it to Giovanni. "Here. This is what I usually pay the kitty sitter—twenty dollars per visit."

"Oh no. I take no money from you." Giovanni touched

her hand. "You are almost like family to us. This is no problem for me to do for you."

"Oh, Giovanni, I can't expect you to do this for free."

"Please, *signorina*, I am happy to do this. Less than fifteen minutes two times a day? Please. You can spend time with your family and not worry."

"Are you sure?" Frankie was almost pleading with him.

"*Assolutamente!* Absolutely."

"But when I go on my cruise, you will let me pay you. I insist."

"I will not take your money. *Capisce?*" He almost looked stern.

"*Capisce!*" *Baloney*, she thought. *I'll buy him something during the trip. I'll figure it out.*

"OK. We are good, *sì?*"

"*Sì!*" Frankie replied. She walked him to the door.

Giovanni turned and put his hands on both of her shoulders and kissed her on each cheek, European style. "Bravo! *Molto bene!* You have a nice visit. I see you Saturday. *Ciao, bella!*"

"*Ciao*, Giovanni!" Frankie let him out, shut the door, leaned against it, and slid down to the floor. "*Mamma mia!*" Then she realized she had been blushing. Probably the entire time he was there.

Chapter Eight

Saturday after Thanksgiving
Ridgewood Country Club, Paramus, New Jersey

The Ridgewood Country Club sits on 257 acres of land with a twenty-seven-hole golf course. Founded in 1890 and moved to its current location in 1926, it has the honor of holding a position in the National Register of Historic Places. It boasts Norman-style architecture, with a tower and porches nestled against a backdrop similar to the landscaping of Northern France. It was everything one could imagine a country club to be.

Saturday was the annual Harvest Ball at the club. The past few years, it had been less of a ball and more of a lavish cocktail party. It seemed as if the days of evening gowns and tuxedos were a relic of the past. It was just as well. No one appeared to want to attend a gala. They were stuffy and expensive and a lot of work. Between ticket sales, catering, silent auctions, live auctions, and entertainment, the event barely paid for itself even while trying to raise money for the local food bank.

Then one year, someone proposed that the club do something different. Something more casual. The ticket price was still $250 per person but no "rubber chicken dinners" and many fewer speeches. The charity got more money, and everyone had a much better time.

Dorothy was all atwitter, anticipating the oohs and aahs and congratulations that would be forthcoming. She fidgeted with her five-carat diamond engagement ring. Granted, she had bought it herself. Rusty had said that he was waiting for a check to clear. Despite the warning signs, she could see nothing amiss. Or maybe she was in denial. Dorothy wanted a companion in a stable and secure relationship. She consoled herself with the notion that people often had financial difficulties. Rusty was no different. At least that's what she kept telling herself.

She spotted Rusty speaking to one of the waitresses. She could swear that he was flirting. How could that be? They were going to announce their wedding plans tonight.

She dashed over to where he was standing and linked her arm through his. "There you are, darling," he said, flashing her a big smile. "This is Megan. She used to work at a club that I frequented in the city."

"Hello, Megan. What brings you to our neck of the woods?" Dorothy tried to sound casual.

"I'm with the catering company. We do a lot of parties in the tristate area."

"Well, you do get around, now don't you?" Dorothy couldn't help herself. Her soon-to-be-husband was almost fifteen years her junior. Megan could have been an ex-girlfriend for all she knew. Dorothy was starting to feel uncomfortable. She had never felt threatened or jealous before. But then again, she had never seen Rusty interact with a young woman before. It was always with her friends and members of the country club. But something about the situation just wasn't sitting right with her. It was if someone had flipped a switch, and the lights had gone on. She tried to shake it off, attributing it to nerves and excitement.

"Rusty, darling, shall we go make our announcement?" She practically dragged him away from Megan.

"Good to see you, Megan," Rusty said over his shoulder.

He turned to Dorothy. "What was that all about?"

"Whatever do you mean, dear?"

"You were jealous." Rusty bristled.

"I was no such thing." Dorothy sounded convincing, but still, what had happened was unsettling.

The president of the club walked over to the podium and asked the band to take a short break.

"Ladies and gentlemen. I am happy to announce the engagement of one of our dearest members, Dorothy Blanchard, to Russell 'Rusty' Jacobs!" Applause and cheers filled the room.

Dorothy smiled and waved to the crowd. As they made their way back to one of the high-top tables, Lloyd Luttrell stopped to congratulate them.

"Oh, Lloyd. So nice to see you." She kissed him on the cheek. "Rusty, this is Lloyd Luttrell. He represented me in my divorce."

Lloyd held out his hand. "Good to meet you, old chap. Hopefully, we'll never be on opposite sides of the table." Lloyd chortled and took a sip of his cocktail.

Rusty was nervous. His hands were sweating. He forced a chuckle in return. "Oh no. Dorothy and I are soul mates."

Lloyd almost spit out his drink. Now he understood Amy's concern for her mother. About a half hour later, when Dorothy was speaking to some of the other women and showing off her ring, Lloyd approached her. "Ah, the newly betrothed. May I steal her away for a moment?" he said to the other women, who smiled their consent.

"What's on your mind, Lloyd?" Dorothy was calm. Neutral.

"Would you do me the honor of having lunch with me next week?"

"I'll check with Rusty and see when he's available," Dorothy answered blankly.

"Actually, I want to take *you* to lunch. Just the two of us." Lloyd sounded casual enough.

"Oh. Well, of course, Lloyd. Anything in particular on your mind?"

"No. It's been a while, and I thought we could catch up before you're swept away." *Smooth*.

"Why, that would be delightful. Shall I call your office and speak to Louise?" Dorothy was referring to his assistant.

"Splendid. I am looking forward to it," Lloyd replied, and shook her hand gently. As he walked away, he resisted the temptation to do a "yes!" arm pump. Lloyd was also divorced. Twice. He knew all too well how those things go down. Fortunately, he was a master at litigation.

The party started to wind down, and the guests were saying their good-byes and toodle-oos when Rachael approached Lloyd. "Mr. Lloyd Luttrell. So good to see you." She gave him a peck on the cheek.

"Rachael. How are you? Ryan? Are your folks here?" Lloyd asked.

"All is well in my world. Ryan is great. Yes, Mom and Dad were here briefly but left about an hour ago. After they said their congrats to Dorothy, they split."

There was an awkward silence between them as if each of them knew the other's agenda. Rachael decided to unseal the vacuum with a little small talk.

"Amy, Frankie, Nina, and I are planning a cruise between Christmas and New Year's. We're all very excited about it."

"I hope none of you end up needing a lawyer!" Lloyd joked.

"Well, you never know with the four of us. Coochie-coochie." Rachael gave a little rumba move.

"Rachael, you always were a ball of fire." Lloyd smiled.

"And I ain't stopping anytime soon." Rachael grinned.

Lloyd reached into his pocket and pulled out a Cartier business-card holder. He handed one of his to Rachael and gave her a wink. "Just in case."

Rachael tapped the card in her hand. "But aren't you a divorce lawyer?"

"Yes, that's my specialty, as you know. But if you are ever in trouble, you can call me, and I'll do my best." He gave her shoulder a little squeeze. "You gals have fun and try to stay out of trouble."

"Will do. And maybe not." Rachael let out a loud laugh and gave him another kiss on the cheek.

"Bye for now." Lloyd turned and made his exit. He was jazzed that he had been able to get Dorothy to agree to have lunch with him. He handed the valet his parking stub, nodded, and smiled at the other departing guests. He would wait until he got in his car to phone Amy and let her know that he had made contact with her mother and a lunch was planned. He pulled his car to one side of the massive driveway of the country club. He quickly typed an e-mail to his assistant for when she got back in on Monday. He let her know to expect a call from Dorothy and to accommodate whatever date she had in mind. Clear his schedule as needed. He also instructed her to make a reservation at the Village Green and send over a bottle of the Gaja Winery's Gaia & Rey chardonnay so it could be chilled, and a bottle of Jadot NSG Les Boudots, in case Dorothy preferred red. This was going to be a very personal tête-à-tête. After he hit SEND, he phoned Amy. He knew that there was a three-hour time difference, so it was only eight o'clock in California.

"Hello?" Amy answered on the second ring.

"Amy. Lloyd Luttrell here."

"Well, hello. How are you?"

"I'm fine, thank you. I wanted you to know that I was able to talk your mother into having lunch with me next week."

"That's wonderful!" Amy was overjoyed. Someone had her mother's back.

"I see what you mean about her fiancé. Rather ingratiating fellow, eh?"

"You're being kind." Amy laughed nervously.

"I had only met him briefly, and at the time, I didn't realize he was a few years her junior."

"All the more reason I suspect he's a ne'er-do-well," Amy replied.

"I hope I can give her something to think about, assuming she doesn't throw a glass of wine in my face." Lloyd chuckled.

Amy laughed. "I doubt that. She's always thought very highly of you."

"The feeling is quite mutual," Lloyd said casually.

"Thank you so much for doing this."

"The pleasure is all mine," Lloyd reassured her. "You do realize that if she decides to take my advice, I won't be able to discuss it with you. Attorney-client privilege."

"Of course. I just want someone besides me to give her food for thought."

"Understood. I will, however, let you know if it went well, or not," Lloyd assured her.

"Thanks so much." Amy gave a huge sigh.

"You are very welcome. Enjoy the rest of the weekend."

"You too, Mr. Luttrell."

"Call me Lloyd." He smiled as he ended the call.

Chapter Nine

The Next Morning
Ridgewood, New Jersey

Rachael couldn't wait any longer. She looked at her clock. It was still 6:00 A.M. in Santa Clara. She figured Amy was up and getting ready to go to the shelter. Amy picked up on the first ring.

"Geesh. Took you long enough." Amy chided Rachael.

"Yeah. Sorry. By the time I got home, I was beat. Greg and Ryan had a bit of a tiff. Something about a video game, and Ryan had a meltdown. I'll find out more details later, when Ryan comes down for breakfast."

"That's not like him, is it? To have a meltdown?"

"Not usually, but he's at that age when he's forming his own opinions about things." Rachael sighed. "And I don't think he likes Greg's new wife, Vicki."

"Even the name sounds pretentious." Amy snickered as she sipped her morning coffee.

"Actually, she's not pretentious at all. 'Indifferent' would be a better word to describe her. She pretty much stays out of the way when Ryan is there. Anyway, I had to go pick him up at midnight. Greg and I will chat about this at a later time. I'm too pooped to go through one of our usual blame-game conversations. He thinks I spoil Ryan. And maybe I do in a way, but I don't ever want Ryan to think he is unloved just because his parents can't get along. You know how kids can blame themselves for their parents' splitting up. They think it's their fault somehow."

"You don't have to tell me," Amy said sympathetically. "When I was younger, I thought my father stayed away because of me. But that didn't last very long because he was very loving when he would get back from his business trips. When they finally decided to get a divorce, I was already a freshman in college, so I knew for sure it wasn't my fault."

"Ryan is OK today. When I asked him about the incident, all he said was 'Daddy wouldn't let me play my game. He wanted me to go to bed. But it wasn't my bedtime.' I guess Greg wanted some alone time with the missus."

"You'd think Greg would want to spend some quality time with his son." Amy sighed. "What about the cruise? Isn't Ryan supposed to stay with Greg that week?"

"Yes, but my parents are standing by in case there's another dustup."

"Oh good." Holding the phone under her chin, Amy breathed a sigh of relief as she fed the cats. "It would be a shame if you had to miss the cruise."

"No way! I need it more than ever. Ernie turned out to be a total dud."

"I would suggest you stay away from men for a while, but we know that's just not in your DNA. Plus, the whole reason for this trip is to try to have fun with them. It's better if you are unfettered. No guilt." Amy was busily getting herself ready to leave for the shelter.

"Guilt?" Rachael let out a big laugh. "That, too, is not in my DNA!"

Amy chuckled. "OK, girlfriend. I don't have a lot of time. Spill. What went down last night at the club? Pooches and other furries await."

"You are a wonderful person, you know that?" Rachael said with admiration.

"Aw, that's sweet. Thanks pal, but . . . so?" Amy was anxious to find out how the evening with the hoopla of her mother's announcement had gone.

"Oh right. The big reveal. It was kinda meh. I noticed that Mr. Charm was getting very cozy with one of the waitresses. Then your mother quickly glided over and hooked her arm in his."

"Interesting." Amy stopped what she was doing and paid closer attention.

"Yeah. The woman was a little older than us, but she seemed to know Rusty pretty well; she was making googly eyes at him. Your mother was very reserved, but I could tell that she wasn't thrilled. I know that look." Rachael had known the Blanchard family most of her life, so she was quite adept at sensing Dorothy's moods and body language. "Later that evening, I saw Lloyd Luttrell take her aside and speak to her."

"Yes, he did." Amy pulled on her sweatshirt. "He called me after the shindig and told me he will be taking her to lunch this coming week."

"¡Mucho gusto!" Rachael replied. "I wonder how she'll take Lloyd's advice."

"My mother always liked Lloyd as a person and a lawyer. She said he was a true gentleman."

"I agree. He actually gives lawyers a good name," Rachael said. "And he's handsome, too, in that 'silver fox' kind of way."

Amy snickered. "Don't you go getting ideas about him."

Rachael laughed. "Be serious. If anything, I go for the younger type."

"Yeah, and look how well *that's* turned out." Amy gave a chuckle.

"Oh stop," Rachael prompted. "I've decided to turn over a new leaf."

"Looking for gardeners now?" Amy couldn't help it. Rachael had given her a big opening.

"Very funny. You might want to try doing stand-up comedy if this biotech thing doesn't work out," Rachael chided.

"Ha. Ha. Listen, I've gotta dash. Two hundred four-legged, OK, a few three-legged critters are waiting for me. Love ya!"

"OK, *chica*. Love you, too," Rachael replied. "See you soon." She hit the END button on her cell phone.

Rachael poured herself another cup of coffee. She thought about all the teasing she had been getting from her friends. Maybe she needed to reevaluate her approach. What was it that kept driving her to have a boyfriend? Any boyfriend. Was she that insecure in her personal life? She surely didn't lack confidence in other areas. Why was she so hell-bent on having a partner? Not that there was anything wrong with having a significant other. Maybe that was the word that was missing. "Significant." It was as if she were trying to fill a void in her life. She was deliberating about her motives when Ryan came into the kitchen.

"Hey, Mom. Sorry about last night." Ryan was an astute child. He knew it was out of character for him to have a temper tantrum. He had outgrown them. Or so everyone thought.

Rachael patted the stool next to her. "Come. Sit. Tell me in more detail what happened." Ryan climbed up on the stool and looked down at the floor. Rachael picked up his chin. "It's OK, honey. I won't be mad."

Ryan hesitated a minute and looked up. "I think Dad was having an argument with Vicki."

"Oh?" Rachael was intrigued. "Were they arguing in front of you?"

"No. They were in the bedroom, but I could hear yelling."

"What were they saying?"

"I couldn't hear many words, but I think Vicki was slamming drawers or something."

"You must have caught a few words, no? You're a good catcher on your baseball team." Rachael was trying to be reassuring and gentle at the same time.

"She said a few bad words." Ryan looked down at the floor again.

"I see. Do you want to tell me what those words were? You don't have to say the word, just the first letter is OK. I know you're a good speller."

"He called her the 'B' word and said she was being selfish."

Rachael thought that wasn't too far from an apt description. "Do you know why?"

"I think she wanted to go to a party or something." Ryan shrugged. "But Dad said he couldn't go."

Rachael realized that the fight was about Ryan. Vicki loved to spend Saturday nights with her friends at a gin joint in the next town, and having Ryan at the house was cramping her style.

"So why did your father ask you to go to bed early?"

"Vicki locked herself in the bedroom. Dad was trying to talk to her through the door." Ryan heaved a big gulp of air.

"It's OK, honey. You can tell me anything." Rachael was

encouraging and calm on the outside, but on the inside, she wanted to strangle Greg. And Vicki. That was one of the stipulations in the custody agreement. No arguments or disruptions during visits. "Then what happened?"

Ryan shrugged. "I went into the hallway to ask Dad if I could watch a movie, and he told me to go to my room."

"Well, that wasn't very nice."

"I guess."

"Then what happened?" It was like pulling teeth. "I promise I won't get mad."

"I went to my room and started to play a video game. I guess the noise was bothering Vicki."

"And?" More extractions.

"She said the 'S' word."

"How?"

"She said she was sick of hearing that 'S'."

"I see. So what did your father do?"

"He came into my room and told me to turn it off." A tear ran down Ryan's cheek. "Mom, I didn't mean to make everybody mad."

Rachael put her arm around her son. "I know, honey. Sometimes grown-ups get mad at each other and take it out on other people."

"But I didn't do anything wrong." Ryan started to cry.

Rachael hugged him closer. "That's right. You did nothing wrong. So tell me, when did you have your temper tantrum?" She smiled at him.

Ryan shrugged again. "I was getting bored, so I took my video game and went under the covers. I didn't think she could hear me." Ryan paused, looking a little sheepish.

"Go on."

"Then Dad came into the room and saw what I was doing and started yelling at me."

"What did he say?" Rachael's blood was boiling at this point.

"He said, 'I thought I told you to turn that thing off.' But he used the 'F' word."

Rachael was so angry she could spit. "OK, sweetie. I don't want you to worry about any of this. Eat your breakfast and go play whatever game you want." She wiped his tears, kissed him on the top of his head, and ruffled his hair.

He gave her a big hug. "Thanks, Mom." He wiped his nose on his sleeve. Rachael shot him a look. "Oops. Sorry." He pulled a small step stool next to the kitchen sink and began to wash off his shirt. Then he washed his hands and held them up. "OK?"

"OK." Rachael gave him a warm smile. She realized it wouldn't be too long before he didn't need that step stool anymore. He could almost reach the single-lever faucet now.

Rachael counted to ten to cool her jets. She was furious with Greg. When Ryan sat down to eat his breakfast, she left the room, picked up her phone, and began to dial Greg's number. Then she thought better of it and dialed her mother's phone number instead. Rachael had decided to pay the couple a personal visit.

"Hello, dear," her mother said. "Everything all right?"

"Hey, Mom. Everything's fine." Rachael didn't want to get her mother involved. She wasn't a fan of Greg's to begin with. "I need to run an errand. Can you come over for about an hour and look after Ryan?"

"Of course. But isn't he supposed to be with Greg and what's-her-name?"

"Vicki." Rachael kept calm. "Yes, but something came up, and Ryan's here. He's eating breakfast, then he's going to play a game, and I thought it would be easier if you came by."

"What happened? Why isn't he with Greg?" Rachael's mother was like a dog with a sock in its mouth. When it came to Greg and Ryan, she wanted no stone left unturned.

"Long story. Well, not really. I'll fill you in when I get back."

"OK, dear. I'll be over in a few minutes." But she wasn't going to let go just yet. "Are you sure everything is all right?"

"Yes, Mom. Everything is fine," Rachael fibbed, but she was going to make sure everything would be fine in the future.

"I'll see you in a bit."

"Thanks, Mom." Rachael ended the call and ran to her room to get dressed. She didn't want to look like a disheveled divorcée. The more together she looked, the better she would feel. She wanted Greg and the missus to know just how serious she was. Serious, yes. But anger was something she would have to keep at bay if she wanted to make her point. It had taken a long time for Rachael to realize that no one pays attention to your words when you're screaming at them. She pulled on a pink cashmere sweater, leggings, and a pair of boots with a two-inch chunky heel. It dawned on her that maybe she was insecure because of her diminutive stature. It had never occurred to her that she might be compensating for something she perceived as a flaw. *Interesting.* She took a good long look at herself. That would be the end of any such thoughts from now on. She was fit and attractive. Smart, funny, and successful. No man could make her feel any differently. She was the master of her destiny. At least when she was given the choice. Everyone always had options. Sometimes they weren't ideal, but there was always a choice. She slicked her hair back to a stylish pixie. Thinking of Amy's hair, she wondered how she would look with a wild color. Nah. Even though she was a dancer, she still had a business to run in a very upscale community. She had to deal with overbearing dance moms and senior citizens. It was important to maintain the decorum of a thoughtful professional. She could always tint her hair for a recital if she wanted. The doorbell rang, signaling her mother's arrival. Rachael swiped on red lipstick and slipped on a pair of pearl stud earrings. She took another look. Perfect for the mission she was about to embark on.

Ryan answered the door. "Hello, Lee-lee!" That was the nickname Ryan had given her when he was little. No one knew where he got it from, but it stuck. And Rachael's mother thought it was cute. As much as she loved being a grandmother, she wasn't keen on the words "Grammy," "Granny," or "Grandma." "Lee-lee" was fine with her.

"Hello, Ryan." She bent over to give him a hug. "Your mom told me you were playing a game."

"Yes! I beat my own score!" Ryan was pleased as punch with himself.

"What are you going to do next?"

"Try to beat myself again," Ryan said with delight, and ran back upstairs. The house was a two-story colonial with two bedrooms on the second floor and a bonus room that opened up to the kitchen area with a railing. Ryan could have friends over and Rachael could monitor them without being a helicopter mom. It gave the appearance of privacy to the kids but she could hear everything that went on. The master bedroom was on the first floor adjacent to the living room, which afforded her some privacy. Whether she wanted some quiet time or she wanted to "entertain" the boyfriend du jour. But she was incredibly careful and selective. Only once had she had a man spend the night at her place, and Ryan was at his father's that particular evening. Rachael may have been boy-crazy, but she was one heck of a mother hen when it came to protecting her son from anything that could cause him confusion or harm.

Rachael went into the kitchen, where her mother waited patiently for an explanation. "Hi, Mom!" Rachael gave her mother a peck on the cheek. "Thanks so much for doing this."

Mary-Jean Newmark gave her daughter a suspicious look. "You're welcome. So what is this all about?"

"I have to run an errand. Shouldn't be too long." Rachael grabbed her tote bag, keys, and headed toward the door.

Her mother got up from the stool and blocked Rachael from moving any further. "I know you too well. You always spend Sunday mornings reading the paper and having your favorite coffee. What gives?"

"There was a little kerfuffle with Ryan and his father last night." She put her hands up. "Before you get a knot in your panties, Ryan is fine, but I am going to have a chat with Greg."

Rachael tried to get past her mother but to no avail. "Mom, please. Let me go do this, and I promise I will fill you in when I get back." She looked her mother straight in the eye. "Please, Mom. While I still have my wits about me."

Her mother stepped aside. "OK, but I am holding you to your promise, young lady."

Rachael gave her a salute. "Yes, ma'am!" She scurried out the door before she lost her nerve, or before her mother could try to stop her again.

Rachael hopped into her SUV, took one more look in the mirror, and said aloud, "You got this, girl." On the way to Greg's, she rehearsed what she was going to say. And she was determined to remain calm and collected no matter what Greg might try to throw in her face. He had no room to talk. He married Vicki five minutes after the divorce was final. Or so it seemed. But one thing was for certain. There were rules when it came to Ryan, and if Greg couldn't stick to them, then there would be new rules, and Greg wouldn't have a whole lot to say about them. She appreciated how important it was for a son to have a relationship with his father, but Greg needed to act like one. Any issues he had with Vicki should be dealt with beforehand or afterward. Not in front of her son. That was it. Simple.

She took several deep breaths as she approached the driveway of the small cottage Greg shared with Vicki. One of the other rules was that Ryan have a designated bedroom since he was supposed to spend one night a week there and every other weekend. It wasn't Ryan's fault the house was small enough to hear everything going on. Greg was lucky he had a roof over his head. And that was only because of Ryan. Otherwise, Greg would never see his son.

Rachael checked the mirror one more time. She turned off the engine and proceeded to the front door, where Greg was waiting. "What are you doing here?" His tone was tense.

"Good morning to you, too." Rachael was cool. "Got a minute? We need to talk."

Greg closed the door behind him and stood on the front porch. "What about?" he asked gruffly.

Rachael took another breath to remain calm. "The fact you have to ask is ludicrous, but it doesn't surprise me."

"Always the pleasant charmer." His sarcasm wasn't lost on her.

"Please, Greg. Can we have a civil conversation?"

"That would be a first," he said, sneering.

Rachael shook her head. "As they say, 'there's a first time for everything.' This is about our son. *Your* son. Can we please be civil?"

Greg folded his arms across his chest. "If you insist."

"Ryan was very upset last night."

"You're telling me." Greg snorted.

"Maybe that's because you were very dismissive?" Rachael asked calmly, waiting for him to explode.

"Look, he . . ."

Rachael immediately interrupted him. "He did nothing, from what I understand."

"Who you gonna believe? An eight-year-old who has a vivid imagination?" Greg was as ornery as ever.

"Let me see if I have this straight. You and Vicki didn't have a fight, she didn't lock herself in the bedroom, and she didn't complain about Ryan's playing his game?"

"I told him to stop. He defied me."

"What did you expect him to do to entertain himself?" Rachael was proud of her demeanor. Very matter-of-fact and at a normal volume. But the words inside her head were screaming, *You imbecilic peckerhead!* "You didn't put on a movie for him to watch. You sent him to his room, then you got angry with him, which seemed to be displaced aggression."

"Wow, listen to you, Dr. Phil." Greg was goading her, but she wasn't taking the bait.

"You had an argument with Vicki, and she was being unreasonable. So you took it out on your son."

"Oh, is that how it went?" Greg eyed her.

"Pretty much. Tell me where I'm mistaken." Rachael folded her arms in turn.

"What happens between me and Vicki is none of your business."

"Thank goodness for that." Rachael stepped back. "Here's the deal, Greg. This is your one and only warning, so pay attention. If I ever have to rescue my son from a hostile environment again, it will be supervised visitation going forward." She looked up at him. "With my mother."

Those words alone made him blanch. He was about to argue with her but thought better of it.

"Understood?" Rachael maintained her stare.

"Got it." Greg turned on his heel, went back into the house, and slammed the door.

Rachael walked back to her car with the biggest grin on her face. That was probably the most civil conversation she had had with him in, well, she couldn't recall. She was enormously proud of herself and couldn't wait to share this with her mother. Mary-Jean would be so proud of her daughter.

Chapter Ten

Two weeks later—mid-December
Santa Clara

Amy's phone chimed the sound she had assigned to her mother's phone number. It was Beethoven's Fifth. *Da-da-da-dum*. She was anxious to find out if her mother had lunched with Lloyd the week before. And if she had, would she share it? The answer came quickly.

"Hello, Mother." Amy sounded cheerful.

"Hello, dear. How is my little girl?"

Amy held the phone away from her ear and looked at it quizzically, wondering who this delightful person on the other end could be.

"I'm fine, Mother. Are you OK?"

"I'm as right as rain." Dorothy was uncharacteristically jolly.

Amy rolled her eyes, anticipating another "Wonderful World of Rusty" story. "Glad to hear it. What's new?"

"I broke off my engagement with Rusty," Dorothy said, a little too much gusto in her voice.

Trying not to stammer, Amy responded. "But? But? Why?" She was also trying to hide her excitement.

"I had lunch with Lloyd Luttrell last week. He gave me a lot to think about."

"Oh? Do tell." Amy was trying to sound like she wasn't prying.

"I won't go into details right now, dear, but I wanted you to know that I've kicked Rusty to the curb, and you won't have to throw a bridal shower for me." Dorothy laughed at her own joke.

"Really?" Amy dragged out the word.

"Yes, really, darling."

"Are you going to clue me in?" Amy's curiosity was through the roof.

"Let's just say that Rusty and I had a difference of opinion. Lloyd gave me a lot to think about. And I am totally fine with my decision."

For a moment, Amy thought her mother had been drinking. Her mother wasn't a big drinker, but she wasn't a teetotaler, either. In fact, Amy could not remember if she had ever witnessed her mother drunk.

"Mother? Are you sure you're OK?" Amy was dubious.

"I'm just fine, my dear." Dorothy paused. "I know you were not a fan of Rusty, but for a while he made me feel important. It's something I rarely felt with your father. My insecurities, I suppose."

That was the word Amy had contemplated. "Insecurity." *That must have been one helluva lunch*, she thought.

"I understand now, Mother. Remember, I was in college when you got divorced. I knew nothing about what an adult relationship should look like. To be honest, at this rate I don't know if I ever will." Amy cracked a smile.

"You will, my dear. Just never settle for less than you want or you deserve. Granted, sometimes there is a gap between the two, but you are smart, cute, responsible, and loving."

Amy held the phone away from her for the second time. Could this really be her mother on the other end?

"Mother, you have rendered me speechless."

"Amy, honey, I know I haven't always been the most approachable sage for you. We women are extraordinarily complex, and sometimes we get caught up in our own mental calisthenics. I hope we can bond better in the future. We need each other."

Tears were rolling down Amy's cheeks. "I love you, Mom."

"I love you, too. And I liked that you called me 'Mom' instead of 'Mother.' To be quite honest, I hate 'Mother.' It reminds me of Norman Bates in *Psycho*."

Amy hooted so loud both cats jumped. "Why didn't you ever tell me?"

"Oh, I don't know. I suppose I thought it was more respectful, but then I kept remembering Norman Bates." Dorothy chuckled. "I suppose I just didn't have the heart to tell you."

The two women roared.

"Listen, *Mom*." Amy emphasized the word. "I am incredibly happy you sound happy. I cannot tell you what a relief this is. I know I will have a much better time on my cruise knowing you are not going to marry Rusty. I'll reserve my other adjectives for now. It's too soon to be bawdy."

Dorothy laughed with more gusto than Amy could ever remember.

"Yes, we can save the name-calling for a later day. Onward to new things."

"I'll drink to that." Amy once again thought perhaps her mother had been hitting the bottle.

"I shall, too."

"Have you started already?" Amy pretended to tease her.

"Not yet. A little later perhaps."

"What are you doing later?"

"I'm having dinner with Lloyd Luttrell."

Another astonished "Really?" came from Amy's mouth.

"Yes. He's a good friend and wants to discuss a few things." Dorothy was cautious in her enthusiasm. She didn't know exactly what Lloyd wanted to discuss, but just being in his company was delightful. He was attentive, witty, and smart. Being handsome with a full head of silver hair didn't hurt. Dorothy had to admit that Lloyd wasn't at all bad to look at.

"Whatever you say, *Mom*." Amy was elated. She knew that her mother was going to be OK.

Back in Ridgewood, Lloyd Luttrell was planning his dinner with Dorothy. He was taking her to Latour, a wonderful French-American restaurant. It had a quaint atmosphere, furnished with antique furniture and oil paintings. He was salivating thinking about the menu. Should he order the beef Wellington or the lamb? Decisions. Decisions. One thing was for certain, he was going to have the chocolate ganache for dessert. Once again, he was contemplating what he should do about wine. He knew he was having beef, so a cabernet sauvignon was on the ticket, and recalled Dorothy's having enjoyed the Gaja, so he'd send over another bottle as well. Lloyd hoped he wasn't giving her the impression he was going over the top, but Dorothy was a fine woman and needed all the support she could get. Too many women get "catfished" by younger men, especially good-looking charmers. He finished his grooming with a light splash of Hugo Boss aftershave. Just enough to smell fresh but not too much to knock her over.

He picked out a pale purple tie to go with his burgundy shirt and burgundy-and-navy-plaid blazer. Dark navy trousers finished his ensemble. Casual, yet elegant. He picked a simple Cartier watch to complement his look. He wondered if he should add a matching pocket square. No. Too formal. He then gave the tie a second thought. No tie? Too casual. He didn't want to scare off Dorothy by implying the dinner was some sort of date. Although, a man could dream, no?

Chapter Eleven

December 21
New York City

Frankie made her way through the throng of onlookers, tourists, and other office workers at Rockefeller Center, uttering a lot of "excuse me, pardon me, sorry" as she inched her way to the revolving door of her building.

The city was bustling for the holiday season, during which eight hundred thousand people pass the famous Norwegian spruce each day, over 125 million tourists visit the plaza over the entire season, and seven million people flock to the city for the holidays.

This year, the majestic tree, weighing over nine hundred pounds, was eighty-nine feet tall with over eighteen thousand lights and a magnificent star made of three million Swarovski crystals. Below the regal spruce was the rink, decorated in garland and large ornaments, where anyone could ice-skate to holiday music.

On the promenade, twelve eight-foot luminous, winged, robed, and haloed angels with six-foot golden trumpets lined the Channel Gardens running from Fifth Avenue to the plaza.

Each angel was slightly angled toward the tree. The view from Fifth Avenue was glorious.

Across Fifth Avenue, opposite the promenade, is Saks Fifth Avenue, whose entire building was covered in thousands of lights, creating the look of an ice castle. At night, the building came alive with animated brilliance. The bare-limbed trees lining the avenue were ablaze with miniature white lights, and giant stars were draped overhead from one side of the street to the other.

On the next corner, across from Saks Fifth Avenue, is the famous St. Patrick's Cathedral. Hundreds of poinsettias were placed throughout the church while choral music played constantly. Nine blocks north, on Fifty-Ninth Street, was the world's largest menorah. No matter what you believe in, you could feel the spirit of the season and find joy in the magical wonderland.

Frankie squeezed her way through the lobby, trying not to spill the two cups of coffee she held in a cardboard box. As she approached the security desk, she handed a cup to one of the guards. "Cappuccino with two shots of espresso, one sugar."

Sam smiled at her. "You know the secret code." Frankie smiled back. "Looks like today is going to be a doozy."

"You got that right. With the long weekend, it's going to take a few of these to get me through." He held up the cup and gestured a toast. "Thanks, Frankie. Have a good one."

She winked back at the man who had been working at Rockefeller Center for over sixty years. She had no idea how old he was, but Sam was as much a fixture at Rockefeller Center as the life-size toy soldiers who stood guard by the famous tree.

Frankie wriggled her way toward the elevator, clutching the box holding her coffee and muffin. More "excuse me, pardon me, sorry" as she scrunched into the car. As she looked around the stuffed elevator, she wondered if the weight-limit sign near the panel of buttons was merely a suggestion. When she reached the fourteenth floor, she gave another round of "excuse me, pardon me, sorry."

Her first stop was the conference room, where the giant television was tuned to one of the morning shows. One of their authors was doing a cooking demo for a new book, *Five, Ten, Fifteen or Twenty.* Frankie wasn't thrilled with the title even though it was exactly what the book was about. Five ingredients, ten minutes to prepare, and fifteen or twenty minutes to cook.

Congenial greetings and nods went around the room. Frankie tossed her coat on an empty chair along the wall, took a seat at the table, and cracked open the tab of her coffee cup. She hated drinking from a cardboard container. She felt it changed the taste of the coffee, but she didn't think she had time to go to her office to grab a mug and get back in time. Matt, her assistant, glanced at Frankie and left the room to get her the mug. In a few minutes, he returned and handed Frankie her favorite mug, the one with the black cat on it.

Frankie was not a demanding boss in the sense of being unreasonable. She did, however, expect people to do their best, be honest, and conscientious. She made sure she was always available and approachable to her staff. Even a mistake could be remedied if handled properly. She gave Matt a nod. She was glad she had chosen him from all the other candidates. He was eager to learn and often worked past five o'clock to read the media news feeds.

Everyone turned toward the TV as the camera panned in on the dish Judy Jackson was working on. It was some sort of zucchini casserole. As she mixed the five ingredients, she chatted with the hosts of the show. Judy had been a best-selling cookbook author for many years, but over the past decade, cookbook sales were dropping owing to the ease of getting recipes off the Internet. But when the novel coronavirus up-ended life, people confined to their homes began cooking and baking, and the demand for new ideas increased.

With many people working from home and trying to school their children, there wasn't a lot of time to prepare a meal. That's when Judy came up with the idea for the book. Rachael Ray had done something similar years ago, so this was actually a new twist on an old idea.

The camera cut away from the kitchen area and focused back on the hosts. "We'll be back with Judy in fifteen or twenty minutes," the sappy male host said with feigned en-thusiasm.

Frankie took a sip of her coffee. "So far, so good. Let's hope it doesn't turn out like mush." A few nervous giggles were heard around the table. A show like this could make or break the sales of a cookbook, especially since it was being broadcast live. No room for error.

Frankie took the few minutes to rush to her office to see if she had any messages. Matt was right on her heels. He handed her several "While You Were Out" slips of phone messages.

"Those came through earlier today," Matt said.

"Thanks." She flipped through the slips. Nothing earth-shattering.

"Your mother called asking if you could stop at Leonelli's and pick up some pastry. I called them. They said if you place the order by the end of the day, they'll have it ready for you Monday morning."

"You are a peach," Frankie exclaimed. "OK. We'll handle that after Judy. Let's get back to the conference room." Frankie lived a few short blocks from Leonelli's, which is where Marco bought his desserts for the restaurant. The two scurried back to where Judy was about to reveal her master-piece.

The bubbling casserole looked festive. Round slices of zucchini with bits of red bell peppers in the shape of wreaths topped the dish.

"Looks yummy." The bubbleheaded blonde hosting the show peered at the food.

"This is one way to get your kids to eat vegetables," Judy exclaimed, as the audience applauded.

Everyone in the conference room gave a group sigh of relief and commended each other for a job well done. It was a good beginning to a day that would finish with an in-office lunch and early dismissal. It had been several years since the company hosted a holiday party. Someone finally realized that not only did it cost a lot of money, but that people got drunk, said or did stupid things, and everyone would be missing an evening that could be put to better use preparing for the holidays. The company decided to arrange for sandwiches and salads, cookies and brownies, and nonalcoholic beverages to be delivered from Pret A Manger. Each of their floors had a large conference room, which is where the lunch would be served. The buffet would start at one o'clock. It gave people an opportunity to mix and mingle with coworkers, grab something to eat, then go home, go shopping, or hide out somewhere.

Frankie thought it was a solid idea. As beautiful and wondrous as the holidays are, there is a whole truckload of stress that goes along with them. Buying the right gift. Paying for the right gift. Who gets a gift? What about cards? To send or not to send? What kind of cards and to whom? Decorations. How much? How little? That's a lot of questions. Then there's the food dilemma. What to eat? Where to eat? When to eat? How much to eat? Frankie shook and patted the side of her head as if she had water in her ears, attempting to rid herself of the angst.

Frankie was very levelheaded and quite capable of handling a crisis situation. As long as it didn't involve blood. She tried to take things in stride, but even with her "superpowers," she occasionally needed a break to recharge. She was very much looking forward to the cruise with her gal pals. Even though she had no idea what to expect out of it, she had every intention of enjoying it to the max.

Frankie went through her e-mail in-box, then the traditional in-box that sat at the corner of her desk. She clipped a few pages from the print editions of *Library Journal* and *Publishers Weekly*, and added a Post-it note to circulate to the editors of the books whose ads appeared. As much as computers and the Internet provided every piece of information you could want, need, or hope would go away, Frankie still liked the feel of a magazine in her hands. Just like she preferred a printed book over an e-book. There was something about the tactile feel of them. Reading something in print required one to use more than one sense.

She glanced around her office to see if there was anything else that needed her attention. She would be gone for almost two weeks. The longest she had ever been away from her office except during Covid-19, when everyone worked from home every day. Things were still operating at the "new normal," with people alternating days of office time and working from home. For Frankie, being able to walk to work on a nice day meant she spent most of the work week in the office at Rockefeller Center. She enjoyed the personal interaction with other people.

Checking the time, she saw that it was almost one. She picked up her phone and buzzed Matt. "Hey, can you come in for a sec?"

"Be right there."

When it came to holiday bonuses, it was up to each department head to divvy up the money. And each year, the sums were measlier than the previous. How do you explain to someone who had worked above and beyond that they're getting half of what they got last year, while the business reports that earnings were up for her employer? Evidently, the executives felt that working from home saved their employees commuter costs. Frankie had complained to human resources earlier that week. "What does that have to do with anything? People were doing their jobs. That's what they get paid for." She lost the argument, and she wasn't about to confront the CEO about it. One wrong move, and you could easily become persona non grata. She groaned, thinking about it. She loved her work but hated her job. *Yep. This cruise can't come soon enough.*

Matt gave a light knock on the door frame.

"Come in," Frankie said.

"Everything OK?" Matt asked.

"Yes and no. But before you get worked up, it's not about you."

"Whew."

"I don't have to tell you that the company can be cheap." She grimaced and rolled her eyes, something she was known to do. "The good news is that we actually got bonuses. The bad news is that it's less than last year." She handed Matt a check for $1,000.

"Wow, Frankie. I wasn't counting on anything because of how bad the economy was earlier this year." Matt was profoundly grateful. He was in his early twenties, brand-spanking-new from a Midwestern college, and sharing an apartment with three other guys. Frankie knew the scenario all too well.

Then she passed an envelope across her desk. It looked like a Christmas card. Frankie wanted to give Matt a little something extra for Christmas. She knew he would appreciate anything she would give him, but she also knew $100 would be largely appreciated. Yes, she remembered her early days in publishing.

"Open it later." She stood up from her desk. "Come on. There's a roast beef with cheddar on a multigrain roll with my name on it." She wasn't kidding. Everyone got to order what they wanted, and the assistants marked the small boxed sandwiches with their names. They even placed the sandwiches in alphabetical order. Frankie was proud of her crackerjack team.

As people entered the room, they shuffled to the buffet table to pick up their lunch, then to the conference table to sit. Some stood against the wall, munching down on the gourmet fare. She waited for the din to subside as people stuffed their faces. Pret A Manger could turn an average sandwich into a mouthwatering pleasure.

"Good afternoon. Just a brief message of thanks for your hard work during a tough year. I appreciate each and every one of you, and I hope you have a good, safe, and wonderful holiday." She raised her glass of sparkling water.

Shouts of "Hear! Hear!" "Thank you, Frankie!" "You're the best, Frankie!" came from her staff.

She almost got choked up. "Remember, I'll be gone for a while, so I expect everyone to behave." Laughter filled the room. "And if there is an emergency, lose my number, please." She laughed, and everyone followed.

By two thirty, the room began to empty as people returned to their offices or cubicles to wind down the day. It was going to be a long weekend, since Christmas fell on a Tuesday that year. People were expected to be back on the twenty-sixth and work weekdays until the last day of the year. Knowing little would be happening at the office, Frankie had decided that the thirty-first would be a day her staff could work from home, giving them two long weekends. Her hope was that nothing would blow up while she was away.

She grabbed her tote, put her coat on, and headed for the elevator, waving and wishing everyone a "Happy Holidays! Merry Christmas! Happy Hanukkah! Happy Kwanzaa!

Happy New Year!" Once, she had come up with something she thought covered all of them: "Happy ChristmasKwanz-Hanukkah." Too bad it never caught on.

The elevator door opened, and she got in with several of the bean counters from the accounting department. "Good afternoon, gentlemen." Frankie flashed a bright smile all the while thinking *the grinches of publishing.* She chuckled to herself. Frankie loved her "thought balloons." They enabled her to keep her temper and confine her less-than-polite words to thoughts. She would envision a puffy cloud over her head, as in a cartoon, with the words she really *wanted* to say but knew that she had better *not.* They nodded politely and responded with some banal greeting or other. She chuckled again. *Joyless creatures. I wonder if they get coal in their stockings. Then again, they probably don't even have stockings.*

She was glad when the elevator car reached the lobby. She had been amusing herself thinking about their playing the roles of the Ghosts of Christmas Past, Present, and Future, and she had almost burst out laughing. Frankie was the first to exit the car. She turned and gave them a big "Ho, Ho, Ho. Happy Holidays!" Following that, she spun on her heel in a comical manner, knowing they would think she was a kook. She figured they already thought that of her anyway.

As she passed Sam, she handed him a hat box that contained a box of truffles from La Maison du Chocolat. He had commented one time when she was carrying a shopping bag from the luxury chocolatier for one of her authors. He told her his wife loved them but they "were a little pricey" for his wallet. He gave her a surprised look. Frankie winked. "Just make sure she shares at least one of them with you. Merry Christmas!"

"Merry Christmas to you, Frankie. Enjoy your cruise. Many thanks." He gave the box an appreciative nod.

Frankie spun on her heel again and joined the throng of

people pushing their way through the revolving door. She headed west toward Avenue of the Americas, which every real New Yorker called Sixth Avenue.

At the corner of Fiftieth and Sixth stood the legendary Radio City Music Hall, decorated with wreaths and garland, the marquee lit with the legendary words: RADIO CITY HOLIDAY SPECTACULAR STARRING THE ROCKETTES.

On the other side of Sixth Avenue, giant ruby-red ornaments sat on the large fountain in front of the Exxon Building, surrounded by trees with sparkling white lights. It was one of the most photographed holiday decorations in the city. No one was exempt from the festive charm. Even the food vendors went out of their way to decorate their food trucks. You couldn't cross any corner without spotting a vendor with scarves, caps, mittens, and gloves that screamed "Joy to the World."

Frankie decided to walk the twenty-six blocks back to her apartment instead of taking a cab. She turned left on Forty-Seventh Street, heading back east and passing all the diamond dealers and jewelry exchanges. The entire block glistened and gleamed with diamonds of all shapes, sizes, and colors.

Once she got back to Fifth Avenue she turned right and headed downtown. It was a pleasant afternoon, and walking gave her a chance to see more of the decorations. Even though she saw them every day, it made her happy to see them over and over again. On the cruise the following week, the decorations would be quite different. Palm trees with colored lights. Not something she was used to. She was getting as much New York holiday magic in as possible.

Frankie wanted to take one more stroll through the Winter Village in Bryant Park behind the New York Public Library. It, too, was a flurry of bustling activity with decorations, a large tree, food and beverages, and over a hundred boutique shops. It also had an ice rink but not as large as the 122-by-60-foot rink at Rock Center. She grabbed a hot pretzel from a vendor, looked through a few shops, and decided she should head back to her apartment. It was around five o'clock, and she was pooped. She pulled out her cell phone and hit the app for Uber. Twenty-minute wait. She could be home in less time if she kept walking. She adjusted her tote and shopping bags and marched down Fifth Avenue until it intersected with Broadway. She crossed Madison Square Park and was finally in front of her apartment building. She didn't realize how bone-tired she was until she dropped her bags in the front entry, kicked off her shoes, and flopped on the sofa. Bandit came out from the bathroom and waited for less than a minute before jumping onto her lap.

"Hey, pal. How did your day go?" She scratched under his chin. "Mine was good. Busy. And I walked home." He looked at her as if to say, "So? What about my dinner?"

"Yeah, I get it. Food. You and me both, pal." She opened a can of flaked tuna for Bandit and peered inside the small refrigerator. Butter, some wimpy celery, suspicious-looking yogurt, and a few bottles of water. "Looks like it's Marco's again."

She hit the speed-dial number for the restaurant and ordered a Caesar salad with grilled chicken. Easy and not too fattening. She chatted with Marco briefly and graciously ended the call. She had to pack for the cruise and wrap presents for her family.

She had been engrossed with her gift-wrapping and jumped when the buzzer rang. Giovanni hadn't been around in a couple of weeks. Marco said he had gone to Italy to visit his fiancée for a week but would be back in time for Christmas. Frankie was crestfallen when she heard that Giovanni was engaged. She didn't know why she had that reaction. Perhaps it was because there would be no chance that her fantasies about the handsome man would come true. Frankie shrugged off her disappointment and focused on the days ahead. A lanky twentysomething delivered her food. "Hello. I'm Antonio. Marco's nephew."

"Nice to meet you, Antonio. Do you live in New York?"

"I live in New Jersey, but I stay with my grandmother when I'm working at the restaurant. School is out, so I can help the family."

Antonio opened the insulated carrying bag and handed her the salad. She dug into her purse for her wallet. "Marco said, 'It's on the house.' Merry Christmas."

Frankie shook her head. "You guys are too good to me." She handed him a twenty-dollar bill. "Enjoy."

"No. I can't take this," Antonio protested.

"Yes, you can. Merry Christmas!" She spun him around by the shoulders and gave him a friendly shove toward the door.

"Giovanni is coming back tomorrow. He said not to worry. He'll take very good care of *il gatto*. I mean your cat." Antonio smiled and gave her a little bow. "Merry Christmas! Have a nice vacation." Yes, that was her plan.

Monday morning, she went to Leonelli's and picked up her mother's pastries for Christmas Eve dinner. It was the traditional Feast of the Seven Fishes, also known as La Vigilia. It could be any combination of fish including lobster, calamari (squid), shrimp, swordfish, whiting, sardines, anchovies, baccala (dried cod), clams, and mussels. Depending on the selection, the fish would be brought out in different courses. Then came the *mista* salad, with greens, tomatoes, fennel, cherry tomatoes, drizzled with a dressing of roasted garlic and olive oil. Her mother would also make stuffed mushrooms and serve them with the salad, along with broccoli rabe and green beans *à la Parmigiana*. A dish of linguine with clam sauce would follow.

Like Thanksgiving, the meal would last for a few hours. After the table was cleared, everyone would go to Midnight Mass. When they got back from church, they would have their dessert.

Christmas Day started out with opening presents in pajamas while sipping Frankie's father's famous eggnog. It was served in small, red, rounded tumblers. Her dad believed there was a glass for each different beverage. She rather liked that idea and tried to implement it in her small kitchen cabinet.

Christmas dinner was simple. A ham, sweet potatoes, salad, and string beans. Any leftover ham came in handy later in the evening when someone wanted to fix a sandwich. It was a much more relaxed day, with everyone recuperating from the massive feast and the two-hour-long church service. By the time they had gotten home from Mass, it was after two in the morning. A few bites of cannoli and everyone crashed into their beds. Frankie preferred her family's tradition over that of other families, who had to be in several places on the same day after going to church. She knew that would be a nonstarter if she was in a relationship. No one was getting in a car and driving anywhere on Christmas Day.

Chapter Twelve

With both Frankie and Rachael in Ridgewood, it made sense for them to take the same flight to Miami. Frankie's dad loaded his trunk with her luggage. "I hope Rachael doesn't have too many suitcases!"

Frankie groaned. "Oh, you know she will." Leaning toward the dramatic, Rachael had an outfit for every meal and occasion.

"She already told me she was bringing three changes of clothes per day."

Her father chuckled. "With all those wardrobe changes, will she have time to enjoy the sightseeing?"

"If there are men involved, yes." Frankie knew Rachael's reputation for chasing men was no big secret. "Although I sensed something different in her voice during our last phone call."

"Maybe she's more mature now." Her father was half-serious.

"I think she finally put on her big-girl pants and stood up for herself."

"I never knew Rachael not to stand up for herself."

"Yes, but that always included yelling and slamming doors." Frankie mused. "She had a confrontation with Greg over Ryan, and she kept her cool. Greg backed off as if she had hit him with pepper spray."

"Words are powerful if you use them in the right context with the right tone."

"I know, Dad. You always said that people will listen once you stop yelling, screaming, or crying."

Bill Cappella looked over at his daughter and grinned. "At least something got through."

A short while later, they pulled in front of Rachael's house. Frankie jumped out and jogged to the front door, where Rachael was waiting. They hugged each other and jumped up and down. "I can't believe we're doing this," Rachael said with gusto.

"I know," Frankie responded. "I haven't taken a vacation in ages. And I'll be away from the office for almost two weeks. I know I'm going to dread opening my e-mail in-box when I get back." Frankie made the face of a crooked smile and rolled her eyes.

"What about your assistant?" Rachael asked, as she began to haul her luggage onto the front porch.

"Matt? He's great. He'll go through the physical in-box, but he won't touch my e-mail. You never know if there will be sensitive stuff in it."

"Right. That makes sense." Rachael tugged at the fifth and final suitcase.

"Wow. You weren't kidding about a change of clothes for everything. You do realize you're going to have to pay extra for your bags?"

"Yep," Rachael remarked.

Frankie pondered if all of it would fit in the Lincoln Corsair her father was driving. "We may have to tie you to the roof," Frankie teased.

"That would be fun," Rachael replied, as if she knew what riding on the roof was like. "Like Mitt Romney's dog, eh what?"

Frankie's father began to rearrange the luggage in an attempt to make all of it fit and decided to put a few things in the back seat with Rachael.

"You gals ready?" he asked, as he got into the driver's seat.

"You bet," they said in unison.

The three of them sang along to the Christmas carols playing on the radio. The trip to the airport only took about forty-five minutes, given the light traffic. When they pulled in front of the United Airlines doors, Frankie's dad called a skycap over to help him unload. "Happy holidays, sir," the man wearing the blue uniform said. "Where to?"

"Miami," Frankie answered.

"And then viva la Caribbean," Rachael added.

Rachael and Frankie showed the man their tickets. He counted the bags. There were seven in total, not including their carry-on totes. "How long you going for?"

"A week." Rachael batted her lash extensions at the man.

Frankie gave her a light elbow to the ribs. Rachael whispered back, "I'm practicing."

"Girlfriend, you don't need any practice." Frankie chuckled.

The skycap tagged the bags and handed them their tickets. "You'll have to pay for the extra luggage at the ticket counter, or they may hold them hostage in Miami." The man grinned.

"No worries. Thanks," Frankie said, and smiled back.

Frankie's father pulled out two twenty-dollar bills and handed them to the man. He knew the bags were heavy and cumbersome, and tips were how most of them make their living. They barely made minimum wage.

Frankie gave her father a big hug and a kiss. "I'll call when we check into the hotel in Miami. But don't expect to hear from me once we're out on the high seas." She laughed. "I'm turning off and tuning out. Unless there's an emergency. Then send word to the ship." She handed him a card that had contact information for the cruise line in case there was something urgent and the passengers couldn't be reached by cell phone.

Rachael also gave Mr. Cappella a hug. "Thanks for the lift. *¡Hasta la vista!*" Both women gave a wave as they entered the terminal. Security clearance took little time. They were fortunate to be flying on a light travel day. Most people were where they wanted to be or where they had to be.

The flight was uneventful and landed at Miami International Airport on time. After they got their luggage, they asked a skycap to find them a taxi, and he wheeled their bags to the curb. When they exited the building, the hot wet air hit them in the face. "Wow. I forgot how humid it is here," Frankie remarked.

"Glad I got that Brazilian hair straightener," Rachael shouted over the sound of a jet coming in for a landing.

Frankie tipped the skycap the same amount her father had at Newark. He was very appreciative and looked for a vehicle that could accommodate all of their luggage. "You staying for a while?" he asked.

"No. We're going on a cruise. Grand Cayman, Belize City, and Cozumel."

"Very nice." He shoved their bags into the back of a minivan. "You all have yourselves a good time."

"We intend to," Rachael exclaimed. Frankie hoped Rachael wouldn't burst into a Mexican folk song.

As the van carried them to the hotel, they couldn't help noticing palm trees with Christmas lights. Frankie chuckled. "It's all coming back to me now. It hadn't occurred to me during my first year of college that there wouldn't be normal Christmas trees. But then I saw dozens of palms with lights. It was kind of kitschy, especially with glowing plastic flamingos wearing Santa caps. I couldn't wait to get home."

A half hour later, they arrived at the hotel. Rachael paid for the cab since Frankie had paid the tip for the skycap. They were always compatible that way. No one ever pulled out a calculator when they were out together. "It will all come out in the wash," Rachael would say.

A bellman greeted them as they got out of the van. "Good afternoon. Welcome to Vie Vay." He eyed the number of bags that came out of the van. "Will you be staying with us long?"

"Just for the night," Frankie replied.

"We're cruising tomorrow," Rachael added.

"Very good," the young man responded. "Please check in at the front desk. I'll bring your bags to your room as soon as you get the key."

The two women checked in, and the bellman followed them to their suite. They were all going to share a large, two-bedroom suite. Amy was going to share one bedroom with Rachael, and Nina would share the other with Frankie. "What time are the other two getting here?" Rachael asked.

"Their flights are supposed to get in around the same time, so they'll hook up at the airport and share a cab here." Frankie put the keycard into the door. She handed the bellman ten dollars, and Rachael handed him fifteen.

"That was the easiest twenty-five dollars he'll make today." Rachael snickered. "I'm going to change my clothes."

"Already?" Frankie looked a little surprised.

"I always feel gross after I fly. I don't know if it's the stale air, even though they say it's fresh. Or maybe it's the close proximity to people. And then there's the humidity? Whatever, I'm slipping on a cool sundress."

"That sounds like a plan," Frankie concurred, as she entered her room and Rachael went into hers.

"This is going to be so. Much. Fun." Rachael began peeling off her shirt and jeans. "I don't know how anyone can wear jeans in this climate."

"Funny you mention it. I wore jeans the entire time I was here in college. Granted, sometimes they were cutoffs, but I don't think I'd be wearing them now. It seems so much hotter here," Frankie mused. She opened her small carry-on and pulled out a crinkled cotton midi dress. "I'm glad this is supposed to look crinkled," she said, holding it up.

After they changed into more comfortable clothes, they decided to take a walk. "But if it gets too hot, I'm diving into the nearest bar for a cold iced tea," Rachael stated.

"You mean as in Long Island iced tea?" Frankie was aghast, referring to the alcoholic drink that consisted of vodka, rum, gin, tequila, and sour mix.

"Oh no. Not yet. I don't want to start this trip schnockered or with a hangover."

"Good thinking," Frankie answered.

They both switched handbags to something more summery and tropical. Rachael had a pink straw bag that matched her pink sundress and pink sandals. Frankie's midi dress was white, and she opted for a plain natural straw tote and a pair of natural espadrilles. Frankie resisted the urge to tell Rachael that she looked like a Popsicle stick. A cute one, no doubt. Maybe she should say something, especially when Rachael slipped on a matching pair of sunglasses.

Using one of Rachael's favorite words, Frankie said, "OK,

chica. I think that's more than enough pink. You're starting to look like a Popsicle stick."

"Too much?" Rachael asked casually. "Good. That was the whole idea." She gave a little samba dance on the sidewalk.

Frankie rolled her eyes and laughed. "I should have known." Within minutes, Rachael was getting catcalls from men driving by. They were also beeping their horns.

"See? I'm practicing." Rachael grinned.

"And you are doing a splendid job."

As they passed a little Cuban café, Frankie stopped and said, "Let's get a Cuban coffee. I haven't had one in a long time." She looked at Rachael. "Although I don't think you need any caffeine."

"Oh stop. I'm doing just fine. That is, unless I'm embarrassing you." Rachael gave her a sideways look.

"Me? I do well enough on my own, thank you," Frankie said in a self-deprecating way.

"*Imposible*," Rachael answered in Spanish.

"I know we haven't spent a lot of time together over the past ten years, but believe me, I've pulled a few whoppers."

"Care to share?" Rachael asked sincerely.

"Oh, there was the time when I didn't see the ice in front of my building and landed on my ass. In front of my boss." Frankie took a gulp. "That wouldn't have been so bad except my wool skirt went up around my waist."

"You were wearing underwear, I presume?" Rachael eyed her.

"Of course I was. Even tights. But it was embarrassing, nonetheless. Who wants to have their boss see you butt-plant yourself on the sidewalk at Rockefeller Center?"

"Good point." Rachael mamboed her way between the tightly positioned tables. A young Latino man approached them. "Good afternoon. What may I get you?"

Rachael was in a feisty mood. "That all depends on what you have to offer." She gave him a wink.

"Don't pay any attention to her. They only let her out of the institution once a month," Frankie said with a straight face. The man looked perplexed until both women burst out laughing.

"Sorry. I'm just having some fun." Rachael calmed the alarmed waiter. "Café Cubano and a *pastelito, por favor!*"

Frankie held up two fingers. "*¡Dos, por favor!*" She stuck out her tongue at Rachael. "See, I can speak Spanish, too."

The waiter brought the coffees and pastries a few minutes later as Rachael and Frankie talked about life, where they had started, and where they were now. Both agreed life could be challenging, and it was how you chose to deal with it that mattered. Hanging on to anger and resentment was a waste of time and valuable energy. Frankie was enjoying their conversation. Her interaction with Rachael over the past decade had been minimal. A few lunches every other year. You really couldn't get into many deep exchanges. It was refreshing. Rachael had turned out to be a very successful, even-tempered woman. Her wild streak was still there, but she had learned to channel it better.

"So what was up with the boyfriend merry-go-round this year? I mean, we know your penchant for flirtations. Were you still this way when you were with Greg?" Frankie asked, hoping she hadn't stepped over the line.

"This year was my year to prove to my mother that there were a lot of frogs out there and finding a good partner wasn't as easy as one would think. Did people really settle years ago? Or were people different?"

Frankie thought for a moment. "I think people are more contemplative as to what makes them happy and aren't willing to settle for something that won't. Look at your own life.

You couldn't suck it up and pretend everything was 'happily-ever-after' anymore. Enough was enough."

"You got that right, sister." Rachael took a bite of her creamy *pastelito*.

"Seriously. When you start to look around and see so many unhappy faces, you have to think 'Wow, is that guy miserable, or what?' I see it at work all the time. People always say, 'I can't wait to retire.' " Frankie shrugged. "What's ironic is that over the past thirty years, thousands of self-help books have been published and millions of copies have been sold. True, many people seemed to have gotten 'in tune,' "—Frankie used air quotes—"but I don't think that very many people actually did anything about it. Probably made them even more miserable."

"*¡Exactamente!*" Rachael exclaimed. "I was so miserable being married to Greg. But I think part of the problem with people in general is that they settle. They think they're doing the right and proper thing. Look how many people get married right after high school or even college. I waited a couple of years, but I should have waited longer. I settled because of the pressure I was getting from my family. And you're right. I couldn't suck it up anymore." Rachael looked at Frankie. "What? You have that look."

"What look?" Frankie asked.

"The one where you are pondering the great questions of life." Rachael winked.

"I was wondering what percentage of positive outcomes actually came out of all those books. You know, from way back to *I'm OK—You're OK*, *The Celestine Prophecy*, *The Power of Letting Go*. There are a zillion of them."

"And I think I read all of them." Rachael took another sip of her coffee.

"Hmmm. Come to think of it, there's only been one big

bestseller. You probably read *Girl, Wash Your Face*. That was a good one actually."

"Yep. Read it. It's about believing in yourself instead of the lies you're told. But that's been a common theme for years. As I said, I've read all of them. All right, I am obviously exaggerating, but I've actually read well over a hundred."

"And look. You are your own woman. You have a successful business, and are on a vacation with some of your favorite gal pals."

"Here's to that and here's to us." Rachael clinked her demitasse cup against Frankie's.

"Yes. Here's to us." Frankie agreed.

Miami International Airport was bustling by late afternoon. Amy checked the overhead monitors and saw that Nina's flight had already arrived and had a luggage carousel assigned. Amy heaved her large rolling bag off the slow-moving ramp and proceeded to the baggage claim area, where she would meet up with Nina.

From the crowd, she heard "Doll-face!" and recognized the voice immediately. Amy waved as Nina zigzagged her way through the crowd, trying not to run over anyone's toes with her suitcase. Nina let go of the bulky bag and gave Amy a big bear hug. "Lovin' that hair." She tousled the light pink bob.

Amy gave her a squeeze. "I can't believe we're really doing this. I can't wait to set sail for the glorious Caribbean." Amy was all atwitter.

"Come on. Let's grab a taxi." Nina glanced down at Amy's suitcase. "Is that all you have?"

"Yes. Believe me, it is packed to the gills. But the woman who helped me pick out the clothes put together a lot of mix-

and-match items. I'm so excited!" Amy's pink cheeks were just a deeper shade than her hair.

They inched their way through the other passengers who were eager to retrieve their belongings. As soon as the sliding doors opened, Nina exclaimed, "Oh, there goes my hair!" She let out a big guffaw.

"You have great hair!" Amy reassured her.

"If you like lots of curls. And, boy, am I gonna have them in a few seconds!" They waited for the light to change in the crosswalk. Nina nodded to the gentleman in the yellow vest who was directing people to different lines and shuttles. She tilted her head in the direction of the taxi stand. He pointed to a stanchion where several people waited their turn.

"Whew, it is humid, isn't it?" Amy started to feel the perspiration trickle down her neck. "I'm not used to this."

"Me either! I don't know how Frankie managed to finish four years of college in this steam bath."

After fidgeting for several minutes, it was their turn. "Vie Vay, please," Nina instructed the driver.

It was rush hour, and though the traffic was lighter than usual, it was still terribly slow. The cab driver was telling them how much the city had grown in the past several years and how worried he was about future hurricanes. Nina wondered how many times he had recited his soliloquy. The women chatted about what they were planning on eating and drinking and what sites they would visit when the ship docked at each port.

"I want to do that sting-ray-petting thing," Amy said whimsically.

"Ew, I don't know if I want to pet anything with the name 'sting' in it, unless it's the musician!" She laughed.

"Oh, it's supposed to be supersafe," Amy assured her. "I read all about it." Amy was the brainiac, and research was her thing.

"I'll check the ship's activity list to see what else is available."

"There are other types of snorkeling, horseback riding, charter boats, but who wants to get on another boat after being on one? You know what I mean?" Amy asked innocently. "Anyway, George Town is a tender port, which means the ship doesn't actually dock at the port. We take a smaller boat to the island."

Nina smiled. "Leave it to you to get every detail down."

"Nah. Just a few tidbits."

The taxi pulled in front of the hotel, and the driver helped the women with their luggage. A bellman approached them.

"Hi. We're checking in for the night." Amy's enthusiasm was palpable. "We're meeting our friends and going on a cruise."

"Oh yes, I met them earlier today." He looked at the two suitcases and the carry-ons. "That's all you've got?"

"Yes," Nina answered.

The bellman let out a low chuckle. "You should see what your friends brought."

Nina and Amy looked at each other. "Rachael."

"Follow me." The bellman escorted them to the front desk and waited for them to get their keycards.

Amy could barely contain herself. "I am so excited."

"Yes, we can tell." Nina gave her a wink.

The three clambered into the elevator, and the bellman wheeled their suitcases to their suite. Loud knocking followed.

"Let us in." Squeals of laughter were greeted by Frankie and Rachael.

"Don't you have keys?" Rachael asked.

"Yes. We just wanted to make a scene." Nina jerked her thumb in Amy's direction.

"I can't believe we're doing this," became Amy's mantra.

"Me either," Frankie replied, giving the pink-haired genius a kiss on the cheek.

The bellman stood patiently as the women hugged each other, all talking at the same time. Finally, Nina realized he had been standing in the hallway waiting for instructions as to where he should unload his cart. "Sorry. We haven't seen each other in a while." She dug into her tote bag and pulled out a ten-dollar bill and handed it over to him.

Frankie chimed in. "Nina, your stuff goes with mine." She indicated for the bellman to put Nina's suitcase in her room. Amy, you'll go with Rachael. That's if there's enough room for your stuff!" She laughed.

"Ha. Ha," Rachael retorted.

"Enjoy your cruise, ladies. I'm off tomorrow, so someone else will help you with your bags." He noticed they weren't paying any attention, so he disappeared down the hallway.

The two-room, two-bathroom suite felt like a rich-girl sorority house. And the giggles and laughter made it even more so.

Nina wanted to do a quick change before dinner. Amy did the same. Within a few short minutes, the four of them were ready for some Peruvian food.

The restaurant was within walking distance of the hotel, but they all agreed that the humidity was stifling.

"How on earth did you survive this sweatbox for four years?" Nina asked.

"It didn't seem as bad back then," Frankie replied.

"In point of fact, it wasn't," Amy chimed in. "Some people, especially some politicians, may deny global warming and climate change, but facts are facts. There are hot spots all over the country where the temperature has risen 1.8 degrees Celsius. In the last ten years, the temperature has climbed faster than it has since the Ice Age."

"Great. We're doomed." Nina smirked.

"Just sayin'," Amy replied with confidence.

"Sure feels hotter," Frankie noted.

"One more factoid. The humidity in Miami has grown to an average of 87 percent a day."

"No wonder my hair looks like I stuck my finger in an electric socket," Nina remarked.

The women laughed and picked up their pace.

A beautiful Peruvian woman greeted them at the hostess station. "Good evening. Welcome to Pollos and Jarras. Will there be four for dinner?" she asked in an accent Rachael recognized from her brief romance with Paulo. She spoke to the woman in Spanish, telling her how much she had loved visiting Peru.

"Such a show-off," Nina muttered jokingly.

"Huh?" Frankie was distracted by the Christmas decorations. "Check it out. Look at all the owl ornaments. They're made from gourds." She pointed to the artificial tree, where over a dozen were hung. "At least it looks like a Christmas tree." She snickered. "Wow, look at this one." It was a hand-carved gourd with miniature nativity figurines.

"Cool. And these dolls."

The hostess was pleased that her guests appreciated the traditional décor. "Yes, those are Andean angels." She gestured toward a table in the corner, where several were displayed on a shelf. "Please." She motioned for them to sit.

"Gracias," Rachael replied. As soon as the woman was no longer in earshot, she continued. "She said this is a special table reserved for particular guests of the owners. So there." She put on a stubborn expression.

"We knew you would come in handy." Frankie clapped Rachael on the shoulder.

"I may have to charge you guys for translating." She motioned for the handsome waiter to come over and proceeded to order drinks for everyone in Spanish. A lot of chatting went on between them as Rachael's three friends chuckled and shook their heads.

Frankie leaned in. "For real. She is going to come in handy."

"*Sí, cuatro* Pisco Sour! *¡Ceviche, aji de gallina, y lomo saltado! ¡Por favor! ¡Nosotros compartiremos!*" She flashed him a dazzling smile.

"OK. Clue us in." Nina spoke first.

Rachael propped her elbow on the table and coyly placed her fingers under her chin. She batted her eyelashes again. Nina was about to blow a gasket. It had been a long day. Sensing Nina's annoyance, Frankie gave her a slight kick under the table. The kind your mother gave you if you were misbehaving in public. Not enough to hurt. Just enough to say, "That's enough."

Nina took an exceptionally long inhale and returned the kick to Frankie.

Both women were trying not to giggle at this point.

Rachael began to explain. "The Pisco Sour is the traditional Peruvian drink. It's made with Pisco, a type of brandy, but it's a far cry from a well-aged cognac." She tossed her head back, being completely animated. "Anyway, it's similar to grappa, but the cocktail itself is made with lime juice, simple syrup, egg whites . . . you even get protein with your drink . . . then it's finished off with bitters."

"Sounds interesting." Amy pondered the concoction.

Rachael continued with less flamboyance but still excited. "We'll start with ceviche, marinated shellfish, and then *aji de gallina*, a shredded chicken dish in a bit of a creamy sauce." She took a breath. "And we'll have *lomo saltado*. It's a stir-fried beef with chilis, tomatoes, and onions, with a dash of soy sauce. It's served with either potatoes or rice."

"Yum. Sounds delicious," Frankie cooed.

"Do you think we could get some bread?" Nina asked. "I'm really hungry. I don't want to drink that potion on an empty stomach."

"Good idea. I've hardly eaten all day, myself. Airport food on the run isn't the best," Amy concurred.

Rachael looked over in the waiter's direction and gave him a nod. He hurried over to the table. *"¿Podemos comer pan, por favor?"* she asked casually.

"¡Sí, señora!" He nodded and took two steps backward before he turned to the kitchen.

Rachael gave the others a wink. "I *am* handy, ain't I?"

The waiter returned immediately with a basket containing a variety of breads. *Pan de maíz,* made with corn; *pan chapla* with anise seeds; and *pan chapata,* similar to Italian ciabatta bread.

The women dug into the basket as if they hadn't eaten in days.

"These are so aromatic," Nina exclaimed, as she sniffed a piece of the *chapla.*

The waiter returned with their Pisco Sours. Everyone clinked glasses. "Here's to a fabulous voyage."

"I'm going to be a blimp by the time this trip is over." Amy ripped a chunk off the *chapata.*

"Now, ladies, we mustn't think of such things while we are on vacation. Including work." Frankie was matter-of-fact.

"Agreed," Nina said after she swallowed a piece. "Besides, I have no one to talk to anyway."

Everyone stopped gabbing and munching. "What do you mean?" Amy asked.

Frankie was the only person who knew the situation and placed her hand on Nina's arm to give her moral support. Nina addressed the group. "They canceled the show."

"What? Oh no." Amy gasped.

"That's terrible. Did you have any idea it was going to happen?" Rachael asked.

"There were some hints and signs. Two of the major players wanted to go on to other projects, and the network didn't think it was worthwhile to try to replace them. Replacing a secondary character, like me for example, is done all the time, but not the stars."

"So what are you going to do now?" Amy was almost fretful.

"I'm flying to New York after this. I have a meeting with a screenwriter who is developing something for television."

"Will you be in it?" Amy asked.

"No. He wants me to help him write the script." Nina went on to explain, "We worked on a few things a couple of years ago, and he liked my suggestions. In fact, he once told me I should consider writing for TV, but I was wrapped up in the show." She shrugged.

"Would it be a paying gig?" Rachael, the reformed business manager, queried. "Sorry. Don't mean to be nosy, but I know what can happen when you're not paying attention to the cash flow."

"Oh, believe me, I know all about cash flow. It seems to flow in one direction," Nina quipped.

"So what's the plan?" Frankie interjected. She and Nina hadn't gotten that far in their earlier chat.

"I have enough money to last me for a few months. If this gig with Owen pans out, I'll get paid well enough to move back to my parents' house!" Nina cackled. "Actually, I had been thinking about my career and what I had to do next."

"And?" Rachael egged her on.

"And I realized I had to do *something*. Anything besides what I had been doing." Nina took a sip of her cocktail and gave it a sour look. "Well, the name is apropos. Anyway, I reached out to Owen and said I was looking for a change and remembered what he had said to me."

"Sounds like he's interested." Frankie's face lit up. "Are you seriously thinking of moving back East?"

"Yes, I am. My folks spend a good part of the year in Florida, so I would have the house to myself for at least five months. By then I should have a better idea of where my floundering career is going. And Ridgewood is an easy commute to the city.

"I'm fairly sure it's a done deal with Owen. I don't want to jinx it, but he said the job is mine if I want it. It's a matter of whether or not I like the concept and where he's taking the story, blah, blah, blah."

"Who cares where he takes the story!" Rachael exclaimed.

"I agree." Frankie spoke up. "It's an opportunity for you to hit reset, and you'll have time to figure out a plan as you go. We know that no matter how much we plan, God often has a totally different idea in mind for us."

Rachael cackled, recalling her failed marriage. "If not Him, it would be your parents." Her easy laughter was contagious, and the other women joined in.

"Well, this is very exciting news." Frankie put her arm around Nina's shoulders. "We'll be able to hang out. Especially if you're working in the city." Frankie raised her glass. "Here's to Nina's new adventure."

"Hear. Hear," Amy cheered.

"*Salud,*" came from Rachael.

"*Buona fortuna,*" toasted Frankie.

Nina's eyes welled up with tears. "I am so, so happy we reconnected and that we're going on this trip."

"*Chica,* we are *already* on this trip. *¡Fabulosa!*" Rachael was excited, too. She would have a few gal pals to hang around with. Women who knew her. More importantly, who understood her.

Nina broke into a huge smile. "There was a reason we met at that reunion. The one I almost skipped. Isn't it funny, though? I was going to New York to audition for a part that I didn't get but I met up with you guys, and here we are."

"Serendipitous, I would say." Frankie raised her eyebrows a few times.

"Oh my goodness." Amy watched the parade of food heading in their direction. "That looks scrumptious."

"And it smells divine," Frankie said.

The waiter plated the food on individual dishes, dividing it among the four of them. They had to resist smacking their lips.

Nina rubbed her hands together, ready to dig in, but Frankie stopped her. "Do you mind if we give thanks?"

Nina broke into a big smile. "I think that would be most appropriate."

The women clasped hands and bowed their heads. Frankie spoke softly. "Thank you for this wonderful meal, our health, our families, our good fortune, and all the love. Amen."

"Amen, sister," Rachael exclaimed. "Now let's eat."

Moans and groans of delight echoed among them. The waiter watched from several feet away and smiled in satisfaction.

"*¡Muy bien!*" Rachael gave him the thumbs-up. She remembered that in South America the OK sign we make with our thumb and forefinger has a totally different meaning. Thumbs-up was the way to go.

Almost two hours later, they finished their meal. Amy stretched, her multiple bangle bracelets jangling. "I'm bushed."

"Me too." Frankie stifled a yawn.

"*Yo también*," Rachael concurred.

"As am I." Nina finished the round of exhaustion.

They divided the check and gave the waiter a handsome tip.

"*¡Feliz Navidad!*" Everyone exchanged well-wishes for the holidays.

The women returned to the hotel and called it a night. It was just the beginning.

Chapter Thirteen

Day 1
Port of Miami to Key West

As the women were packing their suitcases, Frankie reminded them to pack a change of clothes and whatever essentials they might need before their luggage got to their staterooms. "This might be a major challenge for you, Rachael. Pick one outfit. One. *Capisce?*"

"OK. Fine."

"Unless you want to be lugging your luggage around, you may want to consider keeping it light," Nina interjected.

Rachael had five different outfits lying across the bed. "What do you think?" She pointed to a pair of red capri pants and a white sleeveless blouse with red piping.

"I suppose you have a tote bag, shoes, hat, and sunglasses to match?"

"It wouldn't be me if I didn't," Rachael proclaimed.

"We'd better check with each other to make sure we're not dressing too much alike," Frankie joked.

"I doubt that will happen." Nina gave her thumb a yank in Rachael's direction.

"Good point."

"Well, none of you have pink hair, so I think I'm safe," Amy added.

"Come on, ladies. We need to shake a leg if we're going to get all of our bags out the door. We're probably going to need two cabs. I'll call the front desk so we don't waste too much time."

Frankie called down and asked for two taxis, probably vans or SUVs. Shortly, a bellman appeared at the door of the suite with two rolling carts. "Ricky, from yesterday, told me you might need these."

"Sharp guy," Nina said. Then she muttered to Frankie, "The nice tip we gave him paid off."

Clark, the bellman, began loading the carts with everyone's belongings. Frankie counted the bags. Each had been tagged with the tickets they needed for the cruise. There were nine, not including their tote bags. She figured twenty dollars should be enough.

As they made their way down the hall, Frankie wondered if everyone and everything would fit in the elevator. Clark made a suggestion. "You ladies take this elevator. I'll meet you in the lobby."

"Brilliant," Nina exclaimed, as the four women entered the elevator and pushed the button for the lobby.

Frankie gazed at her friends. "I must say, we look pretty terrific."

"Watch out, sailors, here we come!" Rachael just had to throw that in.

Frankie looked at Nina. "Should I tell her, or do you want to?"

"Tell her what?"

"That this isn't Fleet Week, and we're on a singles cruise. Not a navy invasion."

"I heard that," Rachael quipped. "Can't I please have

some fun? You know I'm being campy for fun." She looked at her friends. "Right?"

"Right?" she repeated.

Nina started, "Babycakes, we love you, but sometimes you are over the top." There, she had said it.

"I know," Rachael blurted out. "I thought you realized I was just putting on a show. It's fun."

"Fun for?" Nina asked.

"For me?" Rachael questioned her in a kind way. "Am I really being that obnoxious that you can't appreciate the underlying humor in it?"

Nina paused before she answered. "That is an exceptionally good question. I guess I was tossing you into the barrel of 'people who pretend too much.'" Nina paused. "It's the Hollywood thing. Everyone there is over the top."

Rachael thought for a moment. "I never thought about it that way. You must be sick of people like me." Rachael placed her arm on Nina's shoulder. "I'm just trying to have fun, Nina. It's not easy being a mom with a jerk for an ex and trying to run a business. I need to let loose for a few days."

Nina gave her a big hug. "Sorry, babe. I think it's a knee-jerk reaction. *Please.* Have all the fun you want. Maybe it will rub off on me."

Rachael placed her elbow on Nina's back and started massaging her shoulder blades. "I'm working on it. How's this?"

"Oh, honey pie. I think you're on to something."

The elevator's door opened, and the women marched out as if they were on a mission. And they were.

Clark leaned lazily against the two carts outside on the sidewalk, waiting for one of the vans' drivers to open the cargo area. Rachael's things would probably take up most of it.

They dropped their keys in the box and headed in Clark's direction, going two at a time through the revolving doors, laughing like hyenas. Clark and the two van drivers managed to shove the luggage into the waiting vehicles, and the women jumped in. Amy couldn't stop giggling. "I'm so excited."

"We heard you the first half-dozen times," Nina said drolly.

"Oh, stop being such a sourpuss." Amy smacked her on the arm.

"Kidding." Nina broke into a huge smile. "I'm really excited, too. I cannot tell you how much I need this trip."

"The salt air, sun, and fun will do you good." Amy was naturally perky.

"No doubt."

The two vehicles pulled away from the hotel and headed to the port. The cabs took them through a tunnel that brought them to the docks, where over a dozen cruise ships were waiting. Their ship was docked at Terminal A. Within a few minutes, they arrived at the curb, where a porter was waiting with a dolly. He checked the bags to ensure they were properly marked for their cruise and pointed to the terminal entrance. "Right that way, ladies. Enjoy."

Amy dug into her bag and pulled out a twenty-dollar bill and handed it to the porter. They must have dropped over one hundred dollars so far in tips. But they weren't going to worry about it now. Each knew in advance that this wasn't going to be a cheap getaway. They were going to spoil themselves. They all deserved it.

The port terminal was similar to an airport's. Once they went through security, they approached the area for passenger registration, where they were handed their keycards.

The attendant told them the ship would be ready to board in an hour and they could relax in the lounge area. There would be an announcement when they could board.

Amy resisted the temptation to repeat her mantra.

"Go ahead. I know you want to say it," Nina teased.

"But it's true! I am so excited." Amy clapped her hands with glee.

They found seats in the lounge area and plunked themselves down. Frankie could feel the tension start to leave her body. It had been a grueling year for publishing. Nina stretched out her long legs, allowing herself to relax. Rachael was checking out all the other people in the area, and Amy was snapping photos. She caught Nina in a yawn. "You better delete that right now, young lady. We will have no candid shots during this trip." She was half-serious.

"Back to being Miss Cranky Pants?" Amy made a face.

Nina laughed. "No. Miss-Please-Don't-Take-My-Photo-Unless-I'm-Ready-and-Smiling Pants. Deal?"

"Deal," Amy replied, with a big fake frown. Nina leaned back in the chair and closed her eyes. She peeked for a second to make sure Amy wasn't trying to be Annie Leibovitz, the famous photographer. "You can relax." Amy put her phone back into her tote bag.

"That's a good idea," Frankie said, nodding to Amy's gesture. "Let's try to unplug ourselves as much as possible."

"I'm all for that," Nina muttered, without bothering to open her eyes.

"I'll have to check my e-mail from time to time," Amy said sheepishly.

"Why? Can't they make biological warfare without you?" Nina muttered, her eyes still closed.

"Ha. We don't do that," Amy protested. "At least I don't think we do." She tapped her forefinger to her chin. "Come to think of it, they don't really tell us who the end user is." She made a scrunchy face. "Well, all the more reason I hope I get this job I've been waiting to hear about."

Nina bolted upright. "Job? I thought you had the dream job. Gobs of money."

"To be honest, it's lost its shine. I'm bored. B-O-R-E-D. Bored."

Amy was interrupted with an announcement. "Now boarding the *Medallion of the Seas*."

"Ha," Amy chirped. "Speaking of board. Let's go."

The women were giddy as they made their way up the glass gangway, where they were welcomed by the happy sounds of steel drums playing. The captain and several crew members formed a reception line, greeting the passengers as they boarded. "Welcome to the *Medallion of the Seas*."

"Glad you can join us." Everyone was smiling and shaking hands. "We're here to make your trip enjoyable."

"Your staterooms should be ready in an hour. And your luggage should be delivered shortly thereafter," the bosun said in a deep baritone voice. "Complimentary cocktails are being served on the Sundeck Lounge."

"Ooh-la-la," Rachael responded.

"You just can't turn it off, can you?" Nina chuckled and shook her head.

"Watch and learn, *chica*," Rachael said slyly.

"I could use a few pointers, myself," Frankie added.

As expected, Rachael took the lead. "Can you direct us there, sir?"

The bosun was in his late fifties, trim and proper. "Follow the railing." He indicated with a nod. "You can't miss it. Enjoy."

"Oh, we shall." Rachael was close to doing a rumba dance, but Nina gave her a tug.

"This way, missy." Nina put her arm around Rachael. "I really do need some lessons in flirtation."

"You? Why do you say that?" Rachael was surprised that this successful actress would need help in that area.

"Because being in the business I'm in, one cannot flirt

without thinking it through to the point where you just don't bother."

"I don't get it," Rachael replied, nodding and smiling to the other passengers.

"I guess I'm just outta steam."

"Not to worry. We'll fix that." The sounds of the music continued, and Rachael moved to the rhythm.

As they were reaching the open deck area, Amy stopped short.

"What?" Nina asked. "Everything all right?"

"Huh. I thought I saw someone who looked like my father."

"Your father?" the other three said in unison.

"Must be the sea air." Amy shrugged it off. "Or maybe it's guilt for not spending any of the holidays with him." She snickered. Ready to change the subject, she turned to Rachael. "So tell me, what's the difference between ska, reggae, and calypso?" Amy asked.

"Ska originated in Jamaica sometime in the early fifties. The groups often had horn sections. The group The Specials had a hit single about ten years ago called 'A Message to You, Rudy.' You'd recognize it if you heard it. *'Stop your messing around . . . Rudy, a message to you.'*" Rachael moved her hips as she sang the lyrics. "In the late sixties, reggae, which is a slower version of ska, came along. You know the Bob Marley song, 'One Love, One Heart'?" Again she sang the first verse. "That's reggae."

"But we're not going to Jamaica." Amy looked confused.

"No, but reggae, ska, calypso are considered music of the Caribbean. When we get to Mexico, you'll hear something different, like mariachi, then meringue in Belize."

Frankie chuckled. "Boy, Rachael, you *are* coming in handy."

Rachael wiggled her hips. "*¡Con mucho gusto!*"

There were several dozen people milling about the deck. A

different steel-drum band was playing music similar to what they had heard when they boarded the ship. There were several bars set up, each with colorful flags and floral arrangements of white orchids and gold ribbon. The area was flanked with large wooden teak planters filled with exotic flowers. Gold and silver stars dotted the display. Hints of the holidays were all around, but without the palm trees with Christmas lights.

The four women approached one of the bars and introduced themselves to the bartender. His name was Roger.

"Good afternoon, ladies. May I present our signature drink?" he asked in a Caribbean accent.

"It looks very pretty," Amy cooed.

"And it is delicious, I can assure you." He smiled and handed each of them a pink frothy drink topped with a small colorful umbrella and matching straw.

Frankie took a sip. "I'm liking this already."

Rachael leaned in. "So, Roger, what is your favorite part of this cruise?"

"Watching people enjoy themselves." Roger grinned.

"Excellent answer," Nina replied. "That's what we need. Enjoyment."

"Oh, I am certain you lovely ladies will find much enjoyment. And if you cannot, then we will have to throw you overboard." He let out a huge laugh. "We don't want anyone leaving this ship who hasn't had a good experience. Unbelievably bad publicity." He laughed again.

The women walked around, leisurely eyeing up the competition and the men. Rachael muttered a few "not too bad"s as they smiled their way through the crowd. They all greeted each other as if they had a secret salutation: *I know you're probably mortified that you are on this cruise.* A few raised their eyebrows in acknowledgment of the covert greeting. It was almost comical.

Nina found herself looking at a couple of men and laughing. At one point, she felt compelled to approach one of them, and say, "I'm not laughing at you." She made a slight sweeping gesture with her hand. "I'm laughing at all this."

He smiled back. "Yeah. What are we doing here? You seem normal."

Nina burst out laughing. "Clearly, we haven't met. I'm Nina."

He chuckled in return. "I'm Richard." He looked at her again. "I don't want to sound forward, but you look familiar."

"I get that a lot." Nina smiled slyly, not wanting to totally identify herself. Heaven forbid someone posted a photo of her on a singles cruise. It was bad enough that the show had been canceled. She didn't want to be the source of mockery on a show like TMZ or one of those other horrid tell-all gossip shows.

The second mate of the ship was weaving his way through the crowd, announcing that their staterooms were ready.

Nina smiled at Richard. "See you around the campus." She raised her tropical drink as a toast.

"Sooo . . . who was that?" Rachael pried.

"That was Richard," Nina said with a matter-of-fact tone.

"And?" Rachel continued to press her.

"And he said he thought he recognized me, and I didn't want to get into it." Nina took the last sip through the straw, making a gurgling sound.

"I can understand that, especially now that the show is canceled and you don't know what you're doing next," Frankie said.

"*¡Exactamente!*" Nina winked at Rachael. "See, I can speak Spanish, too."

"Well, I'm proud of you. You actually walked up to a man and said hello," Amy said.

"I didn't want him to think we were laughing at him."

"Good icebreaker." Frankie snickered. "We set sail in four hours." Frankie looked at her watch. "Shall we?"

"Yes, we shall," Nina answered, followed by Amy and Rachael.

The ship was massive but not as large as the mega liners. The signage was clear, making it easy for them to navigate their way to their staterooms. Each of them had her own, with a veranda. The staterooms were large enough to accommodate two people, but they all agreed it would be worth the extra charge to have some privacy at the end of the day. Seven nights with another person in a relatively small space could get on your nerves.

The staterooms were elegant, each with a queen-size bed, sofa, large-screen television, and dresser with a minibar. The bathroom was modern and efficient, with enough room to turn around. The balconies had two chairs and a small cocktail table. As Frankie had suspected from what she could see in the brochures, the stateroom was about the same size as her entire apartment.

All their staterooms were in a row, so they had easy access to one another. Their challenge would be keeping their doors closed. The other challenge would be keeping the noise down. Not that they planned on having a fraternity-house-type party. Nope. It was just that they had a habit of laughing a lot. Laughing loudly. And laughing for hours.

Their luggage hadn't arrived at their staterooms yet, so they decided to follow the advice of the agent and change into the clothes they had packed in their tote bags. Before they had left the hotel, they discussed wardrobe options, taking care to not dress alike. Not that they didn't have their own individual taste in clothes. But any one of them could show up wearing navy blue with polka dots. It could be a sundress, jumpsuit, blouse, duster, or bandana.

A manifest on each of their dressers listed the activities for the evening, restaurants, and entertainment. A "Welcome Mix and Mingle" cocktail party was being held in the large atrium from five to six. Guests had a variety of options for dinner between six and nine. There were a number of activities posted from nine until midnight, including:

- Karaoke
- Dance Lessons with the world-renowned Henry Dugan
- Darts
- Trivia Contest
- Magic Show
- Piano Bar
- Disco

There didn't appear to be any forced fun. Yet. But none of the items on the list seemed appealing to most of them, so they decided to play it by ear. Rachael, on the other hand, fully intended to take advantage of Henry Dugan's presence on the ship. Once they were finished with dinner, the others would decide what level of humiliation they would force upon themselves.

It was only two, so they had plenty of time to explore the ship. The plan was to return to their staterooms to change into something a little jazzier for the evening once their luggage was delivered.

All four women exited their staterooms at the same time, practically bumping into each other. They were so caught up in their exuberance that they didn't notice another passenger exiting his stateroom as well. They practically knocked him over. Naturally, that caused even more commotion, creating more giggles and guffaws. The poor guy thought he was being ambushed by a gaggle of geese.

Frankie was the first one to regain her composure. "We are so sorry." But it was one of those situations where the harder you laughed, the more you laughed. The gentleman couldn't help but snicker as well. It was nice to see cheerful people.

"No worries. We're here to have fun. I believe it's manda-
tory. The name is Peter. I suppose we'll be seeing a lot of each
other." His smooth voice was enticing.

Frankie pointed to her sternum. "Frankie."

"Amy." She raised her hand.

"Nina."

"Rachael."

"Good to meet you all," Peter replied.

"You say that now," Frankie joked.

He chuckled and gave a little salute. "Off to the festivities."

Rachel was looking up at the ceiling.

"What are you looking at?" Amy asked.

"Looking *for*, dear. Looking *for*. I am looking for mistletoe."

"Oh, jeez." Nina linked her arm through Rachael's. "We
are most definitely going to have to put you on a leash."

They walked the entire length of the outside deck, smiling
and greeting the other guests. "This isn't too bad," Nina admitted. "When do we actually set sail?"

"I think sometime around five." Frankie recalled reading
that in the brochure.

"Wow. There's a chunk of stuff to do." Amy was dizzy,
thinking about all the activities ahead. Not necessarily those
that were listed on the manifest. But she knew that tomorrow
there would be an entire list of new things once they reached
Key West. The first night was just a warm-up. At least that's
what she hoped. One thing was certain. She was going to pet
a stingray when they landed at Grand Cayman.

They followed the signs to the deck for the atrium, to
check out the lay of the land. It was a large area, similar to an
indoor mall, surrounded by shops and cafés. White poinsettias were in abundance. Some were stacked to look like
Christmas trees, with gold stars at the top. It was like a small
holiday village floating on the open sea.

Frankie and Nina spotted an interesting gift shop with

handmade jewelry. Frankie gave Nina a nod. "We're going to check this place out."

Amy stopped abruptly once again. "I think I'm hallucinating."

"What's the matter?" Nina asked.

"I could swear that I saw my father again. Something just doesn't feel right."

"Get off the guilt train," Rachael proclaimed.

"Like I said, must be the sea air." Amy sighed.

"We haven't left the port yet, sweet cakes," Nina reminded her. "Maybe you're a bit jet-lagged. It's been a busy couple of days."

"Yeah. Maybe. I think I'll go back to my room and take a nap."

Frankie gave Nina a sign indicating that she would go with Amy.

Nina nodded in agreement.

"I'll go with you," Frankie offered.

"I'm OK. But I think a nap would be good. We have a couple of hours. See you guys back in the staterooms." Amy turned, and Frankie followed her. Amy seemed a little spooked.

Nina looked at Rachael. "Interested in some local artistic baubles?"

"Sure. Why not." They headed to the shop with the sparkly jewelry in the window.

As Frankie and Amy were walking back to their staterooms, Amy caught Frankie's arm. "I never finished telling you guys that I'm a candidate for an associate professorship at MIT."

"Really? That's fantastic." Frankie was genuinely pleased. She knew that Amy loved Cambridge and Boston and missed the East Coast.

"Yes. Maybe that's why I'm feeling a little, I don't know, weird."

"You're nervous. That's normal." Frankie put her arm around Amy. "So tell me about it."

"I haven't been thrilled about where I am now. We can work on developing a product and never know the end result. Too many secrets. It's unnerving. As beautiful as Santa Clara is, I've always felt like a duck out of water there. I have too much Northeast in me." She giggled. "If I get the job, I'll start as an associate professor. The downside is that the pay is only about half of what I'm making now. The upside is that I can find an apartment for a lot less than I'm paying. I've tucked away some money, so I'll be OK for a while. If I get some papers published in academic journals, I'll get merit pay and eventually be a full professor."

"You've really given this a lot of thought," Frankie noted.

"Yes. I'll be closer to my folks, too." She rolled her eyes.

Frankie smiled. "I know you love them."

"Most of the time." Amy snickered.

They came to their staterooms. "You sure you're gonna be OK?" Frankie looked her straight in the face.

"Yes."

"Just knock or send me a text. I'll be right next door." Frankie went into her stateroom and sent a quick text to Nina and Rachael.

Amy is OK. I'm in my room. Knock when you get back. Luggage is here.

Frankie got a quick thumbs-up emoji from them. She spotted one of her suitcases on the stand and the other next to it on the floor. The crew had obviously delivered the luggage while the women were touring the ship. Frankie busied herself unpacking and trying to smooth out any wrinkles in her clothes. She had a plastic spray bottle in her bag. She filled it with warm water and proceeded to spray one of her dresses and smooth it out. A half-assed steam job, but it worked. After she finished putting her clothes away, she went out on the balcony and opened a bottle of Pellegrino water. Even though the ship hadn't left the dock, she was feeling the tension ease out of her body. The calypso band, the special cocktail, and the laughs had fired up her endorphins. She checked her watch again.

Frankie could hear the jocularity in the hallway coming from Rachael and Nina as they got closer to her door. She stuck her head out. "I think Peter asked to have his room changed."

Rachael skidded to a halt. "Seriously?"

"Nah. But I wouldn't be surprised!" Frankie chuckled.

Amy opened her door. "Hey. Keep it down," she joked.

"You feeling all right?" Nina asked, as she dug her keycard out from her straw hobo bag.

"Yes. I have something I want to share with you guys." She motioned for them to come into her room, and she proceeded to tell them about the possibility of her new job and relocating. Amy's enthusiasm was always childlike but in a good way. Her exuberance was infectious.

"How exciting." Rachael clapped her hands. "We'll only be an Amtrak ride away. Yay."

"I don't have the job yet. I have an interview scheduled when we get back. So, yes, I'll be jumping on the Acela to see what I can do with my life."

"This is pretty wild, girls." Nina leaned against the dresser. "You realize I'm also going on a job interview right after we get back? And I may be moving home?"

"That is kinda cool," Frankie mused. "And we're all together again to encourage and support each other."

Rachael got a little teary-eyed. "Getting back together with you guys has been the best Christmas present I've had in years."

"Maybe that's because you're Jewish and celebrate Hanukkah." Amy cackled as did everyone else.

"Good point." Rachael smirked. "Greg was Presbyterian, so we always celebrated Christmas. Ryan liked opening a pile of presents on one day." She paused. "We had a menorah at the house, of course, when I was growing up, but my family was more spiritual than religious."

"That was a big trend even before I started in publishing. There were spiritual books coming out every minute. The Dalai Lama, Thích Nhất Hạnh, Deepak Chopra. All very spiritual and well-respected men. It wasn't so much about religion but living a full, inspired, conscious life." Frankie sat at the edge of the chair. "They taught how to incorporate essentials of kindness and compassion in our daily lives, regardless of religion. Very inspiring stuff," Frankie ruminated. "The messages are not dissimilar to Christianity. 'Love thy neighbor.' Too bad so many of the precepts of common decency have been replaced with the garbage on the Internet and social media. Ugh. Drives me nuts."

"Yeah. I read a lot of Chopra when I first moved to LA," Nina added. "I needed all the spiritual guidance I could get in Tinseltown." She smiled. "They don't seem to have many traditional churches there. A lot of cults and New Age stuff, but most of it was total garbage. Smoke and mirrors. Now you see it, now you don't. Your money, that is. Many of these groups just wanted your money. But enough of that. Tell us more about the job."

"As I told Frankie, it's a position as an associate professor. I would be teaching undergraduates. It's bioengineering innovation and design, including ethics for engineers."

"You lost me at engineering," Rachael joked.

Amy laughed. "I like the ethics part of it. That's something I've been struggling with at my job. We could have been building some kind of chemical weapon for all we knew. Once we finished one aspect of the work, it would be handed over to someone else. The result was that no single person had the whole picture at any given time. Only the guys in the gray suits."

"Gray suits? I didn't think anyone wore suits out there," Rachael observed.

"That's what we called the dudes who would fly in from Washington, D.C.," Amy replied. "They weren't FBI. Maybe CIA, but we were never sure. Anyway, I really hope the position comes through. I don't know how many other people are being considered."

"You are the smartest person I know," Frankie claimed. "You were also one of their top students. Landing you would be a coup for them."

"I hope you're right." Amy smiled.

Nina gave her a hug. "Let's hope all of us find what we're looking for and what we need."

"Amen to that," Frankie remarked. They all did a high five.

Rachael was giggling.

"What's so funny, girlfriend?" Frankie gave her a sideways look. "I know that laugh."

Rachael opened the small shopping bag she had been carrying and pulled out a small bunch of leaves. "Mistletoe. It could come in handy."

"You are too much," Frankie said. "I think you should be wearing a big sign: WARNING! DANGER!"

Nina nodded her head in agreement. "I tried to talk her out of it, but . . ."

"Now to other important issues. What are we wearing to this meet and greet?" Frankie asked. "I've already unpacked and spritzed my dress to get out the wrinkles."

"I guess the rest of us should unpack," Nina suggested.

"Good idea."

"Amy, I am praying that everything works out for you." Frankie gave her a big hug. Then she turned to Nina. "And you, too, girlfriend."

Rachael frowned. "What about me?"

"What is it that you really want?" Frankie asked.

"Good question." Rachael let out a guffaw. "I'm going to have to work on that one. Hey, you haven't told us what your goal is either."

"I'm working on that, too." Frankie smiled. "OK, ladies. Time for our beauty makeovers." She didn't want to ponder the big question of life at the moment.

The group disbanded, each going to her own stateroom to get organized and ready for the evening's festivities.

Chapter Fourteen

That Evening

Frankie chose a sleeveless cobalt-blue jumpsuit and a pair of silver, low-wedge sandals. She completed the outfit with a large, simple, silver bangle bracelet and silver hoop earrings. She pulled her hair back in a ponytail and slicked the flyaway ends with pomade. One more coat of nude lipstick and lip gloss. She took a look in the full-length mirror and gave herself a thumbs-up and a wink. She grabbed a small straw shoulder bag. Just large enough for her keycard, lipstick, and breath spray.

You just never knew how close you might get to another person.

She left her cell phone in the small safe in the closet along with the few pieces of jewelry she had brought and cash. She was really going to try to unplug for as long as possible.

Frankie went into the hall and knocked on the doors to everyone's stateroom. In synchronized motion, they opened their doors at the same time. All of them looked dazzling in their own unique way.

Rachael was wearing watermelon-printed capris with a

bright lime-green tank top. She was two inches taller with her high-wedge espadrilles. She carried the pink purse she had had the night before. Nina commented. "You're wearing the same purse? You sure you're OK?"

"Really. I think comedy must be your forte," Rachael shot back. "I had to compromise on a few things. Handbags were a challenge."

"You know I'm kidding. You look fab. Luscious, in fact." Nina was intent on keeping Rachael's confidence up.

Nina had opted for white jeans and a bright lime-colored tunic. Her hair was pulled back from her face with a lime-and-gold headband that matched the trim on the sleeves and front of her top. She wore flat sandals so as not to tower over the rest of the women.

As Frankie predicted to herself, one of them was wearing navy-blue polka dots. It was Amy, with a miniskirt tied with a sash and a white tank top. She had a white melamine bracelet and matching earrings. Open-toed booties completed her cute, funky look.

"You look adorable," Rachael commented. "No fashion police necessary."

As the four of them started toward the elevator, Peter was exiting his stateroom. "Good evening, ladies. You all look lovely." He stopped for a second. "Is it OK that I compliment you? One never knows these days. Everyone being all PC and the rest."

"You can compliment me all you want." Rachael was the first to answer.

"Thank you, Peter. You look quite dashing yourself." Frankie was being sincere. She guessed Peter to be around forty. Thin, in an elegant way. Not too skinny. More sinewy. He had a full head of dark hair with a touch of gray at his temples. He was wearing a blue pinstripe button-down shirt with navy slacks.

"You all look so tropical," Peter noted. "I'm afraid I'm still looking a little too corporate."

"Nonsense. You look fine," Nina added.

"Heading to the meet and greet?" he asked.

"We are indeed. Care to walk with us, or have we scared you off?" Frankie was half joking.

"I'd be pleased to walk with you. Where are you ladies from, if you don't mind my asking?"

Rachael took the lead. "I'm from Ridgewood, New Jersey. Nina is from LA, Amy from Santa Clara, and Frankie lives in New York City. We grew up together in Ridgewood and decided to vacation together. And you?"

"I'm originally from Chicago, but I now live in Auburn, Massachusetts," he replied.

"What do you do for a living?" Rachael was quick to cut to the chase.

"Boring stuff really." Peter smiled.

"What kind of boring stuff?" Amy asked, as the five meandered down the long corridor.

"I'm an accountant. Can't you tell by the shirt and pants?" Peter said in a self-deprecating way.

The women chuckled. Amy was next to speak. "Well, I work in bioengineering. Can't you tell by my pink hair?"

Peter chuckled. "I never connected pink hair to bioengineering. Obviously, I need to get out more often."

"A man with a sense of humor," Frankie remarked. "We may just keep you."

"Don't scare the guy away," Rachael jumped in.

Peter gave a light laugh. "You ladies seem like a lot of fun. I just might take you up on that offer."

"You can be our wingman," Rachael added.

"And you ladies can be mine. I've never done anything like this before. It's a bit intimidating," Peter admitted.

"You've got that right," Nina quipped. "We figured there was safety in numbers. If we got stuck in any uncomfortable circumstances, we could bail each other out."

"You've put a lot of thought into this trip," he remarked.

"I did this at the last minute. I decided that I didn't want to spend another New Year's by myself watching Ryan Seacrest make a fool of himself. I thought being with a bunch of drunken strangers would be more interesting," he scoffed.

"So, have you picked out any activity for tonight?" Frankie asked.

"Karaoke is definitely out of the question. I'm a pretty good dart player, though, I must admit."

"Really?" Nina asked curiously. Darts was something they would play on the set when they had a lot of free time. She couldn't remember who had started it, but quite often they would be outside their dressing-room trailers tossing darts. After one of the production assistants got nicked in the foot by a stray dart, someone brought a magnetic board to the set. Every once in a while, someone's photo would be on the bull's-eye. "I'm not a bad dart thrower myself."

"Don't you think it's a bit odd to have something lethal on the first night?" Peter remarked.

"Good point. Maybe they're magnetic darts. We used them at work," Nina added.

"What kind of work requires a dartboard?" Peter asked quizzically.

"The kind I don't have anymore."

Peter looked puzzled.

"Let's just say I'm between jobs right now."

"Oh. Sorry?" Peter wasn't sure how to respond.

"It's OK. I was in need of a change."

He peered at her. "Were you in that show? *Family* something?"

"Yep. That was me," Nina replied. "This is the last season, but an announcement hasn't gone out yet. Not that it matters." She pushed the DOWN button at the elevator.

When the car arrived, Peter put his hand on the sliding door so it wouldn't close too fast. He gestured for the women to enter. Amy pushed the button for the atrium deck. As the elevator descended, they could hear the subtle music of a reggae group as they got close to the atrium deck.

As the doors of the elevator opened, the prolonged loud blast from the ship's horn sounded, signaling that the ship was leaving port. Rachael exclaimed, "Here we go, kids."

Nina gave Peter a look. "Don't mind her. They only let her out . . ."

Peter finished the sentence with a grin, "Of the institution a few times a year. I can understand why."

"Great. Another comedian." Rachael pretended to pout.

"Do you mind if I hang with you lovely ladies for a while?"

"*No problemo*, wingman." Rachel spoke with confidence.

There were several waiters and waitresses who hailed from a number of international locales. All spoke impeccable English with the slightest of accents. They wore crisp white uniforms with sailor caps that bore the ship's logo. They carried trays of hot and cold hors d'oeuvres and offered them to the guests. A large table was set up in the middle of the large space. It held an incredible assortment of cheeses, fresh fruit, olives, breadsticks, a variety of toasted breads, crackers, and Marcona almonds. Pineapples carved to accommodate ferns, birds-of-paradise, and anthuriums completed the display. It was an array of tropical beauty.

Frankie and Amy headed to the bar, and Nina walked over to say hello to Richard, the man she had met earlier.

Peter handed a plate to Rachael, who was swaying with the music. "You dance?"

Rachael smiled up at him. "I own a dance studio."

"That explains your rhythm. Oops. Not sure if that was appropriate."

"Oh please. Say whatever you want. We're on vacation. From everything. Work. Politics. The news. Personal drama."

"That sounds good to me," Peter replied. "So I don't suppose you'll be taking any dance lessons."

"I've been an admirer of Henry Dugan for a long time. I read that he goes on cruises and gives lessons to raise money for charity. I was thinking of going and pretending I don't know how to dance." Rachael giggled. "And then grab him and make him tango with me."

"You are quite the firecracker, aren't you?" Peter found Rachael amusing.

"I've been called worse." Rachael picked a few cheeses and a slice of mango.

Peter snickered. "I find that impossible to believe."

Rachael chuckled. "And you are a gentleman, too. Frankie's right. We just might keep you."

Peter was happy he had met up with the four women. They were easy to be with, each charming in her own way.

Rachael thought that having Peter around would make the women appear to be in demand. Or was it the other way around? Time would tell.

Amy and Frankie ordered drinks for everyone. The bartender accommodated them with a small tray to carry the beverages. Frankie and Amy made their way to a high-top table, where an impeccably dressed woman stood by herself. She appeared to be around fifty. "Mind if we join you?" Frankie asked.

"Please. I feel like a wallflower standing by myself. I'm Marilyn."

"Nice to meet you, Marilyn. I'm Amy, and this is Frankie."

"Are you traveling together?" she asked.

"Yes. We have two other friends with us." Frankie nodded in the direction of Nina, then to Rachael, who was heading in their direction. Peter followed.

Frankie explained. "Back in June, we reconnected at a high-school reunion and decided that if we didn't have dates for New Year's Eve by Thanksgiving, we would do the dreaded singles cruise."

Marilyn laughed, almost spitting out her drink. "I was very apprehensive about doing this, but my kids bought the trip for me for Christmas. I got divorced earlier this year, and they thought it was a good way for me to start a new year. Kick the old one behind."

"That was thoughtful of them," Amy said innocently.

"I suppose so, but it's a bit intimidating when you're by yourself."

Peter approached the table. "Did I hear that word 'intimidating'?" He nodded at the other three women. "Peter Sullivan."

"Marilyn Mitchell. Nice to meet you. Are you part of this group?" She was referring to Frankie, Amy, and Rachael, then nodded in Nina's direction.

"No. We've just met. They shanghaied me." Peter smiled. "I'm kidding, of course. In truth, I crashed their party."

"Actually, he was invited," Rachael corrected him.

"Yes. They asked me to be their wingman."

Marilyn smiled. "I guess everyone could use a good wingman or copilot."

"Stick with us, Marilyn," Rachael invited.

"If you dare." Frankie faked a warning. "Tell us. Where are you from? What do you enjoy doing? What were you forced to do?"

Marilyn blinked several times, then ticked off her answers.

"From New York. Fine dining. Museums. Music. I am *forced* to travel to Italy and France."

"Oh, that sounds terrible," Frankie joked.

"I am a buyer for Bloomingdales. Ready-to-wear. *Prêt-à-porter*, as they say. Menswear."

"I'm in New York, too. Grand Marshall Publishing."

"They've been around a long time." Marilyn knew the company. GMP, as they were referred to, was recognized for blockbuster novels, political exposés, and famous biographies.

"Sometimes I feel like I've been around a long time, too." Frankie smirked.

"Ah. No shoptalk," Rachael reminded her.

"Right. Sorry. It's just that it's been quite a roller-coaster year."

"Now zip it," Rachael admonished.

"Yes, ma'am." Frankie smiled. "I'm going to fix a plate. Be right back." She moved in the direction of the delectable offerings, smiling and saying hello to every person who made eye contact with her. *Why not? Wasn't everyone here to kind of, sort of, maybe meet someone?* She was happy no one was wearing a name tag. That would have been over the top for her. Everyone peering at each other's chest. And under these circumstances, that could solicit some unwanted and lewd ogling. The brochure indicated it was *a voyage of interaction with single professional adults.*

Frankie spotted Nina coming toward the cheese table. "So?" Frankie asked in a mischievous manner.

"What?" Nina smiled. "Oh that? Just practicing." She picked up a plate and began choosing some of her favorites. Humboldt Fog, Sottocenere, Stilton, and a swath of baked brie with apples. A few breadsticks and slices of crisp Fire-hook flatbread topped her plate. "I'm hungry."

"I can see that. So am I." Frankie thought for a moment. "We didn't really have lunch. Good thing we had a late breakfast."

"I could dive right on top of this table," Nina joked.

"And I'd be pushing you off and taking your place."

"I'm bigger than you." Nina stood on her toes to accentuate her point.

"But I'm quicker." Frankie snatched the piece of melon from underneath Nina's fork. "Ha."

"Speaking of food. We should probably see where and when we can eat. Should we invite Peter?" Nina asked.

"Sure. Why not? He seems like a pretty nice dude. Besides, you may need an accountant soon with all the money you're going to make writing that sitcom."

"From your mouth to God's ears." Nina looked toward the heavens.

"How does your family feel about your tentative plans? They must be over the moon you'll be around. *When* they're around, that is."

"My mother is thrilled there will be someone to keep an eye on her plants. She nearly had a cow last year when the person who checked the house each week forgot to water her banana plant."

Frankie chuckled. "The plants will be happy, and I will be happy to have you nearby."

"I'm going to fix a plate for everyone to share at the table."

"You're always feeding everyone," Nina teased.

"Not so much in my apartment." Frankie sighed. "I've been getting a little stir-crazy lately. Sure, it's a great neighborhood, a relatively easy walk to work in nice weather. But. I feel like it's time for a change of scenery. It seems all I do is go to work, come home, order food. I don't dare go any-

where on the weekends with all the 'bridge and tunnel people' descending upon Manhattan."

Nina remembered the term people from the outer bor-
oughs of Manhattan were called.

"You love your work, no?"

"Yes, but I'm not liking my job. If you get my drift. There
are so many layers of bureaucracy since GMP bought up half
the publishing industry. Did you know that an editor cannot
buy a book from an author without a committee meeting?"

"Seriously?"

"Yes, and get this. Two of the people on the committee
have to be from human resources. It's totally ridiculous."
Frankie sighed.

"I just don't know what else I would do with my life. I've
built a good career, but . . ."

"Those 'buts' can be a real pain in the butt." Nina chuckled.

Frankie juggled two plates of cheese. Nina carried hers
and a handful of napkins.

When they returned to the table, the others were engaged
in lively conversation. Nina elbowed Frankie. "This doesn't
stink," implying it wasn't so bad.

"Yeah, but your cheese does." Frankie nodded toward the
Stilton on Nina's plate.

Everyone was swaying to the subtle island rhythms coming from the five-piece combo.

Frankie brought up the subject of dinner plans. "Does anyone have any idea what cuisine they're in the mood for? Peter?
Marilyn? Would you care to join our rowdy ensemble?"

"I would be delighted," Marilyn said first.

"Who's your wingman?" Peter stepped back and made a
sweeping gesture with both hands.

"Goodie," Amy said with her spunky attitude. "Where are
we going?"

"I could use a big hunk of beef," Nina blurted. "Oh, I

hope no one is vegan or vegetarian," she said, expecting she might have offended someone.

"I could go for a steak," Marilyn said, squashing any concerns on her behalf.

"Count me in." Peter was on board.

"I'll go over to the hostess station. Be back in a flash."

Frankie crossed the now-crowded room, still smiling and greeting everyone within eyeshot. She found the Prime Steakhouse at one end of the atrium and approached the hostess. "Good evening. Can you accommodate six for dinner?"

The hostess looked at the book. "Of course. Can your party be ready in fifteen minutes?" The tall, exotic woman smiled at her.

"Yes, we can. Name is Frankie."

"Thank you, Frankie." The hostess noted it in her book. "We shall see you shortly."

Frankie was salivating from the aroma of something cooking on a grill. She picked up her step and half danced her way back to the other side of the atrium, where her band of friends waited. "We're good to go. Fifteen minutes."

"Fantastic. Thank you for inviting me along." Marilyn was happy she had company. She was beginning to feel less like an outcast.

"Absolutely," Amy chimed in. "The more the merrier."

"We should probably finish our drinks and head over. It will take a couple of minutes to get through the crowd."

Nina said she wanted to say good night to Richard and would catch up with them in a minute. Rachael raised her eyebrows several times, and Nina shot her a look. As they crossed the expanse of the atrium, Frankie noticed that the ages of the other guests ranged from early thirties to mid-fifties. Everyone looked respectable, smartly dressed, and showered. Frankie smirked to herself. Personal hygiene was one of her pet peeves. Or rather, the lack of it. Besides, this wasn't one of those one-evening speed-dating events, although that was on the manifest for the next day. This, she reminded herself, was an expensive getaway. Then she thought about Rusty. There might well be a few of them roaming the ship, looking for lonely widows or divorcées. She shook her head to get rid of the negative thoughts. *Fun. Only fun things.* Besides, Dorothy had dumped him. Nonetheless, Frankie decided she would fire up her radar where Marilyn was concerned. She wasn't going to get in her business, but she would keep an eye out. Women had to have each other's backs. It was good to have that kind of camaraderie.

The group waited for Nina to catch up, then they were seated by the hostess at a large round table. The steakhouse was also decorated with a plethora of poinsettias. But this time, they were red with gold bows.

Peter went around the table and pulled everyone's chair out for them. "You are quite the gentleman, Peter Sullivan. Tell me, why are you here again?" Frankie joked.

"I've been divorced for a couple of years. And as I said, I didn't want to watch the ball drop and all the hoopla that preceded it, by myself. I thought a vacation to a few places I hadn't visited before would be a nice distraction. I also liked the idea of a singles cruise, believe it or not. I figured it was better than being around couples, or have kids running all over the place."

"The brochure was pretty clear about adult professionals."

Marilyn added, "But my son and daughter insisted I do this. They really didn't give me much of a choice."

Frankie patted Marilyn's hand. "Well, I'm glad they did. And I hope you will be, too."

The hostess handed everyone an oversized menu. "Your server will be here shortly to discuss the specials."

"Thank you," Peter said, and addressed the rest of the

table after glancing at the menu. "Specials? I cannot imagine what could be missing."

"My mouth is watering." Nina's voice was heard behind the huge menu. "Creamed spinach. Stuffed baked potatoes. And look at all the meat selections."

Comments and murmurs about the cuts of beef, chops, and a large selection of shellfish went around the table.

The waitress appeared and asked if they wanted to start with a cocktail. They agreed on wine instead. Peter asked for the wine list. A few moments later, a sommelier appeared. "Anything in particular you prefer, sir?"

Peter lowered his menu to ask the women what they wanted. Amy wanted white but the rest preferred a pinot noir or a cabernet sauvignon with their meal. He ordered a modestly priced bottle of Meiomi, which he intended to pay for as a thank-you to the women for including him. He knew that one bottle wouldn't be enough for five people. That would equal a glass per person, so he instructed the sommelier to have another one ready when the main course was served.

The specials were surf and turf, or a three-pound lobster stuffed with crabmeat.

They ordered appetizers of shrimp cocktail, little-neck clams, grilled octopus, and escargots. Amy ordered the lobster and the others opted for different cuts of beef.

The conversation was lively as they shared ideas as to what they wanted to do and see in each port. Several minutes later, the appetizers were brought out.

"Shopping," Nina said. "Everywhere."

"Snorkeling and petting a stingray in Grand Cayman," was Amy's contribution.

"I want to visit the ruins in Cozumel," Frankie added. "Also the ruins in Belize City. They're both from the Mayan civilization. Actually, it's only about an eight-hour drive from Belize City to Cozumel."

Rachael looked at Peter. "What do you have planned?"

"Fishing in Grand Cayman. Maybe some cave tubing or kayaking," he replied.

"I saw that there are several helicopter tours. One goes to Lighthouse Reef in Belize. It's the place that Jacques Cousteau said had the most beautiful reefs in the world," Amy added.

"Helicopter? Not for me," Marilyn said. "Maybe the Butterfly Botanical Gardens in Cozumel. I also want to see the San Gervasio ruins, where women paid tribute to the goddess of love and fertility. Clearly, I'm past the fertility part, but the love aspect might come in handy. After all, that's why my kids sent me on this trip." She laughed. "I'd also like to go to Tulum."

"I may take the chocolate tour in Cozumel," Rachael added. "Although I want to do some horseback riding on Grand Cayman."

"There sure are a lot of things to do. Too bad we're only going to be in each port for one day," Amy said.

"That's the nature of these trips. Get as much in as possible." Peter swirled the last of the wine in his glass and motioned for the next bottle to be served. He excused himself and went toward the back of the restaurant, where he pulled the waitress aside, then quickly returned as the servers brought the gigantic platters of the main courses to the table.

"I'm so glad we decided to do this instead of eating in the main dining room." Frankie cut into her meat. Perfectly cooked.

"Yes. Thank you for suggesting it and including me," Marilyn said. "I was dreading entering the main dining room alone. I travel all over the world and never have a problem going out to dinner myself or eating in the hotel restaurant, but there is something . . ." She hesitated for a moment, and Frankie jumped in.

"Intimidating!"

"That's the word of the day, so it seems." Peter grinned.

"I'm glad we formed our own posse. We can check out the main dining room tomorrow night. We'll be able to sit together and not be 'intimidated.'" Nina used air quotes.

"I think there are going to be a few activities in the main dining room tomorrow night. Speed dating. I think." Amy was digging into the lobster claws with the small seafood fork. She looked up and caught the waitress's eye and mouthed, "More butter, please."

"Speed dating." Marilyn mused. "That's something I haven't tried yet."

"You may not want to," Nina interjected.

"Oh, stop," Rachael said. "We're here to have fun. Besides, who knows what kind of comic relief material Nina can glean for the script."

"Excellent point," Nina said. "I will be taking copious notes."

"Tell me. How does it work?" Marilyn asked.

Frankie explained. "Depending on how many people participate, hopefully an equal number of men and women." She chuckled. "Everyone gets a card with numbers that correspond to a table number. Say there are twenty tables. There is one woman per table with an empty chair opposite her. The men take a seat at any of the tables. But before it begins, everyone is handed a card. If there are twenty tables, there are twenty numbered lines on the card. The cards are for you to take notes and check off one of the boxes that say *Interested to meet: as a friend; as a business associate; as a date.* The women do the same thing. If you're not interested in a person at all, you just leave that line blank. It's first names only. Then the host starts a timer. Usually ten minutes. So, you have ten minutes to talk to the person. A bell rings, and the men move on to the next table. At the end of the event, the coordinators tally the scorecards and inform everyone about who wants to see them again and under what circumstances."

"What if no one wants to see you again?" Marilyn asked. "I'd hate to get back a bunch of blanks." She looked a bit dismayed.

"That hardly ever happens. Someone is going to want to spend time with you on one of those levels. The good part is you get to decide if you want to pursue a connection."

"Let me see if I have this correct." Marilyn retraced Frankie's explanation. "I meet twenty men. I make a note as to who I want to see again and under what heading. Friend. Business. Date."

"So far, so good." Frankie nodded.

"Then someone gives me a tally of who wants to meet me again under those same conditions. But what if they want a date, and I only want a friend?"

"That's up to you. If you differ on any of those boxes I would say 'Run'!" Frankie exclaimed.

"I take it you've done it before?" Marilyn said to Frankie.

"We all have," Rachael gushed. "Obviously, it didn't work out for any of us, but it's worth the fun. Especially the gossip afterward." She hooted.

"One time I met a very nice man who told me he was a doctor," Amy confessed. "I thought he was nice, but I only wanted to interact with him again as a business associate. Unfortunately, he wanted to date me. I explained as gently as I could that I didn't want to pursue a relationship with him, and he claimed he understood and business associate was fine with him." Amy shook her head. "Some people will tell you anything to get to where they want to go. Anyway, we met for coffee, and he brought me a red rose. The 'Danger! Danger!'

alarm went off in my head. Once again, I explained that it was a lovely gesture, but I was not interested in pursuing a relationship." Amy dug out another piece of lobster meat and plopped it in her mouth.

"Then what happened?" Peter was also enthralled with the story.

Amy swallowed and wiped the melted butter from her chin. "He sent me an e-card with valentine hearts."

"I guess he didn't get the message the first two times," Peter said. "The guy couldn't take a hint."

"Correct. I had to block him." Amy cracked a claw to emphasize the word "block." "I know it sounds mean, but he clearly wasn't getting it."

"He was probably hoping you would change your mind," Peter said thoughtfully.

"Not a chance." Amy scooped out more lobster meat. "It was starting to creep me out."

"Don't you think it would be awkward if I wanted to see someone again, and he didn't?" Marilyn asked. "The ship isn't *that* big."

"Awkward-schmawkward." Rachael wiggled her shoulders. "I wouldn't worry about it if I were you. There are plenty of men who would want to be in your company."

"What makes you say that?" Marilyn was curious.

"I noticed a few men looking at you when we were walking through the atrium." Rachael smirked and nodded.

"Rachael has man-dar," Frankie joked.

"Man-dar?" Marilyn looked confused.

"Man. Radar. Man-dar." Nina took the lead. "Rachael has always been, shall I say, fascinated by the opposite sex to an inordinate degree."

Rachael wasn't going to let the *Rachael is man-crazy* train leave the station without having something to say about it.

"Marilyn. Don't let these women give you the wrong impression of me," Rachael said with an air of confidence. "I've made it my hobby to find out what makes the opposite sex tick. As much as possible." She turned to Peter. "Don't misunderstand me. Suffice it to say I have had a number of experiences and feel as if I can read their body language."

"Especially if they're all over *your* body!" Amy guffawed and almost choked on a piece of her lobster.

"Ignore her," Rachael said calmly. "I am not a trollop. I've dated."

"A lot," Frankie said, taking her turn. "Rachael's life has been an ongoing speed-dating event."

Nina inadvertently spit her water across the table. Peter roared. Amy stopped midchew. Marilyn hooted.

Rachael looked up at the ceiling and shook her head. "Do you see what I have to put up with?"

"It's all in good fun," Frankie offered. "Rachael is an easy mark for poking fun."

Amy was starting to giggle uncontrollably. "Poke?"

"Ladies. Get your minds out of the gutter." Frankie feigned a reprimand. "We have other guests at our table."

Peter was trying to control his amusement. Marilyn wasn't sure which way the conversation was going.

Frankie tried to calm the jokes and laughter for a moment. "Seriously. We love Rachael. And we love to tease her. We love to tease each other. Really."

"You ladies are a hoot." Peter took another bite of the ribeye on his plate.

"You're a good sport, Rachael." Marilyn lifted her wineglass in a toast. "I'll follow your man-dar advice."

The conversation around the table wound down to small talk about other places they had traveled. Favorite locales. Worst trip. Best trip.

"Here's to this being on the list of 'Best Trips.'" Peter held his glass up in a toast. "Cheers."

"Hear! Hear!"

"*Cin cin!*"

"*¡Salud!*"

"*Skòl!*"

"*Cent' anni!*"

"Has anyone decided if they are going to participate in any of this evening's activities?" Marilyn asked.

"Nina and I are going to the dart tournament," Peter announced.

"I'm thinking about the class with Henry Dugan," Rachael said impishly.

"I might do trivia," Amy answered.

"You'll beat the pants off everyone," Frankie stated with a laugh. "You have an unfair advantage."

"What advantage?" Marilyn queried.

"She's a genius," Nina said smoothly. "Graduated top ten in her class at MIT. She has a PhD in bioengineering."

"That is impressive," Marilyn responded, and chuckled. "I guess I'll be skipping that."

"If they allow teams, you can be my teammate," Amy offered.

"A ringer, eh?" Peter joked.

"Shhhh . . ." Frankie whispered. "We don't want people to know all of our secret weapons."

Peter smiled. "Right. Man-dar. Genius." He turned to Frankie. "What is *your* special talent?"

"I'm the 'pushy-planner-lady.' Also known as 'Miss Bossy Pants.'"

"Yeah, but that's not a secret." Rachael got her digs in and stuck out her tongue.

"I'm an open book," Frankie said. "Why not? I work with enough of them." She chuckled at her own pun.

"Oh, I think there has to be some mystery in there, too, no?" Peter quizzed her.

"Hmmm. I think he's got you on that one," Nina inter-jected.

"And Nina is a comedian," Frankie quipped back.

"That's no big secret either," Amy said innocently. "She was on *Family Blessings.*" Then she realized she had outed Nina.

"Oh jeez. I'm sorry, Nina."

"I thought you looked familiar." Marilyn eyed her. "But then I thought you probably get 'You know who you look like?' a lot."

"I do get that a lot." Nina chortled. "And I usually respond with, 'Really? No one has ever said that before.' "

"See. Comedian." Amy pointed the last piece of lobster at Nina.

"That's terrific," Marilyn added. "But I didn't watch the show very often."

Nina smiled. "Probably never, right? But that's OK. To be honest, if I weren't in it, I wouldn't watch it either. Not my best work, even though it's my best-known work."

"Nina is an exceptionally fine actress. She did a lot of the-ater in high school and college. Moved to LA and got the job in the show," Frankie explained.

"Let's not forget that awful zombie movie I was in. Not my best work either."

"Don't be so modest. You made an excellent zombie." Rachael cackled.

"You're quite an interesting group." Peter folded his arms across his chest and leaned back against his chair.

"We warned you." Frankie smiled.

"You did indeed."

Everyone had devoured the last morsel on their plates. "Can I interest anyone in dessert?" the waitress asked.

Groans went around the table. "Does everyone have an activity?" Frankie asked.

"See. Bossy Pants." Rachael elbowed Peter.

"Amy, Marilyn. I'll go with you to trivia; Nina and Peter, darts; Rachael is going to harass the dance instructor."

The women gave her sloppy salutes. "Aye-aye, Captain."

"Should we meet in the Stargazer Lounge afterward?" Frankie asked.

"Pushy-Planner." Rachael nodded and poked Peter again.

"I think the games are officially over at eleven, but the piano bar and disco are open until midnight. The lounge is open until two." Amy recited the schedule.

"See. Genius." Rachael went to elbow Peter, but this time he saw it coming.

He chuckled. "I'm going to be black-and-blue tomorrow."

He began to rise from the table, assisting the women out of their chairs. "I hope you don't mind. Some women get offended."

Sounds of "Are you kidding?" "Being polite is never a bad thing." "I appreciate it," went around the table.

Frankie hesitated. "What about the check?"

"It's been taken care of," Peter said mildly, and showed the women out.

"That was lovely of you. And generous. Thank you." Marilyn was the first to speak.

Frankie stopped herself from saying, "Oh, you didn't have to do that." An acknowledgment of appreciation was more warranted. Why diminish the gesture with any other comment but one of thanks? She followed instead with, "Yes, Peter. That was wonderful. Thank you very much."

Words of gratitude came from Amy, Rachael, and Nina. Frankie thought they could all learn a little something from Marilyn. Even each other.

"OK. Everyone. You have your orders. See you in the lounge around eleven thirty." More wimpy salutes were aimed at Frankie.

* * *

As predicted, Amy was tearing up the scoreboard for the trivia game. There were about thirty people playing, three per team. Each team would pick a card from a barrel. If they answered correctly, they would get a point. The teams would rotate ten times. The team with the most points at the end won a five-hundred-dollar gift card to be used at any of the shops on the ship.

By the fifth round, people were either moaning or cheering for Amy's team. Frankie thought she saw two men placing side bets.

Amy's team got all of the answers right, with Frankie and Marilyn contributing on a couple of them. They shrieked in delight when they were handed the gift card, and several men offered to buy them drinks. Frankie muttered, "That's one way to get attention. Play trivia with a genius."

"We have time for one." Frankie looked at her watch and gave Amy and Marilyn a look that said, *Don't you dare call me Bossy Pants in front of these guys.*

Two of the men motioned for a cocktail waitress to come over. "Prosecco, please," Frankie said.

"Me, also," Amy added.

"Yes, for me as well." Marilyn nodded.

The men introduced themselves. They were from Milwaukee. Jeff was a regional manager for one of the big box store chains, and Steve was an insurance adjuster. Perfectly nice gentlemen, but they wouldn't pass the chemistry that would be needed under the mistletoe. It seemed as if many of the passengers were there for the same reason, and not necessarily to find true love. Relaxing on a cruise to exotic places and not feeling like a fifth wheel. Everyone was in the same relationship-status boat. Literally.

* * *

Rachael was all atwitter when she entered the small ball-room. She had been a fan of Henry Dugan ever since she could remember. He created a style of dancing that incorporated jazz moves with ballet. He called it "jazzalett." Everyone thought he was doing the other a disservice. But he felt that if it got more people to dance, then all the better. He was also proficient in every dance technique.

There were only a dozen people in the room. Ten were women. She didn't want to make a spectacle of herself. For real. So she changed her mind about faking out the instructor.

Rachael approached Henry. "Maestro Dugan. It is an honor to meet you. My name is Rachael Newmark."

"Good evening, Ms. Newmark. Thank you for joining me this evening. Tell me, do you dance?"

"Yes, as a matter of fact, I do. I have a studio in Ridge-wood. Salon La Dance."

He clasped her hands. "How fantastic." He had a hint of an Irish accent. "What is it that you teach?"

"Pretty much anything anyone wants to learn. I have twelve instructors. We have classical ballet, ballroom, jazzalett, tap, although that's been on a downswing. I also coordinate dance events for community groups and senior villages."

"That is very impressive, Rachael. We shall dance together on this journey."

"That would be marvelous." Rachael was beside herself with joy. Someone she had admired since she was in grade school was going to dance with her. "When I signed up for this trip, I had no idea you would be on board. Then I was told you do it to raise money for charity."

"Yes. It's a foundation in New York for children who are disabled. We work with their physical therapists and incorporate dance in their regimen. It makes their therapy much more enjoyable."

"That's wonderful. I would love to learn more about it. Perhaps I can involve myself or some of my instructors."

"How very kind of you. We should talk. Perhaps some-time tomorrow evening after we leave Key West?"

"Absolutely." Rachael finally realized she was still clasp-ing his hand.

He smiled at her. "I don't suppose you'll be taking any lessons?"

"Are you kidding? I'll be in every one of your classes un-less you throw me out."

"We have three classes a day, then a little dance recital the last night of the cruise for anyone who wants to participate."

"Can I talk you into a tango?" Rachael figured, in for a penny, in for a pound.

"Tango? That would be divine." He looked around the room and counted; there were three men, including himself, and ten women. He would have to pick a style that could ac-commodate the imbalance of partners. "After class tonight? Here? We don't usually run past ten thirty."

"¡Maravillosa!"

He turned to the group. "I have an idea. Do you know what a flash mob is?"

Some people nodded while others shrugged.

"It's when a group of people break out into a dance in an unlikely place. Like a shopping mall."

A few people nodded. "This is what we are going to do. We are going to rehearse a line dance. Like the Macarena, or the Electric Slide. The final night of the cruise, the captain has one more cocktail party. But before it starts, he makes an announcement on the grand staircase. We'll all be milling about on the balcony above. I'll start up the music, and you'll start dancing down the stairs. What do you think?"

"Sounds great," one of the men said.

"Sure. Could be fun," a woman chanted.

Many more agreeable comments came from the attendees.

"Excellent." He instructed everyone to line up and he began to show them simple moves that would look impressive when done together as a group. The beat of the music helped everyone to stay in rhythm.

An hour and a half later, all ten people had most of the moves down. At least they were beyond embarrassment.

"Before everyone leaves, I would like to share a dance with another instructor. Please sit and enjoy." He motioned for Rachael. Her legs were shaking. She didn't know what to expect.

The maestro pushed a button on his phone and the room filled with the sounds of piano and strings playing music from Argentina. He held out his hand and led Rachael on a ride she would never forget. Dugan was masterful in his cues, and Rachael followed him seamlessly. It was as if they had rehearsed for days. When the song ended, the small group jumped out of their seats and applauded. Rachael was in what felt like a transcendental state. The maestro bowed to his dance partner, and she returned one in kind. He held her by the shoulders. "That was exquisite. I do hope we can dance again on this trip."

"I cannot explain what a thrill this is for me." Rachael was trying not to faint from excitement.

"And I look forward to meeting with you when we get back to New York. I would like you to meet with our committee and the other dance therapists."

"Of course. Of course." Rachael felt like she was floating six inches off the ground. So much for her sense of being too petite.

"We have another class tomorrow morning at eight. The ship docks at Fisherman's Wharf, so we don't have to deal with a tender schedule. I hope to see all of you then. Good night." He grabbed his warm-up jacket and told Rachael to stop by during any of the classes.

She promised she would and danced her way to the Stargazer Lounge.

* * *

After they finished their prosecco, the women excused themselves and bid the nice gentlemen good night. "See you around campus," Amy quipped.

They walked toward the elevator that would take them to the top deck of the ship. The Stargazer Lounge was appropriately named. A wall of windows surrounded the large lounge from floor to ceiling, with glass panels creating a large part of the ceiling. No matter where one sat, one could see thousands of glittering stars over the dark sea. The rest of the ceiling mimicked the night sky with more twinkling lights. It was almost hard to tell where the real stars ended and the interior lights began. Overstuffed club chairs formed dozens of seating areas, and a three-piece jazz combo played softly. Small centerpieces made of twigs, silver stars, and votive candles sat on each table. A round, low-seated bar was in the middle of the room with its own tower of poinsettias. It was a glistening combination of holiday cheer and the evening sky.

The soft atmosphere of the room was broken as Rachael came flying into the lounge area. "You are not going to believe this."

"Do tell," Nina responded.

Rachael went into detail about her meeting with Henry Dugan, the tango, and the possibility of working with his foundation for disabled children.

"Boy, you've been busy," Amy exclaimed.

Rachael still looked dazed over her experience and ordered a glass of wine.

Amy was looking out to sea and remembered something. "Hey, tomorrow is a full moon," she announced to all and sundry. It will be really cool to watch it come up."

"And I'll bet the sunrise will be rather magnificent as well," Peter added.

"I remember camping on Big Pine Key when I was in college. You could watch the sunrise from one side of the key, then walk a few hundred yards at the end of the day and watch the sunset on the other side," Frankie said.

"Looks like we'll have the same opportunity," Peter said.

"If I get up early enough." Nina looked doubtful.

"We could set our alarms, then go back to sleep," Frankie suggested.

"You are always right on top of things, aren't you?" Peter said.

"It's my Bossy-Pants job." Frankie chuckled.

Marilyn gathered her purse and stood. "I think I'm going to call it a night. I'm very happy we met. See you tomorrow, I hope. Good night, everyone."

"Speaking of tomorrow, what does everyone have on their agenda?" Nina asked.

"Of course I will be visiting the Ernest Hemingway Home and Museum. Funny thing. I'm not a big fan of his. A lot of us agree that if he were to submit one of his manuscripts today, he would be rejected," Frankie said wryly.

"Seriously?" Peter interjected.

"A lot of men like his writing, but his novels were relatively short, depressing, and didn't appeal to many women," Frankie explained. "We read him in school because we had to. I want to visit because of the cats. I was there once when I was in college. The thing I found most interesting is that he collected polydactyl cats, which are known as Hemingway cats. They have extra digits on their paws. Almost like thumbs."

Amy chimed in, "I see a few of them come through the shelter, but they get adopted quickly. Which is good. I think I'll do the same thing."

"Dry Tortugas is where I'm heading," Peter said.

Nina said she would probably take the trolley tour and hit

Duval Street. Rachael said she would catch up with them at some point. She wanted to take Henry's class in the morning.

"Should we plan on meeting up for lunch somewhere?" Frankie asked.

"Good idea. I'll scope out the local cafés and text you guys around noon. How does that sound?" Nina offered.

"You gals enjoy your day. I'll probably see you in the evening. Should be a spectacular sunset. I'm going to hit the hay now. Glad I met up with you," Peter said. "By the way, good dart match."

"Oh, how did it go?" Frankie asked. "Did you guys win?"

"We came in second," Peter said guiltily. "It was my fault. I missed a bull's-eye."

"That's only because the other guys were jeering. Threw you off your game," Nina said in defense of him.

"Thanks, Nina. But I'll take the blame. Sneers don't throw me unless someone is complaining about their tax return, and I have to explain why they can't deduct their bowling ball as a therapeutic aid." He gave a smile. "See you tomorrow."

As he got out of earshot, Nina said, "Nice guy."

"Yes. Too bad he's not my type," Rachael said.

"Since when is a man *not* your type?" Nina teased.

"Funny. Maybe I'm becoming a little more discerning now." Rachael seemed more thoughtful than before.

"Wow. That instructor must have pulled some of your strings," Nina noted.

"I can't explain it, but I may have had an epiphany when we were dancing. I've been caught up in validating myself through the attention of men, when it occurred to me that I don't need to get it from someone else. Dancing with one of the world's most renowned choreographers and his inviting me to visit his foundation made me realize that I came this far all by myself. With hard work and tenacity. Not because some guy bought me dinner."

Nina checked Rachael's forehead to see if she had a fever. Rachael playfully slapped her hand away.

"Sometimes it only takes a moment for all the lights in our psyche to turn on and illuminate us," Frankie said, recalling the many self-help books she had worked on over the years. She gave Rachael a hug.

"But that doesn't mean I'm not going to do my 'coochie-coochie' dance anymore, just in case you were wondering."

"You wouldn't be Rachael if you didn't." Nina chuckled.

"OK, kids, time for me to hit the sack." Frankie stretched.

The others concurred and left together for a good night's rest.

Chapter Fifteen

Day 2
Key West, Florida

The ship pulled into the harbor at the crack of dawn. Frankie had set her alarm clock for six thirty to watch the sunrise. She was surprised that it was slightly later than when she was at home. Probably because Key West was farther west and south. According to the almanac, sunrise was at 7:09 and sunset at 5:46. The days were still shorter no matter where you were north of the equator.

There was a slight rap on the door. It was either room service or Nina. She pulled on a bathrobe and unchained the lock. "Good morning, sunshine." Nina was wide-awake and in a fine mood.

"Hey. Good morning to you. Coffee and croissants should be here shortly." Frankie gestured for her to come in. "We'll have our breakfast on the veranda. The morning light was beginning to brighten the horizon. Several minutes later, there was another knock on the door. This time it was room service.

"Good morning. Welcome to Key West, Florida. The

southernmost tip of the United States," the server said with a slight Caribbean accent. "Shall I place this on the veranda?"

"Most definitely. Thank you." Frankie moved out of his way as he hoisted the tray over his shoulder. He placed the coffee and basket of baked goods on the small table.

"May I get you anything else?" he asked cordially.

"No. This is lovely. Thank you." She handed him ten dollars even though tipping was discouraged. Who couldn't use some extra cash in their wallet?

"Oh, thank you very much." He bowed and walked toward the door. "Have a beautiful day."

"I was looking up restaurants for lunch," Nina said. "There's an authentic Cuban place called Conch Republic Seafood Company near Mallory Square. I'll make a reservation for twelve thirty so we'll know where and when to meet. Sound good?"

"My push-planning is rubbing off on you." Frankie stretched before sitting on the veranda chair.

"I think we're all rubbing off on each other." Nina poured her coffee.

"That could be a good thing or a bad thing." Frankie raised her eyebrows.

"So far, so good." Nina smiled. "Look at that sky. Isn't it magnificent?"

Frankie sighed. "It certainly is. Sure beats the cement and exhaust fan I have out my window."

"You've alluded to being antsy about your place." Nina tore off a corner of a baguette, saving the croissant for the next round of sampling the fresh morning delights.

"I know. It's a sweet place, but there isn't a whole lot I can do to change the décor, especially the scenery. Like I said, it feels like I go to work, come home, order food. Thank heaven for Bandit. At least I have him to talk to."

"And he doesn't talk back," Nina said.

"Oh, don't be so sure. He makes funny noises called trilling. It's like a language all its own."

"Huh. And I thought only dogs talked back." Nina took another bite. "These are delicious."

"What time are you planning to go into town?" Frankie asked.

"I may go back to sleep for another hour. Probably around ten or ten thirty."

"Ring me when you're ready. Amy and I will go with you. Rachael has her class, so she'll meet us for lunch. I'll slip a note under her door with the name of the restaurant and time."

Nina wiped the crumbs from her lips and brushed the rest of them onto her plate. "That was lovely. See you in a bit."

"*Ciao, bella,*" Frankie said, as she stared at the water-colored sky painted in pastel shades of pink. Within minutes, the large ball of the sun poked its head over the horizon. It was stirring to see how quickly the sun moved into the sky.

She sat for another half hour, then slipped a note under Amy's door telling her what time they were planning on leaving the ship, and one under Rachael's door with information for lunch. Two hours at the Hemingway House should be enough time. Then they could decide what they wanted to do afterward. One more cup of coffee and half a muffin, and Frankie was ready to shower and get herself together for the day ahead.

Around ten o'clock, Frankie heard a rap on her door. "It's me, Amy." Frankie let her in. "Nina is right behind me."

"I guess Rachael took that class. I haven't heard a peep out of her," Amy said.

"I'm sure that won't last very long." Nina chuckled. She was finally starting to relax. It had taken two days to shake off the concern about her job prospects. The further away she was from the turmoil, the easier it was for her to deal with.

"Everybody ready?"

"You bet." Amy was dressed in a pair of baggy white shorts with a tropical print blouse and red slip-on sneakers. A straw hat with a red ribbon and a straw tote bag completed her outfit.

Nina was wearing a long, flowing, pale blue skirt with an off-the-shoulder peasant blouse. She, too, had a straw hat, but the brim was much floppier than Amy's. Frankie chose a black-and-white polka-dot midi sundress with a white linen sun hat. A white jute bag completed her outfit.

"We look *maravillosa*," Frankie exclaimed. The three women sauntered down the corridor as Rachael was returning from her class.

"Ladies. I had the most wonderful class with Henry. We're working on a routine with several other people. Should be fun. I'll catch up with you at lunchtime. *¡Hasta luego!*"

"*Ciao*," Frankie called, as Rachael blew past them.

"She looks very confident, doesn't she?" Nina remarked.

"Yes. She sure does. I wonder what routine she was referring to."

"Guess we'll find out sooner or later." Amy smiled.

There was a crowd of people waiting to disembark from the ship. They spotted Marilyn in line. Amy waved. As they got closer to each other, Amy asked Marilyn what she had planned for her afternoon.

"As I was heading back to my stateroom, I decided to take a walk on the deck and met a very charming man. He was leaning on the railing enjoying the view. We started chatting, and before we knew it, it was almost one in the morning. He invited me to have lunch with him today in town."

"How nice." Frankie was pleased.

"Cool beans," Amy added.

"Glad to hear it," came from Nina. "Enjoy."

As the women departed, they went in the direction of their various destinations, promising to meet up later.

Nina, Amy, and Frankie discussed Marilyn's meeting someone. "Wow. I thought that stuff only happened in the movies," Amy mused.

"I hope she's OK," Frankie added.

"What do you mean?" Nina asked. "She's going to lunch with someone from the boat."

"You're right. I just get the sense she's a little vulnerable. The wound is still fresh. I wouldn't want some slick dude sweeping her off her feet. Amy, you know what I'm talking about," Frankie stated.

"I do. But we managed to fix that situation."

"True. But we don't know any of Marilyn's family or friends. After this cruise, we may never see her again. As much as I'm a Pollyanna, I still get the willies from time to time," Frankie admitted.

"Living in New York can give anyone the willies. Even if you think you have your paranoid thoughts under control, it's in your subconscious," Nina pointed out.

"I know you're right." Frankie sighed.

"Is there something you're not telling us?" Nina pried. "You seem a teensy-weensy melancholy."

Frankie took a beat. "OK. Here's the thing. I didn't want to say anything before because I felt ridiculous."

"About what?" Nina flinched.

"You know how much I love the food at Marco's, and his family?"

"Yes. His brother is cat-sitting for you, right?" Amy added.

"Well, I never took much notice of Giovanni. He was always in the background, running things when Marco would be talking to customers. Giovanni would also deliver dinner when I ordered out."

"So?" Nina peered at her closely.

"So . . . one night he stopped by to pick up the key and he was handsomely dressed, clean-shaven, beautiful black wavy hair slicked back. He was stunning." Frankie was starting to get embarrassed.

"And?" Amy pressed.

"And, of course, my legs turned to jelly. His slight accent and his, I dunno, his aura, blew me away. Probably because I wasn't expecting it."

"So what's the problem?" Nina asked.

"He's engaged. I found out just before we left. His cousin Antonio delivered dinner and told me Giovanni was in Italy visiting his fiancée, and I was not to worry because he would be back in time to take care of Bandit."

"Oh, honey. That stinks." Nina put her arm around Frankie.

"It's silly. I never went out with him or anything, but when I heard he was engaged, I was terribly disappointed." She shrugged and sighed.

"Well, at least you found someone who piqued your interest. That's a step in the right direction." Amy tried to put a positive spin on her friend's woes.

"I agree with Amy. And this is why we are on this trip. To forget about life for a while, meet people, and have fun. All of us seem to be going through some kind of transformation, so let's just go with it. At least for now." Nina was being very encouraging.

"Thanks. You guys are the best." Frankie put an arm around each of them.

"We should probably stop all this groping. The men will think we're not available." Amy snickered.

Frankie turned to Amy and planted a nude-shade lipstick kiss on her cheek. Then she turned to Nina and deposited what was left from her lips to Nina's cheek. Both made a silly

face at her. She dug into her jute bag and produced two tis-
sues and handed one to each of them. "Sorry." She smirked.

"Aw, honey pie. It's OK to have a schoolgirl crush. Heck,
remember when we all adored Drake Bell?" Nina asked.

"Who?" Frankie couldn't remember the name.

"Exactly," Nina said. "He was a TV heartthrob, and we
all had a crush on him."

"I'm drawing a blank. But I do remember Jesse Metcalfe.
He was a cutie; and he's still on TV."

"My point is, we had crushes on people we didn't know,
and now we can't even remember who they were." Nina was
consoling her friend.

"I don't know why I feel so foolish."

"Well, just stop it. Now," Nina instructed her.

As they walked through Mallory Square, they saw that it
was replete with holiday decorations. Older homes had a
more traditional décor, with wreaths, garland, and Santas on
the lawns. Hundreds of palm trees were adorned. Each frond
was wired with green lights, and white lights wrapped
around the trunk. Colorful lights adorned large gumbo-
limbo trees. White lamp poles decorated like candy canes
lined the streets. The gift market was equally festive, with
miniature lights in all the windows. Key West, known for
kitsch, had its fair share of tacky decorations as well. Some
of the Santas were scantily clad in shocking costumes that
would most likely be banned in most other towns. Festivities
abounded. All day and all night.

Nina decided to take the half-mile walk to the Hemingway
Home and Museum. They would do some shopping after
lunch on their way back to the ship.

Amy was reading the brochure to Nina and Frankie. Originally, Hemingway and his wife, Pauline, arrived in Key West
in 1928 and rented a home for three years until Pauline's generous and wealthy uncle Gus purchased the property for

them. The original home was built in 1851 and was in desperate need of renovation, which they completed in the early 1930s. Today, it is a historical landmark, home to forty-plus polydactyl cats. A fishing captain had given Hemingway his first multitoed cat named Snow White, and Hemingway began "collecting" them over the years. In 1940, when he and Pauline divorced, Hemingway moved to Cuba with his third wife, and Pauline maintained the property, cats and all, but Hemingway retained the rights to the home. It was eventually sold at auction for eighty thousand dollars."

"I wonder what that is in today's money."

"About seven hundred grand." Amy calculated the number in her head, and continued, "Get this. His former wife Pauline died ten years before he did, in 1951. They said the cause of death was shock. She was only fifty-six. Her son, Gregory, who had experienced difficulty his entire life with gender identity, had been arrested on a morals charge. Fifty years later, Dr. Gregory Hemingway, sometimes referred to as Gloria, was found dead in his cell in Miami–Dade County Women's Detention Center, where he was waiting to face a charge of indecent exposure."

"That's in the brochure?" Frankie asked, showing her surprise.

"Not the official one." Amy raised her eyebrows.

The women approached the Spanish Colonial estate along with over a hundred other tourists. "I guess we should have signed up for a tour," Nina said. "So, Miss Push-Planner, what should we do next? Wait in line?"

Frankie was forlorn. "I'm sorry, guys. I don't know what I was thinking. This is the busiest time of year. Maybe we can get into the gardens."

"Show us the way."

The property was brimming, with over a half dozen different varieties of palm trees, banana trees, royal poincianas, mimosas, bamboo, and Barbados cherry trees. Bougainvillea climbed the sides of the building. It was a veritable garden of paradise.

"Wow. How gorgeous is this?" Frankie commented.

"Spectacular," Nina said in awe.

"I'll say. 'Spectacular' doesn't describe it. I don't think I've ever seen anything so beautiful. It's a landscape wonderland," Amy said softly. "Oh, look. It's a Hemingway cat. There's another." She realized there were several walking idly on the property.

"Yes, this is the Hemingway House. Therefore, Hemingway cats," Nina said playfully.

"Yep. You're some kind of comedian." Amy bent down to stroke a big tabby. "You know it's in their DNA."

"What is?" Nina asked.

"Polydactyly. That's why there are so many of them."

Nina looked at Frankie. "She's a walking encyclopedia."

"Who needs Google when we have Amy?" Frankie kidded.

After the women spent an hour viewing the exterior, the line for the tour didn't seem to be getting any shorter.

"What do you say we start to head back? Stop at Mallory Square?" Frankie suggested. "We have another hour before lunch."

"Sounds like a plan," Nina agreed.

"I'm really sorry I didn't think this through. I remembered when I was in college you could just walk in." Frankie was apologetic.

"No worries, babe. I'm sure we'll find something to do that won't cause too much trouble," Nina reassured her. "And thanks for sharing your secret crush with us. I'm glad it wasn't anything too dreadful."

"Thanks, pal." Frankie was relieved that she had spilled her latest angst with her friends.

"That's what we're here for." Amy put her arm around Frankie. "No biggie about the tour. I think we saw enough."

As they headed toward the restaurant, a juggling Santa on

a unicycle, wearing a G-string and a flashing cap, deliberately blocked their passage. He gave them a few "Ho-ho-ho"s as he manipulated the Christmas ornaments in the air.

Frankie figured he was looking for some coin so she pulled out her wallet and stuffed a fiver in the stocking hanging from his big black belt. As they were walking away, she turned to the others, and asked, "Anyone have hand sanitizer?"

The three women burst out laughing, and Amy responded with a small spray of Purell.

"You are priceless," Frankie commented. "You are a walking bundle of information, and you have hand sanitizer to boot."

"Goes with the territory," Amy answered. "We're always slathering this stuff. You never know what's lurking in a petri dish." She smiled mockingly.

They were at Mallory Square again with a half hour to spare before they met Rachael for lunch. Nina opted to stop in the ceramic studio, while Frankie chose the candle shop. Amy decided to just keep window-shopping.

A half hour passed, and Nina came out with a beautiful dish in the shape of a lotus blossom. Frankie was carrying several lavender and vanilla candles. "You never know when you'll need a hostess gift," she reminded her friends.

"We still have three more ports to go," Amy reminded her.

"True, but I don't want to have to think about it." Frankie was matter-of-fact.

"What hostess are you gifting?" Nina asked casually.

Frankie answered, "I have no idea, but I always keep a little something just in case." She winked. "You do know that the ship has a mail-room facility that will pack and ship whatever you don't want to haul back, don't you?"

"Oh, that's really good to know." Nina smiled brightly. "I may get another one of these." She indicated the shopping bag she was carrying.

"On the way back from lunch. Rachael should be there any minute. I can't wait to hear about her dance lesson. Let's go." Frankie began to walk in the direction of the restaurant.

The women chatted, commenting on the party-like atmosphere filling the streets, the beautiful foliage, the quaint buildings and shops along the way. But it was mostly the nineteenth-century architecture that they found so interesting. "Did you know that during the nineteenth century, Key West was one of the wealthiest towns in the country?" Amy's factoids came into play. "There were a lot of shipwrecks and salvage companies. They also provided much of the salt used back then. They harvested it from receding tide pools. And they also made a lot of cigars." She giggled. "You know, right now we're closer to Cuba than we are to Miami," Amy continued. "This area was a great asset during the Spanish-American War."

"Who needs a tour guide when we have Amy?" Nina gave her a one-arm hug.

"Too bad we missed Cowboy Bill's Holiday Charity Hayride and the Lighted Boat Parade," Amy continued.

"So how did such a historical and vital area become so, so quirky?" Nina asked.

"They had rumrunners and speakeasies during Prohibition. Lots of piracy and illicit drugs. It was kind of like the Wild West. And its proximity and accessibility made it a safe haven for a lot of illegitimate businesses but a nightmare for authorities. Today, there are more bars per capita than any other place in the country!"

"Such an interesting little town." Frankie smiled at a Santa in short shorts riding a unicycle.

Nina snorted. "Interesting for sure."

As they turned the corner from Whitehead Street to Duval, Amy thought she spotted Marilyn heading in the direction of the Old Town Mexican Cafe. "Hey, isn't that Marilyn?"

"Looks like her. Must be where she's meeting her lunch date." Frankie giggled.

"Should we spy on her?" Nina asked impishly. They all looked at each other. "We can't help it if we happen to be passing by the restaurant. It is, in fact, on our way," Frankie said, with a straight face. "But we'd better hurry. Looks like she may be going inside."

The women hustled, trying to look casual with their fast pace. "We'll just say, 'We're from New York.'" Frankie chuckled.

They were less than a block away when Marilyn entered the café. It appeared she had spotted someone inside and gave a little wave.

"There she goes." Frankie slowed her pace so as not to bump into the throng of people milling about. She tried to look casual as she peeked into the café. "Dang. I can't see where she went."

"Don't look so obvious. She may see us and think we're spying on her," Nina warned.

Frankie turned, "Isn't that exactly what we're doing?"

"Good point, but let's not make spectacles of ourselves."

"What should we do now?" Amy asked.

Frankie nudged Nina. "You're the tallest. See if you can get a better look at whom she's with."

Nina craned her neck but all she could see was a profile, and his face was in the shadow. The only thing she could make out was a full head of salt-and-pepper hair. "Well, he's not bald." She felt like they were gawking a bit more than they should be. "Come on. Let's move it before she spots us."

They hurried past the café and continued to Conch Republic Seafood. "Now what?" Amy asked.

"What do you mean?" Nina replied.

"How are we going to find out who she's with?"

"We have several more days to figure that out," Frankie said, a glimmer in her eye.

"Oh, I know that look." Nina smirked.

"I have no idea what you're talking about." Frankie faked her answer.

"Ha." Nina linked her free arm through Frankie's. "I guess I'm going to have to keep my eye on you, too."

Music filled the streets from open windows and doors. From the outside, Conch Republic Seafood looked like a lively place. There was a covered deck for dining. And drinking. Rachael was pacing in front of the restaurant.

"How did it go?" Frankie asked.

"Great," Rachael answered with gusto. "I am so excited about all of it."

"What did you practice today?" Nina asked, as they approached the front door.

"Um, well, it's a surprise." Rachael had a playful look on her face.

"Hey, no secrets here, missy," Nina reminded her.

"Oh, come on. Henry is working on something, and I don't want to ruin the surprise. OK? Can we leave it at that? Please?" Rachael was almost pleading.

"OK. Fine. But it better be a good surprise." They followed the hostess, weaving their way to the outdoor patio area.

The menu was chock-full of seafood delights, and they decided to share several appetizers. Of course, the conch fritters were a must, along with peel-and-eat shrimp, crab cakes, and baked oysters. They resisted the temptation to order a round of beer. "Save the calories for dinner," Frankie joked.

They exchanged information about what they were able to see at the Hemingway House, but Rachael was much more interested in their spotting Marilyn.

"So you didn't get a good look at him?" Rachael sounded disappointed.

"No, except he has a head of salt-and-pepper hair."

"That describes about forty percent of the men on the boat." Rachael took a huge bite of the crab cake. "Yum. This is delish." After she swallowed a chunk, she asked, "What's next?"

"I think I'm going to stop by the shops at Mallory Square again," Nina said.

"I didn't mean that. I meant what's the next plan for sleuthing?" Rachael's curiosity was aroused.

"I haven't figured that out yet. Who do you think we are, Charlie's Angels?" Frankie let out a loud roar. She motioned for the waitress to bring the check.

"Let's see. It's almost two thirty. Is there anything else you guys want to do or see? Personally, I wouldn't mind going back to the ship and getting some sun," Frankie said. "The ship leaves at six. We should also decide what we're going to do for fun tonight."

"I think we should do the speed dating. It could be a hoot." Amy inserted her idea.

"Count me in," Rachael squealed.

"I guess you won't let me sit that one out, will you?" Nina asked, as if she knew the answer.

"Correct. The only sitting you will be doing is interviewing potential love connections," Frankie told her.

"Love connections?" Nina moaned. "All right. Count me in, too."

"Excellent. I'll sign us up when I get back to the ship. Any ideas for dinner?"

"There's a deck party at six. We should go to that first. How about Asian?" asked Rachael.

"If I ever digest those fritters." Nina rubbed her belly.

The women laughed out loud. "Me too!" Amy patted her stomach.

They split the check, gathered their tote bags and their purchases, and went off to their destinations.

When Frankie returned to her stateroom, she called the number listed on the manifest for activities. She punched the four-digit number. "Good afternoon. Guest services," came a chipper voice over the phone.

"Good afternoon. I'd like to make a reservation for the speed dating tonight," Frankie explained.

"Excellent," Chirpie replied. "Do you have an age preference?"

Frankie balked for a moment. "Uh, I guess. Late-thirties to late forties. Maybe a scooch at fifty but he's gotta have spunk!" Frankie laughed. Chirpie joined her. "There will be four of us." Frankie gave her their names. She waited a moment for Chirpie to record the information. "Can you tell me how many people are attending?" Frankie scrunched, anticipating the response.

"So far we have thirty people. Seventeen women and thirteen men."

"What happens when there aren't an equal number?" Frankie asked.

"The women will sit out a round. But don't you worry. We always end up with a balance," Chirpie chirped. "Please be sure to sign in by eight thirty. Caribbean Ballroom."

Frankie hung up, thinking she might have made a huge mistake. In any event, she was taking down her gal pals with her. She chuckled. *Should be an interesting night.*

Instead of changing into a bathing suit, Frankie decided to wrap herself in a large, sleeveless spa robe and sit on her veranda. She brought a book with her, but she knew she wasn't going to be able to read. There was too much going on in her head. But wasn't the reason for this trip to relax? Put the worries on a shelf for a few days? She grabbed one of the pillows, placed it on the cocktail table, perched herself on one of the chairs, and stretched her legs across her makeshift lounge chair. Even though it was a little awkward, Frankie was able to relax into the quasi-dreamlike state of Theta. The place between dreaming and being awake. Most of us recognize it in the morning when we first wake up. Our surroundings are a backdrop in our dream. And vice versa. We're half here and half there. Wherever "there" is.

Frankie's mind drifted from the conference room at her office to Giovanni's eyes. She came out of her trance with a start. *Why couldn't she stop thinking about him?* Like it or not, she *had* to. She was embarrassed about the way she felt the night her legs went all rubbery on her. She strained to remember if she had flirted with him. She hoped not. And this is probably why she avoided romance. *Well, too bad.* For the moment, she was on a singles cruise. *Suck it up and get over it*, she told herself. She turned her attention to a fishing boat heading toward the dock and imagined what life must be like for the wife or girlfriend of a fisherman. She guessed it wasn't as rough as the life of the women in New England, where they had real widows walks on the Victorian homes. The thought gave her the shivers. She saw two women waving at the fishermen from the dock. They looked happy. It brought a smile to Frankie's lips.

A short while later, she heard a ruckus coming from the corridor. Frankie figured it was her posse returning from their last-minute shopping. She could hear Rachael shrieking with laughter. She opened the door and saw Nina standing on a chair while Rachael handed her a bunch of green leaves. Amy held a roll of tape. "What in the world are you doing?" she called from her doorway.

Rachael held up a shopping bag. "Mistletoe! It was fifty percent off at the Christmas Shoppe."

"So you had to buy the remaining inventory?" Frankie smirked.

"You know me. I simply cannot resist a bargain," Rachael quipped.

"I hope you realize there are security cameras on every level." Frankie pointed to the small round ball that was at the end of the corridor.

"Oops." Rachael covered her mouth with one hand. "Maybe they'll throw me in the brig."

"A brig is for military vessels," Frankie corrected her. "They just call it jail on a cruise ship." Frankie smiled wickedly.

"They really have a jail on board?" Amy looked at Frankie.

"They do. It's the size of a broom closet, with a single bed."

"And you know this how?" Nina eyed her friend suspiciously.

"I did my homework. With our little ensemble, I had to be sure they could accommodate all of us." Frankie let out a laugh. The elevator dinged, indicating that someone was getting off on their floor. Thinking fast, they scrambled into Frankie's stateroom. It would have taken too long for them to find their keycards. Nina carried the chair as Amy and Rachael brushed past Frankie, who was holding the door open for them.

The women collapsed on the bed, laughing hysterically.

Frankie reached into the shopping bag and counted a dozen swags of mistletoe. "So how many of these little things have you planted so far?" She eyed Rachael suspiciously.

"Just one, so far." Rachael sat up. "Too many people were milling about. We'll finish our mission later." She turned to Amy and Nina. "Right, girls?"

Nina moaned. "Am I supposed to be carrying a chair around? That might look a bit odd, don't you think?"

"Good point," Amy concurred. "Nina, what if you wear a pair of wedge sandals? Could you reach a few doorways?"

"Oh, so I'm the one who has to distribute these around the ship? I don't think so," Nina declared.

"Oh, come on. Don't be a spoilsport," Rachael whined.

"Uh-uh. Not me, kiddo. I'm not going to cruise jail."

"How about this?" Frankie had an idea. "We get a long stick and attach one of the bunches on the stick. This way, Rachael can carry it around with her and hang it over the head of every man she sees."

Amy and Nina hooted. "Great idea."

"Very funny." Rachael pouted. "I'm trying to have a little fun. OK, mischievous fun. But it's not going to hurt anybody."

Nina thought for a moment. "If we can cover the security cameras in the elevators, I might be able to reach just above the sliding doors."

"Aren't you becoming a criminal now?" Frankie teased.

"Let's do it." Amy clapped her hands.

"OK. But remember, all for one, and one for all. I hope there's room enough in that jail for all of us." Frankie sighed in resignation. She knew she wasn't going to win this battle.

"Yay!" Amy shouted. "When should we do this?"

"After the speed-dating thing," Frankie suggested.

"Right. That thing." Nina sneered. "I don't know what's worse, getting caught hanging mistletoe or getting rejected by a bunch of guys."

"First of all, they won't put us in cruise-ship jail. That's reserved for someone who does something harmful. And as far as getting rejected, you need to change your attitude, missy." Frankie winked at her friend.

"What's everyone wearing tonight?" Amy asked, changing the subject.

"I'm wearing a long black sheath with a silver necklace," Frankie said.

"Is it formal?" Amy asked.

"No. Just wanted to get a little dressy for tonight. Who knows. I might meet Prince Charming," Frankie added.

"And you've changed *your* tune, too," Nina chided her friend.

"Yep. That's what we're here for. Fun. Sun. And maybe a date," Amy chimed in. "I have a deep purple jumpsuit that will be a little dressy with some accessories."

"I have a pair of navy capris with a matching short-sleeve jacket," said Nina.

Rachael thought for a moment. "And I have a short red fit-and-flare dress."

"I think we shall make a lovely troupe. Who could possibly resist us?" Frankie joked. The others chuckled. "Dinner is at six at the Kunya Siam Thai restaurant. The event is at eight thirty in the Caribbean Ballroom."

"Has anyone seen Peter today?" Amy asked. The others shook their heads. "What about Marilyn?"

"Not since we stalked her at lunchtime," Nina replied.

"Should we call her and see what she's up to?" Amy asked.

"Sure, why not?" Frankie replied. She picked up the house phone and asked to be connected with Marilyn Mitchell's stateroom.

A pleasant voice answered. "Hello?"

"Hi, Marilyn. It's Frankie. How are you today?"

"Very well. Thank you. And you?"

"Just peachy." Frankie was being sincere. "We were just checking to see if you wanted to join us tonight for dinner. We're also going to do that speed-dating thing."

"Thank you for thinking of me, but I already have dinner plans." It was obvious that Marilyn wasn't going to give up too much information.

"That's wonderful." Frankie hitched her eyebrows as she looked at the other women. "How was your lunch?" She was trying to pry info out of Marilyn without being too pushy.

"It was lovely." And that was all she said.

"Glad to hear it. Well, you enjoy your evening. Maybe we'll see you tomorrow. We'll be at sea all day."

"You enjoy the festivities. Thanks again for thinking of me." Marilyn ended the call.

Frankie turned to the others. "She has a date with the mystery man. I'm assuming it's the same guy. She didn't offer, and I didn't want to pry."

"Maybe we can stalk her later," Nina said wickedly.

"Looks like we have a full evening ahead of us. We should get a move on," Frankie suggested.

With that, the women departed to their individual staterooms to get ready for the evening.

Chapter Sixteen

Day 2
Evening

Around five forty-five, Frankie began rapping on everyone's door. "Ready?" They exited their rooms one at a time. "Should I knock on Peter's door?"

"Nah. If he wanted to hang out with us, I'm sure he would have said something. Maybe we'll run into him later."

"Do you think he'll do the speed-dating thing?" Amy asked.

"Only if he's crazy," Nina quipped.

Frankie noticed that Rachael was carrying one of the small bouquets of mistletoe. Amy had the tape. When the elevator arrived, it was empty. Rachael removed her scarf and handed it to Nina to cover the security camera. "You realize they will see you do that, correct?"

"Yeah. But this makes it more fun," Amy answered.

Nina reached up. It was a bit of a stretch, but she was able to drape the scarf over the protruding camera lens. Rachael handed her the bouquet, and Amy ripped off a piece of tape. Another long reach, but Nina managed to secure the mistletoe right above the elevator doors. Amy was trying to control her excitement. "This is fun."

"As long as we don't get into trouble." Frankie eyed Rachael. "This was your idea, remember."

"It's not like we're defacing property. We're enhancing it. This is a singles cruise, correct?" Rachael responded.

The elevator was about to stop on another floor while the women regained their composure. When the doors opened two other women entered, and said, "Good evening."

Amy stifled a laugh. The two other women hadn't noticed the new addition to the elevator car. As it ascended, several more passengers got in. By the time they reached the deck for the Thai restaurant, the car was full, but no one had noticed the green foliage hanging above the doors. Amy, Nina, Rachael, and Frankie excused themselves as they wiggled their way out of the car. They looked up at the mistletoe and shrugged. "We tried," Amy said.

"Depending on how this event goes, we'll either have to put some in every elevator or ditch the idea completely." Rachael looked slightly forlorn.

"Oh, cheer up, cookie." Nina elbowed her. "There wasn't anyone in the elevator you would have wanted to kiss anyway. Remember, be careful what you wish for."

"You're right." Rachael sighed, then perked up. "One of mine has already come true. Dancing with Henry Dugan."

"See? Creative visualization," Frankie added. "Keep good, positive thoughts in your head. A greater power is listening."

"Amen to that," Nina agreed.

Though the ship wasn't enormous, it was large enough to accommodate as many as eight hundred passengers and four hundred crew members. The women's staterooms were conveniently located for elevators and the main deck, but the restaurant was on the far side of the ship. It took several minutes for them to get there.

"This thing is massive," Amy commented, as they passed

several other restaurants, a game room with several ping-pong tables, gardens, and a library. "I'm kind of glad we'll be cruising tomorrow. There's a lot to check out."

"Did you check the manifest for tomorrow?" Frankie asked.

"I have another dance class in the morning. I think I'll sign up to play tennis. The only bad part is that you have no idea whom you're playing against. You're supposed to state your proficiency level, but people fib. I don't suppose any of you would be interested?"

"I'm taking a cooking class in the culinary studio in the afternoon," Amy informed them.

"There's a painting workshop I'm thinking of doing," Frankie said.

"Yoga for me, then going to the spa for a facial and a massage," Nina replied.

"Seems like we're taking advantage of the amenities," Frankie noted.

The Thai restaurant wasn't as large as the steak house but had a view of the ocean. The ship's horn blew once, indicating it was leaving port.

"This is great." Amy looked out at the sunset forming on the horizon. "And don't forget, we have a full moon tonight, too."

"A full moon and speed dating. What could possibly go wrong?" Nina joked.

They asked the waiter for suggestions, and he was happy to oblige. They started with mixed appetizers and a green mango salad. Orders of jumbo shrimp tamarind, red curry chicken, and garlic beef were to be shared. After the waiter left, Nina grunted. "Full moon and speed dating à la garlic and curry. We are going to be odoriferous for that party."

"Oh my gosh. You're right." Amy's eyes widened.

"Love me, love my breath," Rachael declared. "Besides, I have a package of those breath mints that dissolve instantly. I'm happy to share my 'life savers' with you." Rachael used air quotes to emphasize her pun.

As they were uttering sounds of delight, the conversation went back to Marilyn and her mysterious gentleman friend.

"I wonder why she was being so guarded." Nina dipped her chopsticks into the chicken curry.

"Maybe she doesn't want to jinx it," Amy suggested.

"Or maybe she's just one of those private kinds of people. We are, after all, just a bit rowdy," Rachael pointed out.

"You being the rowdiest," Nina teased.

Rachael raised her hand. "Guilty as charged."

"Did she give you any indication that she wanted to hang out with us again?" Amy asked.

"Not really. I said that we'll probably see her sometime tomorrow, but she didn't acknowledge anything specific."

"Well, I hope she's having a good time." Amy helped herself to another jumbo shrimp.

"She didn't sound disappointed or anything. In fact, she sounded fine," Frankie said. "But I am a bit curious about this guy. He seems to have monopolized her time."

Everyone became silent. Then Nina spoke up. "I think we should leave Marilyn alone. She seems pretty savvy. I'm sure she can take care of herself. She's sophisticated and well traveled. If she needs company or assistance, she knows where to find us."

The others grumbled in agreement, all secretly wanting to know what was happening with Marilyn, especially since it seemed to be happening so fast.

"The mistletoe mission is enough trouble for us to get into. Plus, we still have the speed-dating adventure. I vote we limit our escapades to two a night," Frankie suggested.

"Party pooper," Rachael bellyached.

"You won't be happy until we make total spectacles of ourselves, will you?" Nina mocked.

"Correct." Rachael made a face.

Amy pointed out the window. "Look at that sunset. It's spectacular! If we hurry, we can watch the moon come up on the other side of the ship."

"Good idea." Frankie motioned to the waiter to bring the check. They gave him their keycards and he processed the bill.

Frankie left him an extra thirty dollars on the table. She hoped she wouldn't end up in the ship's jail for breaking the rule about no tipping.

They passed through another garden area that led to the pool. Several people were still swimming and lounging about as the full cold moon peeked its way above the horizon.

"I wonder if they still call it the Full Cold Moon in the tropics?" Rachael asked. "Amy, genius of us all. What say you?"

"Since you asked, it's also referred to as the Long Night Moon because it's around the longest night of the year. In the Southern Hemisphere, it's called the Strawberry, Rose, or Honey Moon, as in honey, not marriage. I would guess in this part of the world it may be called the Rose Moon, since it looks a little rosy right now. But that is the extent of my lunar almanac knowledge."

"Very impressive," a voice from behind said. They turned in unison.

"Richard. Nice to see you again." Nina had almost forgotten that she had met someone the night before. Not as in the cute-meet they refer to in romantic comedies. But someone other than her group of friends. She introduced him to the others, starting with Amy. "This is our own walking-talking Google search engine."

"Nice to meet all of you," Richard replied. "Are you going to the event tonight? The one in the Caribbean Ballroom?"

"You mean the speed dating?" Rachael asked.

He lowered his voice. "Not sure if I want to be that obvious." He smiled.

"Isn't that why we're here?" Rachael was getting a bit sassy with him.

"I'm trying to keep a low profile," Richard joked.

"You're not doing a very good job of it." Rachael continued to taunt him.

Nina interrupted the bantering. "Don't mind her. She's the hooligan of the outfit."

"I can see that." Richard gave her a big grin.

"I think we should head down to the ballroom and let the games begin," Frankie recommended.

The group moved toward the elevator. Rachael eyed Richard. He could certainly reach the top of the elevator doors. "We have a little job for you."

"Really? What kind of job?" Richard looked doubtful.

Rachael pulled a small bunch of greenery with white berries from her purse. "Here. Tape this to the area above the elevator doors." Amy took the roll of tape out of her bag and ripped off a piece.

"You want me to put mistletoe above the doors?" Richard questioned the task.

"Yes. Please." Rachael batted her eyes at him.

"You *are* the hooligan of the bunch, aren't you?" Richard took the greenery and the tape and affixed it to the area above the doors. "You realize we're on camera?"

"Yeah. Yeah. And there's a jail on the ship. They can arrest us for decorating," Rachael retorted. "Quick, someone call the foliage police."

Richard laughed out loud. "You gals are a hoot. I'll tell them you held a candy cane to the back of my head, threatening to 'stick it to me.'"

Everyone chuckled. "You're a pretty funny guy yourself," Nina commented.

The doors of the elevator opened. Richard put his arm across the doors, keeping them from getting out. He pointed at the mistletoe. "Excuse me, but I need a kiss from each of you."

All four of them froze. "Kidding." Richard moved his arm away. "But now you can see how much trouble you can cause." He chuckled.

"Yeah, Rachael. See what you started?" Frankie mocked her.

"Oh, shut it." Rachael sauntered out.

They made their way to the registration table, resisting the flight reflex the women were feeling. Frankie grabbed Nina's hand, and Amy clutched Rachael's arm.

Nina muttered to Richard, "Do we look desperate or terrified?"

He laughed again. "I think 'terrified' would probably be an apt description. What are you terrified about?"

"Flunking out at speed dating," Nina replied quietly.

"I doubt that will happen," he said reassuringly.

"If you say so." Obviously, Nina had not picked up on the fact that he just might be interested in *her*.

Everyone was handed a card and a small pencil. Nina counted the women in the room. There were eighteen. Then she counted seventeen men. Pretty good odds, and all of them looked respectable. The women were assigned their tables and took their seats. The moderator spoke into the microphone, giving the instructions. "Because we have such a good turnout, we are going to have to limit the interaction to eight minutes. When you hear the bell, the men will get up and move to the next table in ascending order. So if you are at table ten you will move to table eleven, then come back around until you've been at all the tables. After each session, please mark the cards accordingly. We'll collect them after the event and notify the participants. Any questions?"

A few mutterings but nothing audible. "OK. Your time starts now."

Frankie cringed, thinking that eight minutes is a very long time if you're trying to make conversation. But it wasn't a whole lot of time to get to know someone. Striking a balance was key. She decided on topics that would weed some of them out. "Do you like to hunt?" If the answer was yes, she would cross them off the list pronto. "What kind of music do you like?" Innocuous but important. If they said "goth" or "heavy metal," she'd scratch half their name off the list. Maybe they could expand their horizons. Having a job was key. "What do you do for a living?" She wanted specifics. She remembered one fella she had met online who said he was an engineer. Turned out he worked on car engines. Not that there was anything wrong with that, but "mechanic" would have been more accurate. Then there was the doctor who really wasn't a doctor, who also wanted to be friends but sent the Valentine's Day card.

She realized that if she approached this speed dating like a game, it would be a lot more fun. "What's your favorite movie?" That, too, tells a lot about a person. Any of the Halloween slasher movies would immediately disqualify the suitor. She didn't expect them to express interest in a romantic comedy like *Sleepless in Seattle*, but a good, campy, well-written comedy like *There's Something About Mary* was one of her favorites. It was a good laugh for men and women looking for love.

Nina caught Frankie's eye. Frankie bit her lip, trying not to laugh. One after another, the men sat, asked questions, and moved as soon as the bell rang. Everyone was busily marking their cards. In approximately two hours, the anxiety-provoking event was over. The mood was palpable. There was a sense of relief in the room, not the panic Nina had expected.

"Thank you very much for joining us. We'll have your results to you before midnight. They will be slid under your doors. Enjoy the rest of the evening."

As they were leaving the ballroom, Nina dropped back slightly, wondering how Richard had fared. He was a nice-looking man. Definitely in his favor. He also had a nice baritone voice. Another plus.

They had had the opportunity to speak uninterrupted for eight minutes, which gave her some additional insight into him. And it also sparked some interest. She found out that Richard was an attorney who specialized in environmental law. He was one of the good guys who went after the bad guys. The ones who polluted the rivers and groundwater. He liked to play tennis. Had done a bit of horseback riding when he lived in Arizona. Now lives in Philadelphia, with a dog he rescued from a junkyard. Major plus. She hoped he would check off the same box for her as she had for him.

Frankie connected with two men. One was a writer from Huntsville, Alabama. Fortunately, he wasn't looking for a publisher. He wrote technical manuals for NASA. *Who knew that was a real job?* He had a good sense of humor, but Alabama was a bit of a stretch when it came to fostering a relationship. The second one was a bit quirky. A musician from New Orleans. Another geographically undesirable situation, but she was learning how to be comfortable around men again. She might not have met a love match, but it was good practice.

Amy connected with a guy who collected comic books.

You wouldn't know it by looking at him, if comic-book collectors had "a look." Truth be told, many were nerdy, and some got way too involved with the identities of fictional characters. But fortunately, Evan was in it for the financial aspect of collectibles. He had started collecting graphic novels when he was a kid and was able to pay for his college tuition after selling half his collection. Evan lived in St. Petersburg, Florida. Another geographically undesirable situation. But Amy enjoyed meeting new people. All in all, she had enjoyed the experience. She hoped Evan would mark her down as "interested as a friend." She wanted to see the latest Star Wars movie playing in the theater on the boat, but she knew none of the other women would want to go.

Rachael connected with one guy. He was a software developer from Chicago, but they had a common interest in dancing, and she encouraged him to take Henry's class. She didn't say why or what they were working on, but she assured him he would have fun.

Nina asked Richard if he had enjoyed the musical-chair humiliation. He laughed and said he had enjoyed himself talking to a variety of women and getting to know more about her. But that's all he said. Nothing about meeting up or reconnecting at some point. Maybe he was waiting to see what she wrote down on her card? She hoped so.

The three women waited for Nina to come out to the open foyer area. She was smiling and ushered them off to the elevators.

"Everything all right?" Frankie asked.

"Yes. Keep walking," Nina instructed her friends.

When they were far enough away from the rest of the speeders, she suggested they go back to the Stargazer Lounge, recon and review the past two hours.

As they entered the star-glistening space, someone was

playing "Clair de Lune" on the grand piano. "Oh, that is one of my favorite pieces," Frankie cooed. They made their way to a table as far away as they could so that other people could not overhear them. They waited for the server to take their drink orders, then they huddled close together to share their experiences.

"The one thing we should have thought about is the 'geographically undesirable' locations. Not that where they live is horrible, but a long-distance relationship is hard to maintain even with all the technology we have. Zoom, Skype, FaceTime are all good to fill in some gaps, but it can't hold an intimate relationship together," Nina observed astutely.

"I think it was the simple idea that there would be single people, people like us. Workaholics, failed relationships, wanting to make a human connection," Frankie said, tossing her thoughts into the conversation.

"To be honest, I wasn't particularly banking on meeting Mr. Right. Just meeting *people*. Getting back into the game. Interacting with the opposite sex in a social atmosphere instead of being covered in protective clothing and a face shield," Amy explained.

Rachael cleared her throat. "I like being around men."

The other three gave her a sideways look at the same time. It was a synchronized "No kidding" statement. "Oh, come on. I don't mean it in a salacious way. I mean I like their company," Rachael said, defending herself.

"Until you realize they're jerks," Nina interjected. "It's no wonder the past tense of 'fling' is 'flung.' After you have your fling, they get flung out the door."

The women tried to contain their laughter.

"I'm still happy we're on this trip," Frankie announced. "It's a nice change from the daily grind. The ship is beautiful, the service is impeccable, and I have to say, the food has been top drawer. There is no lack of things to do or people to meet. Even though we haven't made any love connections, it was a good warm-up exercise."

"Warm-up for what?" Nina asked.

"The rest of our lives," Frankie said, waxing philosophical. "Think about it. All of us are about to make big moves. Everyone but me, that is, but that's OK for now. I may not be making a big move, but it's helped me get out of my funk. And that, I hope, will get me to move on, too."

Rachael was about to disagree concerning big moves, but she realized that her big move was literally a dance move. She had met her dance idol. She had danced with him. And now she would be working with him and his foundation. That was a huge move. She was circumspect. "I believe this trip is changing my life for the better." The women raised their glasses and toasted their good fortune and a happy, fulfilling future.

Frankie peeked around the room. She hadn't noticed Marilyn in the lounge when they had first arrived. And now she was leaving with someone. A man. Frankie craned her neck to see who it was, but he was holding the door open for Marilyn, and Frankie couldn't get a good look at his face. "Hey. Marilyn just left with some guy."

"Who?" Amy squeaked.

"I don't know. Couldn't see his face."

"Was it the same guy from lunch?" Rachael asked.

"I dunno. Nina couldn't get a good look at him either. All we know is that he's about six feet tall and has salt-and-pepper hair."

"That describes about a hundred men on board," Nina reminded them.

"Should we follow them?" Rachael was in a mischievous mood.

"Tell you what. You stick to your mistletoe operation, and

Amy and I will tail them. It's a lot easier to duck behind a door if there are only two of us," Frankie commented.

"OK then. Let's go." Rachael checked her bag to see how many bunches of mistletoe were left. "I've got four more in here."

Amy handed Nina the tape. "Let's meet back in our rooms in an hour."

"Sounds like a plan." Frankie got up and scurried toward the door. "Come on, Amy. Shake a leg."

They made a hasty exit, hoping they could catch up with Marilyn and the mystery man without being discovered. The couple went outside to walk along the deck. Amy and Frankie weren't sure how they could stay cloaked, but there were several deck chairs stacked along the wall just high enough for them to squat behind and observe. Marilyn and her suitor were leaning on the railing, but Marilyn's position obscured his face. Amy was leaning as much as she could to get a good look at them when her foot slipped on the deck and she stumbled onto the walkway.

As the couple turned to see what had caused the commotion, the man yelled, "Amy? Amy Blanchard? What are you doing here?"

"Dad?" came the equally shocked response from the young woman sprawled on the deck. He rushed over to his prone daughter and helped her up. Both started talking at once as Marilyn looked on in shock.

"Dad. I thought you were going on a golfing trip?" Amy was in a state of disbelief.

"I was, but Gary came down with some kind of stomach thing and couldn't make it. I didn't know what I should do for the next few days, but since I was already in Palm Beach, I thought I'd check out any cruises leaving from Miami. I realized it was a last-minute thing, but this one still had a few available staterooms. I decided a cruise would be relaxing."

"Yeah. About that, Dad." Amy was now standing with her arms akimbo. "What are you doing on a singles cruise?"

"I could ask you the same question, my dear." William Blanchard smiled at his daughter. "You said you were going on vacation with your girlfriends."

Frankie came out of her hiding place. "Hi, Mr. Blanchard." She waved sheepishly. Marilyn hadn't moved; nor had her expression of total confusion changed.

William Blanchard continued. "And yes, the bonus about this cruise is that it's not filled with sugar-crazed kids or couples mooning over each other." He put his hands on her shoulders. "I thought this would be a nice way to meet new people, relax, and see some sights. Is that all right with you?"

Amy gave her father a big hug. "I am very much all right with it."

Seeing the look on Marilyn's face, Frankie immediately jumped in. "And this is the mystery man you were having dinner with tonight?"

Marilyn began to walk toward them. She gave them a dry, wary look. "If I didn't know better, I would say the two of you were spying on me."

"Uh-oh. Busted," Amy quipped.

Frankie began to ramble about gigolos, lotharios, and how they prey on vulnerable women. They wanted to be sure she was safe.

Marilyn took a moment to digest what Frankie had said. "You mean you were concerned about me?"

"Yes," Amy said. "I just went through a similar thing with my mother." She looked at her father. She jerked her thumb in the direction of her dad. "Not this guy."

"Well, that's a relief," Marilyn said, with an air of skepticism.

"Seriously. After my parents got divorced"—she pointed at her father—"my mother got involved with a guy who was taking advantage of her and her money. Thankfully, she dumped him fairly recently. We didn't want the same thing to happen to you."

William Blanchard resisted the urge to say, "My money, too," but he thought better of it. He didn't want to seem petty in front of Marilyn.

"But we just met." Marilyn was stoic.

"True. But we like you. And we know life can be kind of crummy when a relationship is over." Amy defended herself and her friends. "You seemed lonely, and you clearly didn't want to be on this cruise, so when you suddenly found someone, we didn't know if you were being duped by some suave Don Juan." She looked at her father, then at Marilyn. "Just so you know, he is not that kind of guy. And I'm not just saying that because he's my dad."

Frankie immediately came to her aid. "She's right. I've known Mr. Blanchard all my life. He is kind and decent."

"I think I should go back to my stateroom. This is a bit much for me to digest. If you'll excuse me. Good night." She turned and went back into the main lobby of the deck.

"Marilyn, wait." William wanted to go after her, but he needed to sort this out with his daughter.

Amy looked at her father. "We can sort this out some other time. You go after her." Amy crossed her arms across her chest. "Now. Hurry up. Go. Scoot."

He shook his head in bewilderment. "Fine. We'll talk later. I assume you are registered under your real name?"

"Of course. Are you?" she asked, sneering.

"Yes. Of course." He turned on his heel and hurried to catch up with Marilyn.

"Holy mackerel." Frankie exhaled. "You OK?"

"I'm not sure." Amy grabbed the railing. "I surely wasn't expecting *this*."

"You should be happy your dad is out and about and not

sulking alone for New Year's." Frankie put her arm around Amy's shoulder.

"Of course, you're right. I'm thrilled he's not moping. I think it's just the jolt of seeing him. *Here*. And with another woman. As far as I know, he wasn't much into dating. I think the shock of my mother's divorcing him threw him for a loop, and he stayed away from women in general."

"So it's good that he's finding interest in being social." Frankie turned Amy around and looked her straight in the eyes. "You know, it seems that the older we get, the harder it is to find an acceptable mate. Partner. Let him enjoy his new-found freedom."

"But they've been divorced for years. He should have found his freedom a while ago," Amy whined.

"I didn't mean it in the legal sense. I meant that he is finally comfortable and feels he can be free to engage in social interaction with women."

"I know you're right. When my mother met Rusty, I thought my father was going to have a seizure. Not that he wanted her back, but he was frustrated that she would fall for some ne'er-do-well. I never believed Rusty's story about being related to the Jacobs family in Switzerland."

"See, everything is turning out OK," Frankie reassured her friend. "Come on. Let's go back to my stateroom. I have a bottle of prosecco in the minifridge."

William Blanchard could hardly catch his breath as he hurried toward Marilyn. He could understand her being upset. Who would want to discover someone's daughter lurking in the shadows? Marilyn moved closer to the elevator, William close on her heels. She pressed the UP button, and the doors opened. Two people got out, leaving the elevator car empty. As Marilyn was about to step in, William scooted in behind her and quickly pressed the DOOR CLOSE button so no one could get into the car with them. She stood motionless and silent.

"Marilyn, I feel I owe you an apology, but I'm not sure what I'm apologizing for."

"William, I enjoyed your company very much today. And I enjoyed Amy's last night. Quite frankly, I don't know what to think."

"How about not thinking about it and let me explain as much as I can. You heard most of the conversation. I was supposed to go on a golfing trip, but it got canceled. I didn't want to spend another New Year's Eve sitting in a bar with a bunch of strangers. Nor did I want to spend it in a hotel room by myself. This cruise seemed like a good alternative. Granted, the people on the ship would be strangers. Well, not so much anymore." He gave a soft chuckle. "It was an opportunity to relax, be in warm weather, and be around people like me."

Marilyn seemed to soften a bit. "I suppose I may have overreacted. But you can certainly understand my surprise."

"I do. Please let me make it up to you somehow." William had a pleading look in his eyes.

"I suppose you can start now." She pointed to the mistletoe dangling above the doors.

William took her in his arms and gave her a sweet, gentle kiss on the lips. It didn't linger, but it was enough to say, "Heck, I like you. A lot."

The elevator doors opened, and several people hooted at the couple, who were still in each other's embrace.

William led Marilyn out of the car and pointed at the mistletoe. "Enjoy."

Frankie knocked on Nina's and Rachael's doors. "Come in. You've gotta hear this."

"What's going on?" Rachael asked. She was clad in pink pajamas covered with sketches of musical instruments.

"Everything all right?" Nina looked concerned as she wrapped a bathrobe around her T-shirt and boy shorts.

"Dandy," Amy squawked.

Frankie held the door open as the women shuffled in. "Tell them," she directed Amy.

Rachael and Nina deposited themselves on the sofa. Amy sat on the bed in a big huff. "The good news is that I don't have anything wrong with my brain as far as hallucinating, nor do I suffer from parental guilt."

"What on earth are you talking about?" Nina looked at her with wonder. Frankie bit the inside corner of her lower lip to keep from bursting out laughing.

"Remember when I thought I saw my dad, and Rachael thought it was guilt?" They nodded in agreement. "And the other day, when I was feeling a little dizzy because I thought I saw him again?"

"Yes. Get on with it puh-leeze," Rachael demanded.

"It wasn't a mirage. He's on the ship."

"He's wh-what?" Rachael stammered.

"Are you kidding?" Nina realized it was a rhetorical question.

"I. Kid. You. Not." Amy practically spelled the words out.

"Oh wait," Frankie gleefully interjected. "It gets better."

"How?" Nina asked curiously. As if William Blanchard's presence on board wasn't enough of a shock.

"Marilyn's mystery man?" Amy spread her hands inviting the answer.

"No. You can't be serious," Nina blurted out.

"Yes. And yes I can," Amy replied calmly.

"That is simply unbelievable," Rachael remarked, astounded. "How did you find out? Where were you?"

Amy, with the help of Frankie, recounted their steps, how Amy stumbled, and voilà.

"Were they kissing? Hugging?" Rachael was trying to pull the words out of Amy's mouth.

"Nope. They were leaning on the railing. Chatting. He pointed up at something, then I planted my face on the deck."

"They call that 'face-planting,'" Rachael said.

"Yes. Evidently people do it so often they now have a new word for 'klutz,'" Frankie chimed in.

"And then what happened?" Rachael was sitting on the edge of the bed, waiting for more details.

"Marilyn left, and I made Dad go after her. I told him we could discuss this little vacation snafu later."

"How long ago did this happen?" Nina asked.

"Half hour maybe. As long as it took for us to get back here," Frankie said.

"I wonder if he was able to catch up with her," Rachael mused.

"I should probably call him." Amy lifted the house phone off the cradle. "Mr. William Blanchard, please."

Two rings, and he answered. "Hello?"

"Dad. It's Amy."

"I wasn't expecting anyone else to call me Dad." He was trying to keep the conversation light, all the while knowing he was going to get a tongue-lashing from his daughter for not telling her his plans.

"Very funny," Amy quipped. "I caught a glimpse of you twice, and thought I was having some kind of hallucination. You should have told me your plans."

"You didn't tell me yours either, doll."

"Fair enough. So how can we continue our trip without it becoming awkward? Speaking of which, were you able to catch up with Marilyn?"

"Yes, I was." William wasn't about to kiss and tell, but he certainly wanted to thank whoever stuck that mistletoe in the elevator. It didn't look like it was official. "She was very gracious about the whole thing."

"Are you going to see her again?" Amy crossed her fingers.

"As a matter of fact, I am. We're going to play miniature golf tomorrow after lunch. And then some bocce and croquet. We're doing the circuit as it's listed on the manifest."

Amy heaved a sigh of relief. "I'm very happy to hear that." She gave the thumbs-up to everyone trying to listen in.

"I sure hope Marilyn isn't mad at us."

"Well, she was a bit peeved that you were spying on her."

"Mea culpa," Amy said. "I hope she can forgive us."

"I'm sure she'll get over it." William smiled. His instincts told him she would. "It's almost one thirty in the morning, my dear. Time for me to get these old bones to bed."

"Old bones? That's a bunch of malarkey. I saw you trying to move in on her," Amy teased.

"You what?" All William could think of was that kiss on the elevator. How could she have seen it?

"I'm kidding. I saw you pointing up at something in the sky. I figured that was how you were going to eventually wrap your arm around her."

"That old move?" William chuckled. "Not me. Now say good night."

" 'Night, Dad. See you around." Amy hung up.

Rachael sat with her mouth agape. Nina looked at her. "I don't think you've ever been this quiet, as in ever."

"I . . . I am dumbfounded."

"Imagine how I feel." Amy leaned against the dresser.

"Well, it seems like things are OK between Marilyn and your dad. Now *we* have to mend fences." She picked up the phone and asked for the concierge. "Good evening. Could I please have a box of Jacques Torres chocolates sent to Mrs. Marilyn Mitchell's stateroom in the morning? Do you happen to have an All Things Wicked collection?" She paused. "Excellent. Can you include a note that says, 'Nothing wicked intended except these chocolates. Please forgive us.' Signed Amy, Frankie, Nina, Rachael." She listened for a moment. "Yes, thank you very much." Frankie turned to the others. "It's the best we can do."

"Imagine if she starts dating my dad for real? This will be one heck of a story." Amy flattened herself on Frankie's bed.

Frankie noticed an envelope on the floor near the door. She reached to pick it up. "I completely forgot about this. Go get yours." It was the results of the speed-dating event.

They ran to their staterooms and returned with their envelopes.

Nina was the only one with whom anyone was interested in pursuing a date. For the other women, men were more interested in friendship or business, and there were few enough of them.

Nina's hands trembled as she ran her finger down the card. Then she broke out in a big smile. "Richard would like to see me again. As a date." Nina read it again to be sure she hadn't made a mistake. She handed the card to Frankie. "It *does* say that, doesn't it?"

"It does indeed." Frankie handed it back to her. "With his contact information."

"So now what happens?" Rachael asked. "I am assuming you put Richard down in the same column?"

"Duh. Correct," Nina chirped back.

"Either one can call, text, or e-mail the other one," Frankie said.

"What are you going to do, Nina? Wait for *him* to call *you*?" Rachael was too impatient for that sort of thing.

"I'll sleep on it. If I can sleep. Do you realize how long it's been since I've been on a date with someone?" Nina said thoughtfully.

"Well, I have got to get some sleep." Amy stretched. "This was a lot to process."

The women said their good-nights and went to their staterooms, agreeing to meet for breakfast in the Coastal Café. Frankie made a reservation for nine o'clock. She knew that everyone was going to get a slow start in the morning. Luckily for Rachael, Henry had moved the dance class to eleven.

Chapter Seventeen

Day 3
Cruising to Cozumel

As anticipated, the women made a slow start. Frankie was happy she had ordered coffee to be delivered to her stateroom at seven. She knew her unusually slow pace would stretch the time she needed to get ready. Normally, she was in and out of the shower, hair blown dry, makeup applied, and dressed in an hour. But that morning, it was going to take at least ninety minutes. A half hour of caffeine in her system should help.

They convened at the café and were seated next to a wall of windows. "This is divine." Amy sighed. "I'm so glad we planned this trip. Actually you, Frankie, made the plans. Bravo to you."

"Too bad I didn't plan on your father showing up." Frankie smiled over her third cup of the morning.

"It's fine. I'm over it. The ship is big enough where I doubt we'll keep bumping into each other. Besides, I'm making him give me his itinerary just to be sure." Amy buttered her warm muffin.

"See. You are a genius." Rachael bit into a slice of mango.

"Uh-oh." Frankie ducked her head.

"What?" Nina turned around to see what Frankie had spotted.

"Uh-oh. It's Marilyn."

Amy froze. "Is she with my father?"

"No. She's sitting alone."

"Should we go talk to her?" Rachael asked.

"I don't know if that's a good idea," Amy said.

"I hope she got the chocolates." Frankie sat up a little straighter. A few minutes later, the waiter came over with a slip of paper. It read:

> *Thank you for the chocolates. And the surprise.*
> *All is forgiven.*
> —*Marilyn.*

After Frankie read the note out loud, they looked in Marilyn's direction and waved. No one dared to get up. One step at a time. They didn't want her to feel as if she were being invaded.

Amy was the first to speak. "I'm going to go over to her. We don't want to have any tension."

"She wrote a note," Rachael replied.

"Yes, but it's always that first difficult conversation that takes you to the other side of the issue that's important," Frankie observed.

"Another self-help book?" Rachael asked sarcastically.

"No. My mother." Frankie chuckled.

Amy got up from the table and walked toward Marilyn. She wasn't sure if Marilyn was going to throw a bagel at her or give her the opportunity to speak.

"Hi," Amy said sheepishly. "I wanted to apologize again."

"No need. Your father and I sorted it out." Marilyn gestured for Amy to sit.

"Thank you." Amy took a seat and continued. "It was silly of me. Us. But it was kind of a knee-jerk reaction for me." Amy fidgeted in the chair. "I'm really, really sorry."

"Well, you are all forgiven. As long as I don't find you lurking around deck chairs or hiding behind a poinsettia display." She smiled at Amy.

"Thank you, Marilyn. I promise that you won't see any of us stalking you." Amy laughed nervously. "I better get back to my breakfast before it gets cold. I hope we can see each other under less covert circumstances. Have a really good day." Amy stood and returned to her table.

She was smiling when she sat down. "All good." She looked down at her plate. "Where's my bacon?"

Rachael pretended not to hear her.

Frankie spoke up. "We never heard about your mistletoe mission. How did it go?"

Nina took the lead. "We hung all of them. Rachael insisted we go back to her stateroom to get the rest. I think we hung about a dozen all told."

Rachael leaned back with a smug look on her face. "Come on, Nina, admit it. It was fun."

"Sure, if you don't mind dodging passengers and crew members." Nina was only half joking.

"So where are they?" Frankie cut another piece of her French toast.

"Several elevators, the doorway from the second deck lounge to the outer deck, and the main stairwell."

"The main stairwell? How did you manage that?" Amy asked curiously.

"I tied a string to one of the bunches and hung it over the railing. It's dangling down about halfway against the wall."

"But it counts if you're going up or down the stairs." Rachael grabbed a piece of bacon from Nina's plate.

"Hey, get your own." Nina slapped her hand.

"But this way the calories don't count," Rachael said, mounting a ridiculous defense.

Frankie looked at her watch. "Wow, it's almost ten thirty. Rachael, you have a dance class at eleven, right?"

"Right-o. Better shake a leg." She motioned for the waitress and signed the check assigned to her stateroom. "Not sure what I'm doing for lunch. I mean, we just ate. But I have a tennis match at two."

"OK. We'll see you at dinner?" Frankie asked. "Tonight, we're going to be in the main dining room. Apparently Santa is going to pay us a visit."

"Santa?" Amy asked curiously before taking a last swig of her coffee.

"Isn't he a little late?" Nina asked.

"He's been busy." Frankie snickered. "I think I'm going to walk around the ship for a while. Maybe sit near the pool. My painting workshop goes from two until four."

"Yoga for me is at one," Nina said. "Then a spa treatment from two to four. What time does your class get out, Amy?"

"Five."

"Should we meet up for drinks around five thirty? Dinner is at six thirty."

"When does Santa arrive?" Amy asked, childlike.

"Sometime around nine, I think," Frankie answered.

"OK. Let's plan on meeting at the Leeward Lounge at five thirty," Frankie suggested.

"Sounds good. Unless I have other plans." Nina tweaked her eyebrows.

"Yeah, what are you going to do about that?" Rachael got her last few words in before exiting.

"Nothing yet. I'm still trying to decide."

"The longer you wait, the less likely he'll still be available," Rachael warned.

"I'll take my chances. I think I'll let him chase me until I catch him." Nina dabbed the syrup from her chin.

"I like that plan," Frankie interjected. "You don't want to seem overanxious."

"Oh, I'm anxious all right," Nina said, laughing.

The women signed their checks and headed in different directions, waving at Marilyn as they exited the café.

Marilyn waved back.

As Nina was walking toward the elevators to get to the sundeck, she heard a loud announcement over the PA system. "May I have your attention please. Would Nina Hunter and Rachael Newmark please report to the main lobby." Nina froze. There was no escaping the ship, so she decided it was better if she turned herself in.

Rachael was about to enter her class when she, too, stopped in her tracks. "Oh poo." She knew she was in trouble. "Maestro, as you can hear, I am being summoned to the main lobby."

"Is everything all right?" He sounded genuinely concerned.

"I hope so. My apologies. I'll be back as soon as I can."

Rachael scooted out the door and made her way to the lobby.

The captain and the first mate were standing near the grand staircase. The captain was holding a green clump of leaves in his hand. Rachael saw Nina and hurried to her side. "We're so screwed."

"Maybe not. Let me handle this, OK?" It was more of a statement than a question. Nina approached the captain.

"Good morning, Captain. I'm Nina Hunter. This is Rachael Newmark."

"Yes, ladies, I am aware of your identities, as are all the

security cameras onboard." The captain's tone was even-tempered. "We couldn't help but notice that you have been decorating the ship."

Rachael couldn't contain herself. "It was all in good fun."

Nina touched Rachael's arm as if to say, "Shut up." Then she spoke to the captain. "Sir, how much trouble are we in?"

"As of now, you are on notice. Any more shenanigans, and you'll be walking the plank." There was a twinkle in his eye.

Rachael didn't know how to respond. Her face turned white as a sheet.

"Aye aye, Captain." Nina saluted him. "No more shenanigans."

"Seriously, ladies. We appreciate you getting into the spirit of the season, but we cannot allow our guests to be climbing all over to plant, well, plants."

"Understood. Apologies." Nina wasn't saying much more, and hoped Rachael would do the same.

"But . . . because you took such initiative, I am inviting the two of you and your friends to sit at my table tonight."

"That would be delightful," Nina said appreciatively.

"Oh yes. It would be an honor." Rachael chose the right words.

"Six thirty. Don't be late."

"Thank you, sir. Thank you for being so understanding." Nina extended her hand to shake his.

"This way I'll be able to keep an eye on all of you." He gave them a short salute.

Rachael and Nina made a beeline to the hallway. Rachael took one last look at the grand staircase. The mistletoe was still swaying from the railing above.

Once they were far enough down the corridor, Rachael gasped. "Boy, did we dodge a bullet." She was almost hyperventilating. "And did you see? There was still the one hanging over the railing."

When the elevator arrived, Nina looked up. "And there's another one." She paused. "I wonder if they took the rest of them down?"

"And tonight, I'm not going to ask." Rachael waved as she got off on her floor and rushed back to her class.

Nina knew that everyone on the ship had heard that announcement, including Richard. At least that would be an icebreaker for conversation.

Amy had been heading back to her stateroom when she heard the announcement summoning her friends to the grand foyer. She assumed it could only be because of the mistletoe. When she entered her stateroom, she saw the blinking light on the house phone indicating there was a message. She hit the speed-dial button. It was her father. "Amy? Everything all right? I heard two of your friends being called to see the captain. Please call me back."

Amy instantly called to be connected to his room. She hoped he was still there.

"Hello?"

"Dad, it's me. Everything is all right. Nina and Rachael were on their own mission last night."

"What kind of mission?" he asked.

"They were hanging mistletoe in elevators and doorways. I'm assuming that is what it was all about."

William Blanchard snickered and thought, *So that's whom I have to thank.*

"What's so funny?" Amy asked.

"That's a story for another time. I'm glad everyone is OK. I'll check back with you later. And try to stay out of trouble."

"You too, Dad." Amy clicked off the phone as another call was coming through. It was Nina.

"Hey, girl, yes, we got caught. But get this. All four of us are invited to sit at the captain's table tonight."

"Really?" Amy said in amazement.

"Yes, he said he wanted to keep an eye on us."

"I guess that's a relief, right?" Amy asked.

"I suppose so. I'm going to call Frankie and leave her a message about dinner. And that we're not in the hoosegow."

"Okey dokey! Enjoy the yoga and spa."

"I sure need it," Nina replied. "*Ciao* for now."

"*Ciao*," Amy replied. She wondered when they had all started using that expression. Must be something that had rubbed off from Frankie. She used it all the time.

Chapter Eighteen

With the ever-changing colors of the Gulf of Mexico and the clear blue sky, the trip from Key West to Cozumel was beautiful. The sea was calm, the sun was bright, and the ocean air exhilarating as the ship made its way to the next port. From a distance, the passengers could spot several deep-water charter fishing boats. The long-range stationary binoculars were being put to good use.

Frankie decided to check out the ship's library before her painting class. It was larger than she had expected. It was about as wide as a store in a strip mall and as deep. But instead of being a pizzeria, or a beauty salon, the walls were lined with light maple shelves. Two bays ran down the middle. It reminded her of a small bookstore. There was a large selection of books on fishing and golf, and the countries and port cities where the ship would dock. It also had a good mix of new novels, anthologies, and current-events titles. She thought that unless one was a speed reader, it would not be easy to finish a novel in a couple of days unless one did nothing else. At least that had always been Frankie's experience. Even though she worked in publishing, she wasn't the fastest reader and marveled at the people who could devour a book in a single night.

After her stroll through the library, she stopped at the small art gallery next to the library. It had a number of cultural pieces from the Caribbean on display. Paintings, sketches, ceramics. Most of the items were for sale. She supposed it was for people who needed that last-minute gift before they disembarked for home. She hoped it would give her some inspiration. There was so much visual stimulus around her. It was difficult to know what to look at next. Then there was New York during the Christmas season, brimming with more lights and sounds than at any other time of the year. No wonder she was having brain fog. She still hadn't completely shifted into relaxation mode. The ruckus with Amy, Marilyn, and Mr. Blanchard wasn't a recipe for calm. She was glad that incident was behind them and had ended so well. She could only imagine what had happened to Nina and Rachael at their meeting with the captain. She decided to text Nina. The only time they agreed to use their cell phones was when they were away from each other for several hours. She scrolled down to Nina's number.

All OK?

Peachy. ☺ We are dining with the captain. All of us. 6:30.

Frankie stared down at her phone. *What the what?*

Whatever you say. Talk later.

She continued her thoughts. *This should be interesting. And I wonder why I can't relax. At least they're not in cruise-ship jail.*

The colors in the art went from vibrant reds, yellows, and orange, to soft, calming blues. She was looking forward to Belize City and the turquoise water. According to the School of Atmospheric Sciences, Belize has the bluest water in the world. A few years ago, Pantone, the company known for creating a standard language of color-matching codes, added Belize Blue to their charts. Staring at a round wall hanging, she began to feel the serene effects of the different shades of blue. That's when she decided she would work with that color palette. She took another walk outside before heading to her class.

Nina was able to loosen up a bit at yoga. The massage and facial should really do the trick. She needed this downtime in a big way. Not that she didn't want to be with her friends. It was the show's being canceled, thinking about her meeting in New York, then getting nabbed by the security cameras. Peace, quiet, except for some New Age music, was the ticket for the day.

Amy was her exuberant self as she entered the culinary kitchen. It was exactly like those on the Food Network cooking shows, only a little smaller. She was one of eight other chefs for the day. Each was handed an apron with a matching hairnet. The apron displayed the ship's logo. She looked at the others and recognized one of the men from the evening before. His name was Charlie. Amy thought he was nice but not a love connection. She was happy he had put down the same interest as she did, "friends." At least it wouldn't be awkward working closely with someone whom you might have inadvertently insulted.

They were instructed to pick a partner, and they picked each other. Another good thing. This would be a good opportunity to forge a friendship. At least for the next few days. The menu was simple, but mostly the lesson was about preparing the food and plating it. The fun part was the bananas Foster. Each got a lesson in how to flambé a dessert without setting the kitchen on fire. As they became more comfortable with the long-handled lighters and rum mixture, the instructor announced they would be assisting the other servers in dishing up this delicious plate after dinner. Some of the students oohed in appreciation. A few others gasped in fear. Most importantly, they all had to sign a waiver.

"Not to worry," the chef said in his French-Caribbean accent. "We will be ready with fire extinguishers. Bravo. You will all do very well." He nodded and left the room. His assistant instructed the students simply to show up for dinner. The stations would be arranged around the dining room, with small signs with their names on them.

"Well, all righty," Amy exclaimed. She washed her hands and tossed her hairnet into the trash. "See you later, Charlie. Thanks for being such a good partner."

"Ditto," he replied.

Henry's plan for a flash mob dance was going well. The students' ages ranged from thirty-something to early fifties. The two fifty-year-old women still had their groove on and were keeping up with everyone else. When the class was over, Henry asked Rachael if she would tango with him again. As they danced, he explained more about the foundation. And the more they danced, the more certain Henry was that Rachael would make a great member of their team. And the more time he spent with her, the more intrigued he became.

The afternoon was winding down, and people were returning from their daily activities to their staterooms to change for dinner.

Nina was disappointed that there wasn't a message for her from Richard. Maybe he was waiting for her to call him? Maybe he was too busy calling all the other women who wanted to date him. She shrugged off the negative thought. She was feeling pampered and relaxed. She had just lain down on her bed for a moment when the phone rang, and she jolted upright.

"Hello?"

"Nina?"

"Yes."

"It's Richard. How are you this evening?"

"I'm well. Thank you. I had a battery recharge at the spa. And you?"

"I played a little tennis. With Rachael, as a matter of fact."

"Really?" Nina was surprised.

"Yes. Really. She's darn good," Richard concluded. "Beat the bejeezus outta me." He cleared his throat. "Would you like to meet for a drink before dinner?"

"Yes. That would be nice. What did you have in mind?" Nina hoped it wasn't the Leeward Lounge.

"The Top Deck Lounge?"

"Excellent choice." Nina was relieved she wouldn't be on display in front of her friends. That would be too weird. "Five thirty?"

"Perfect. See you then."

Nina hurriedly knocked on Frankie's door. "I won't be meeting you for cocktails." She gave Frankie a sly look.

"He called?" Frankie was almost shrieking.

"Shh . . . yes. Drinks. Five thirty."

"I wonder what he's doing for dinner," Frankie pondered.

"One step at a time. That will give us almost an hour to chat. We'll see how it goes."

Frankie high-fived her. "I'll let everyone else know."

"Wish me luck," Nina said over her shoulder.

"Good luck. But I don't think you'll need it." Frankie waved as she shut the door.

Frankie was happy. Nina was glowing. Maybe it was from the facial, but Nina's joy was evident. Now Frankie had to decide what to wear for dinner. Captain's table. Formal? Semiformal? It better be the latter. She didn't have anything that she would consider formal. She had already worn the black sheath the night before, so that was out of the question. She pulled on a white sleeveless shirt with a stand-up collar. Black capri pants and sandals with a chunk heel. Frankie was glad she had bought the sea-glass necklace with the matching bracelet and earrings when they were in Key West. She pulled her hair back in a chignon, leaving just a few wisps of hair to make it look less severe. A small clutch purse finished off her outfit. Chic and elegant would have to do.

Peter was leaving his stateroom at the same time. "Peter. Where have you been? Are you avoiding us?" Frankie ribbed him.

He seemed a little sheepish. "No. Not at all." He lowered his voice. "I think I've met someone."

"What do you mean you *think* you've met someone? Did you meet someone or didn't you?" Frankie kept razzing him.

"OK, Miss Bossy Pants, I met a woman, and we've been spending time together."

"That's great, Peter. How did you meet? I could use some pointers."

"She's actually the ship's photographer. Well, one of them."

"Really?" They continued walking together.

"Yes. She's working on her master's degree in photojournalism and doing this during the holiday break as part of a course in candid photography."

"They're pretty obvious about it, no?" Frankie wondered.

"That's just it. She's the stealth photographer. You're not supposed to notice her."

"So how did you manage to notice her?"

"Exactly. I noticed her taking photos of other people when they weren't looking. She caught me staring at her and put her fingers on her lips, telling me to keep quiet. I whispered that she would have to have a drink with me."

"Aren't you the clever one? So how is this working while she's working?"

"I'm the decoy. I distract people."

"Covert operations, eh?" Frankie hit the elevator button.

"One could say. But we're having a hoot doing it."

"I'm glad you're enjoying yourself. But now I know that if I see you, I'd better say 'cheese'!"

"Oh no. Please don't."

"Of course I won't." Frankie patted his shoulder. "You have all the fun you can. That's why we're here."

When the elevator door opened, Frankie looked up to see if Rachael and Nina's handiwork was still hanging about. Barely. It looked as if someone had tried to pull it down, without much success. Frankie shook her head and pointed up. "Rachael and Nina. The mistletoe fairies."

"Cute." Peter snickered. "You ladies are quite funny."

"Oh, that we are." The elevator stopped at the floor for the main dining room.

"See you later," Peter called out.

"Not if I see you first." Frankie flashed a big bright smile.

On her way to the Leeward Lounge, she spotted the drooping mistletoe over the railing of the main staircase banister. She shook her head and smiled.

Amy and Rachael were already seated in a cozy arrangement of club chairs and a round cocktail table near the railing. It was a covered, open-air lounge with a balcony that overlooked the deck below and the ocean. Frankie gave her drink order to the waitress as she passed by.

"So, ladies. Here we are. How was everyone's day?"

They chatted up a storm, talking about Amy's ability to flambé without starting a blaze, Rachael's "mystery" dance class and her tennis game, where she had beaten the pants off Richard. Frankie told them about her Ode au Bleu painting, an abstract with dozens of shades of blue. "You'll see it tomorrow. They're putting them on display in the gallery."

"Well, aren't you fancy?" Rachael said.

"Hey, and tonight I'm going to be part of the dessert display," Amy cooed. "They're letting us help out with preparing the bananas Foster. They need several stations to accommodate all the guests, and we're going to help." Amy swayed her shoulders in rhythm with her words.

Rachael tried to suppress her smile. "You know I can't tell you what I'm up to."

"Yeah. Yeah," Frankie muttered. "It's a *big* surprise." Frankie used her arms for illustration. "We get it."

Amy leaned in toward the center of the table. "I wonder how Nina is doing."

"Don't you even *think* about it." Frankie was mid-sip when she spoke from behind her martini glass.

"Oh no. I wouldn't dream of it," Amy said demurely.

"As if." Frankie placed her drink on the table and motioned for the checks. On their way to the main dining room, Frankie spotted a few more bunches of greenery, courtesy of Rachael and Nina. Each time, she elbowed the women.

The three entered the main dining room, which was replete with holiday glitter, stars, and more poinsettias arranged to look like trees. Frankie imagined there must be a few thousand of them on board. There were also traditional Christmas trees lining the room, but instead of traditional ornaments, the trees were decorated with beautiful blooms of gardenias. Hundreds of them. If this was how they decorated for the captain's dinner, New Year's Eve would be magnificent. Several different theme parties were planned on different decks. Five in total, and a fireworks display was scheduled for the stroke of midnight.

The maître d' checked the book and saw they were to be seated at the captain's table. He nodded and told her to follow him. Nina counted eight chairs at the table. Two were occupied by the captain and the first officer, also known as the first mate.

"Good evening, gentlemen." Frankie extended her hand.

"Frankie Cappella. Thank you so much for inviting me and my hooligan friends. I heard they created a bit of a stir." The captain stood, as did the first mate.

"Good evening. I'm Captain Adrian Sideris, and this is my first mate, Kenzo Tanaka."

Frankie shook both their hands. "Nice to meet you."

"Yes, they did create a bit of a stir, but I appreciated their spirit of the season, although we don't encourage passengers to take matters into their own hands." He directed his comments to Amy.

"It was really all in good fun." Frankie added another act of contrition to the list.

"I'm Rachael Newmark. Yes, please excuse my companions' behavior." She smiled, knowing that she would also be involved in a "passenger surprise."

Kenzo held out Frankie's chair. "Tell me, if we have the captain and the first officer at our table, who is steering the ship?" Frankie asked coyly.

Both chuckled. "We get that question all the time." The captain explained that there was an entire crew of highly skilled personnel watching over the ship's passage. "You can rest assured, we are in good hands." The men assisted the other two women with their chairs.

"Have you been to our library yet?" Kenzo asked.

"We would love to get your opinion or suggestions," Captain Sideris commented.

"I found it to be a very good mix of fiction and nonfiction. I was impressed by the variety and the size." Frankie was being her most charming. She turned to the first mate, Kenzo. "That means sea in Japanese, am I right?"

"Very impressive," Kenzo responded with surprise. "I was aptly named."

Frankie noticed that he had no discernible accent, so she asked, "Where are you from originally?"

"San Francisco," he reported.

She turned to the captain. "And, sir, do I detect a slight Greek accent?"

"Indeed. We grew up on the water."

Rachael and Amy gave short dissertations on what they do and where they live, sparking a conversation about Henry Dugan's Let's Dance Foundation.

Frankie glanced in the direction of the tables on the far wall. "The room is stunning. Are those the tables for the silent auction?"

"Yes. Please peruse the items. They include gift cards for the duty-free shop, the gift shops on board and in the ports, and a number of excursions. Some of them are worth a good bit of money. A helicopter ride over the Great Blue Hole costs over eight hundred dollars."

"Show me where that table is." Amy sprung out of her seat.

Frankie continued to converse with the two officers. "I think it's fantastic. There is an organization called SPUR, Special People United to Ride, in the area where I grew up. It's therapeutic horseback riding for people with special needs."

"It's wonderful to have such organizations. Too often, they depend completely on donations and volunteers," Kenzo observed.

"I'm going to see what Amy is up to and look for something I'd enjoy," Frankie said. "If you'll excuse me." Captain Sideris and Kenzo stood as she left the table.

"I see we are still missing one of your hooligans," the captain noted.

Rachael didn't want to invade Nina's privacy. "She should be joining us shortly. I see there are two more seats."

"Richard Cooper and Peter Sullivan," the captain informed her.

"Oh my goodness. I played tennis with Richard today, and Peter is across the hall from us."

"I trust you haven't corrupted them?" Captain Sideris smiled.

"Maybe just a little." Rachael was being flirty. "I think I'll check out what prizes I want to win. Be right back."

During their cocktail hour, Nina and Richard had a lively conversation about who their favorite comedians were, when it struck Richard why he recognized Nina. "Aren't you the actress who plays Mitzi on *Family Blessings?*"

"Guilty as charged." She raised both her hands in surrender.

"You're pretty cute and funny."

"Not much longer." Nina tried to hide the embarrassment.

"What happened, if you don't mind my asking."

"The show is being canceled. A few of the actors want to do other projects." Nina held on to her dignity.

"What's next for you?" Richard asked casually.

"I'm considering working on a sitcom as a writer." Nina was trying to get used to that idea.

"That could be very cool." Richard was encouraging and enthusiastic.

"I think so." And she did. Finally. She had made up her mind. Even if she didn't like the work in progress, she'd make sure she liked it after getting her hands on it. "I'll be moving back East in February."

"New York?" Richard assumed.

"Close. I'll be house-sitting for my parents for the winter until I figure out where I can go with a Bernese mountain dog." She chuckled. Nina realized that she was very comfortable with Richard. He was easy to talk to, and they seemed to have a number of things in common. Two on the list of "Most Important" to Nina: dogs and humor.

Richard checked his watch. "I don't mean to be rude, but I have a dinner appointment."

Nina's heart sank as she courageously faked not being defeated. The emotional roller-coaster ride was wreaking havoc with her stomach. "As do I. Shall we?" She stood, making sure her legs weren't wobbly. "Where are you headed?"

"The main dining room," Richard said nonchalantly.

Oh great. I get to watch him have dinner with another woman. Nina was not going to let her thought-balloon show.

"So am I," Nina said with confidence. "I wonder if there's going to be dancing."

"I guess we'll find out." Richard made room for Nina to get into the elevator. Both of them looked up at the same time. The bedraggled mistletoe was hanging by a thread. He didn't know how to react. He pointed and hesitated.

"I'm not much for tradition," Nina lied. "But if you are, I would be happy to comply." *Boy, that was so lame.*

Richard tilted his head and gave her a peck on the cheek.

"I'm not sure if that counts."

Nina didn't know how to respond. Fortunately, the doors opened, and two more people stepped in. Neither said a word to the other until they came to the main dining room floor. Talk about awkward.

When they arrived at the station of the maître d', Nina gave him her name. Richard was next.

"This way, please."

Nina was a little puzzled. It appeared that they were being guided to the same table. She was about to say something until she realized they were both being led to the captain's table.

The roller coaster in her stomach continued. She counted herself plus three friends, the captain, the first mate, and Richard. Who was that other chair for? She thought she was going to puke and hoped it didn't show.

They were greeted by the captain and the first mate. "Your friends are perusing the items in the silent auction."

"Excellent idea. Do you mind if I join them for a few minutes?"

"Please do. And sign up for as many items as you want. It's for a good cause," Kenzo indicated, with a sweep of his arm.

Nina didn't wait for a response from Richard. She raced over to the table where Frankie was standing and acted blasé as she gritted her teeth. "OK, let's pretend we're not talking about the guy I just had drinks with."

"OK. I see he's sitting at our table. How did you manage that? You get double rewards for being naughty?" Frankie kept smiling and pointed to items, feigning interest.

"I had nothing to do with it. He mentioned he had a dinner thing here, and we walked in together."

"But isn't that good news?" Frankie made a move to bid on a day excursion to Tulum.

"There is still one empty chair at the table. Maybe it's his date."

"And maybe it's not." Frankie looked up and saw Peter shaking the captain's hand.

"Honey pie, it's old-home week at the table. Hooligans and company."

Nina pretended not to notice Peter taking the seat between Frankie's and Amy's.

"It's boy-girl-boy-girl. Richard is between you and me. The captain is on your other side, then Rachael, then Kenzo. Perfect."

"I am so nervous," Nina admitted.

"Stop. You need to allow yourself to have a good time."

"I know. You're right. OK. Let's bid on some of these things. It's for a good cause."

Rachael sidled up to them. "Hope you're plunking down a lot of coin."

"We are." Frankie picked an excursion to Stingray City off Grand Cayman. She really had no interest in swimming with them, but if she won, she'd give it to Amy. She also bid on a bottle of Dom Pérignon, and several gift cards. She was happy to discover one of the plates she had admired in the gallery was also up for auction. The starting bid was $300. What the heck. It was for a good cause. She wrote down her name with $350 next to it.

Frankie reminded the others that they would have to keep coming back to check on their bids. Each prize was accompanied by a clipboard with lined paper. Its purpose was to provide a list for people to add to their bids. Each item had its value labeled on the sheet, together with an opening bid. There was also a notice of what increment was necessary to outbid the previous person. It could be anything—five dollars, ten dollars, or more. Often, the auction came down to two people bidding against each other and going over the actual value, just for the fun of it. It was important to keep checking the item so as not to lose out.

"We can also keep an eye out from our table." Amy noticed that they were in direct line with the captain's table. "Nina, I think you have the best line of sight."

"Please don't give me a job to do. I'm jittery enough as it is. I can't deal with the pressure." She was only half joking.

"We'll take turns," Frankie said, ending the debate.

As the women approached the table, all four men stood and helped them into their chairs.

"I hope you don't mind," the captain stated. "Chivalry is not dead on my ship. We have total respect for you."

"As much as I am for equal rights and equal pay, a kind gesture is always appreciated." Frankie beamed.

Before the first course was served, the waiter checked to

see if there were any allergies or food concerns. Everyone answered in the negative.

Fifteen minutes later, the first course of lump crabmeat
with a side of avocado toast was served. "I am so impressed
with the food, Captain Sideris." Nina complimented the
staff.

"Thank you. We pride ourselves on the finest cuisine at sea."

"It's quite impressive." Richard added to the conversation.
"You have such a variety of cuisines, and so far, everything
has been delicious and beautifully presented."

"We are, what I like to consider, a floating village. And I
am the mayor." He raised his glass of a dry sauvignon blanc.

Words of salutation went around the table.

When the last morsels were devoured, the plates were
cleared from the table. Shortly thereafter, the second course
arrived. It was a grilled vegetable risotto.

The moans and groans of palate delight echoed throughout the large dining room.

"Sounds like a success," Peter noted. "Tell me, sir, do you
have the same crew all the time?"

"We have a corps of seamen and staff. The main dining
room is part of our jurisdiction, shall we say. The other
restaurants and shops are responsible for their own staffing."

"They are doing a splendid job," Peter indicated.

"I appreciate the positive feedback." The captain turned
to Richard and Peter. "I assume you have all met based on
the conversations, but tell me, did you know about Rachael
and Nina's brush with the law?"

Richard did a double take at Nina.

"The law?" Peter exclaimed.

"At sea. I am the law. International Convention for Safety
of Life at Sea, Chapter 5, Regulation 34-1."

Rachael and Nina gave each other sideward glances and
started to shrink in their seats.

"Fortunately, I didn't have to throw them in the brig. Although it's not officially called a brig on a cruise. More like cruise ship jail."

"What was the offense?" Richard asked curiously. He was, after all, involved in one of the pranks.

"Apparently, they had some issues with our décor."

"Décor?" Peter was bewildered. Then he remembered running into them when they were on their mistletoe mission. "Oh wait, you mean the green stuff?"

"*Akrivós*! Correct." All four women slid down deeper into their chairs.

Richard looked at Nina. "Criminal behavior. I am a lawyer, you know."

"Right." Nina nodded. "I think I'll go check on the auction items."

"I think you need adult supervision." Richard pulled her chair out and followed her to the auction tables.

Rachael tried to give Frankie a kick under the table but knocked into Kenzo's leg instead.

"Ouch." He gave a little yelp.

"I am so sorry." Rachael grabbed his arm.

"Shall we add assault to the charges, Captain?" Kenzo joked.

"I felt my shoe coming off and I was trying to get it back on without crawling under the table." Rachael was becoming a great storyteller.

Frankie bit the inside corner of her mouth. It appeared it was becoming a common occurrence with her. She set her sights on Nina and Richard. Things seemed to be moving along nicely. Richard had a good sense of humor, and he liked dogs. Frankie knew how important that was for Nina.

Frankie didn't want to interrupt her friend, who was with potential date material, but she wanted to check her bids.

Rachael fumbled under the table, trying to make her fib seem real. "I think I'll head over to see how things are going." She was more specific. "For the auction." She knew what everyone else was thinking. Maybe not the captain or Kenzo, but the others for sure.

"Let me accompany you," Kenzo offered. "I am curious to see which of the items are the most popular."

Amy, Frankie, Peter, and Captain Sideris were left alone at the table.

"I trust you are having an enjoyable trip?" The captain gazed into his wineglass.

"It's been wonderful." Amy leaned in. "I'm helping with the dessert tonight."

"Ah. You took the cooking class today?"

"Yes. It was loads of fun."

"And, Frankie, what did you do this afternoon?"

"I took the painting class. My painting will be on display tomorrow." She took a sip of wine as the busboys cleared the table, replacing utensils for the next course.

"That's marvelous." Captain Sideris raised his glass. "Congratulations."

"Thank you. I've dabbled a bit, but I never seemed to have the time to take it on as a real hobby. Besides, my cat, Bandit, would probably think the paints are for him to play with."

"Cats are interesting creatures." He turned to Amy. "And you? What line of work are you in?"

Amy blushed. "I am a bioengineer in Silicon Valley. I volunteer at a no-kill shelter, and I have two cats, Blinky and Hop-Along."

"Bioengineering? Sounds impressive."

"Nah. It's actually kind of boring. We get parts of projects; and then the work we do gets sent somewhere else. Most of the time we don't even know who the end user is."

Frankie chimed in. "Amy is a certified genius. We're hoping she gets a professorial position at MIT. We want her back on the East Coast."

"MIT?"

"Yes, I'm an MIT graduate, a faculty position opened up, and I am one of the candidates."

"Wonderful," Captain Sideris exclaimed. "We don't get a lot of professors on our ship. I'm not sure why."

"They're too busy with their heads in their books." Amy laughed.

The others returned to the table. Nina looked over at Frankie. "I hope you don't mind, but I increased your bid for the champagne by twenty-five dollars. You're on the hook for $150 if no one outbids you."

"It's still a bargain. We'll drink it on New Year's Eve."

"Sounds like a plan," Nina said, hoping Richard would want to share a glass with her.

The third course was being served. It was a Caribbean version of surf and turf. The beef was filet mignon, but the turf part was a combination of shellfish in a slightly spicy Caribbean sauce made with a special blend of green herbs served on wilted greens. The conversation wound down as everyone savored the delicious meal.

"Save room for dessert," Amy blurted out.

The captain smiled at her, knowing already that she was involved in serving the dessert. "Do I suspect you also have something up your sleeve?"

"I'm zipping my lips," Amy said coyly.

"Speaking of zipping one's lips. Rachael, you've been unusually quiet," Nina noted.

Rachael was obviously distracted by something. She checked her watch. Five more minutes. "Who, little ol' me?" She batted her eyes and did her best Scarlett O'Hara impersonation. "I'm simply enjoying the pleasure of your company and the marvelous cuisine."

A small jazz combo was playing soft Latin music in the background when they were interrupted by a loud *bang*. A crashing of drums and a horn section filled the room with sound. It was the introduction to "Boogie Wonderland" by Earth, Wind & Fire, with the first word of the song ordering people to "Dance." Rachael was one of the eighteen guests from different parts of the dining room who jumped up, strutted to the dance floor, and formed a flash mob. They performed the moves they had practiced with Henry in perfect coordination. Not a single misstep. The audience went wild. People were clapping, others were "chair-dancing," and some stood up to rock with the music. Thunderous applause blasted off the walls. Henry was ecstatic over the proficiency of his class.

Rachael was sashaying back to her chair when a voice came over the PA system. "Ms. Rachael Newmark. You're not done," Henry announced from the other side of the ballroom. She stopped short and turned around.

"Me?"

"Please." Henry motioned for her to come back to the dance floor.

"Ladies and gentlemen. I'd like to introduce you to one of my prima students, Rachael Newmark. She will be joining our foundation when we return to New York." Then he took her by the hand and led her to the middle of the floor. The music turned to a sensuous tango. Henry gripped her by the waist, and they became a flowing, fluid, organic work of art. It was spectacular. For the first time since she could remember, Rachael felt that she had been validated. She had talent. Real talent. And she would parlay that into working with a wonderful organization that existed to help others. She knew she could balance both her business and this new opportunity. Yes. Rachael Newmark was her own woman.

Henry spun her around and ended the dance with the traditional deep dip. Again, the crowd went crazy, with a standing ovation. He kissed her hand, and they both took a bow. Rachael returned to her table, where everyone continued to clap. It was a cacophony of questions, praises, hugs, and kisses.

"Wow." Amy squealed. "All I'm doing is setting some rum on fire. You set the whole room on fire."

Rachael was glowing. You would have thought she had won the lottery. And maybe in her mind, she had.

Between the flash mob and the tango, the servers had quickly cleared the tables, preparing for dessert. An announcement came over the PA: "Dessert assistants, please go to your appointed stations."

"There's my cue." Amy scooted over to the table that held the ingredients for the bananas Foster. There were eight serving tables surrounding the perimeter of the dance floor. She spotted her friend Charlie. They gave each other a thumbs-up.

The instructor gave the rehearsed signal for the group to light their mini torches, and the next signal was to light the rum. The dance floor was encircled with a ring of fiery bananas, and oohs and aahs were coming from the audience. Servers scurried to complete the dishes with a scoop of vanilla ice cream and serve the dessert to the guests.

Once dessert was served, the carts were removed. The sound of jingling bells announced the arrival of a jolly old man in a red suit, with someone dressed like an elf. "Sorry, folks, for being a little late. I've been busy delivering presents. We had to deal with a bit of wind, which slowed us down." The audience chuckled. "As you know, the proceeds of tonight's auction items will be going to Maestro Henry Dugan's Let's Dance Foundation for People with Special Needs." The crowd applauded. "I'd like to announce the winners, while my assistant will tally the take." He began to read off the names. "For the stingray excursion, the winner is Frankie Cappella." Hoots came from the table, and Frankie went over to the area where her certificate awaited. Before she had a chance to return, he announced the winner of the

Dom Pérignon. Again, "Frankie Cappella." Frankie settled up with the elf and happily presented Amy with the voucher.

Amy was gushing. "Oh, Frankie. That is so nice of you. Thank you so much."

Santa continued calling off the names as people fetched their items. The process took about fifteen minutes. "The final auction item, a helicopter tour of the Blue Hole, goes to Amy Blanchard."

Amy was beside herself. "Oh my gosh." She was gushing so much, you would have thought she had just been named prom queen. The two things she wanted to do were now on her agenda. She was jumping up and down like a little kid.

Once she settled down, Santa continued. "Ladies and gentlemen, because of your generosity, I am pleased to announce that we have raised over five thousand dollars tonight." More applause filled the room. "Enjoy the rest of your evening. And remember, I've got my eyes on you."

Rachael stood and clapped. "Good thing he wasn't watching us dispensing the mistletoe."

"Indeed," Nina agreed.

The musicians returned to the soft Latin and bossa nova music for anyone interested in ending the evening with a dance. Richard whispered in Nina's ear, "I think they're playing our song."

Knowing they didn't have a song, Nina appreciated Richard's joke and accepted the invitation to dance.

Everyone at the table was sufficiently satiated. It was time to wind it down. The next morning they would be arriving in Cozumel, and they had plenty on their itineraries. Frankie was the first to speak. "Captain, thank you for a most wonderful evening."

"The pleasure was mine." He stood to say good night to his guests. "And please, no more monkeyshines."

"We promise," Rachael said sheepishly.

"I'll try to keep them under control," Peter offered.

They said their good-nights and made their way to the large double doors of the dining room, through the grand foyer, and onto the elevator. Frankie elbowed Rachael and nodded in the direction of the drooping mistletoe. Huge guffaws filled the car.

When they got to their staterooms, Frankie gave Rachael a huge hug. "I am so proud of you. That was incredible."

"Thanks, honey pie. You know, I wasn't sure about this trip, but what a difference it's made. If it weren't for you, I'd be somewhere in the mountains with Jimmy."

"I thought Jimmy was Floyd," Frankie joked.

Rachael thought for a moment. "Floyd? Was there a Floyd? So many men, so little time." She chortled and then hugged Frankie.

"And Amy. You were masterful with that lighter." Frankie smiled at her friend.

"Oh, I'm a real pyromaniac for sure." She smiled back.

"It was a great night," Frankie assured her. "I think Nina might agree, but we'll have to wait until tomorrow to find out, eh?"

Chapter Nineteen

Day 4
Cozumel, Mexico

The turquoise waters of Cozumel welcomed the passengers as the ship docked around eight in the morning. They would have until six o'clock to enjoy the activities before departing for the next stop at Belize City.

Frankie had breakfast delivered to her stateroom at seven while she anxiously waited for an appropriate time to grill Nina about the rest of her evening with Richard. She could hardly contain herself. She couldn't wait. "OK, girlfriend. Spill."

A sleepy Nina answered. "Hey." Then came a yawn.

"Must have been quite a night." Frankie pressed for more information.

"It was lovely. He is so easy to be with." She paused. "Do you have coffee in your room?"

"I do. Come over."

Less than a minute later, Nina knocked on Frankie's door. Both were still in their pajamas. "See, I knew it was a good idea to get our staterooms together." Frankie ushered Nina in.

She poured two cups, added some cream, and brought them out to the veranda. Nina carried the basket of baked goods.

"So?" Frankie peered over her cup.

"So, I really like him."

"Like, really, *really* like?" Frankie was using the old phrase they would use when they really, *really* liked someone.

Nina laughed. "It's been an awfully long time since I've been with a man who acts like an adult, is funny, and loves dogs. And not necessarily in that order."

"You're going to see each other again, I hope, right?"

"Yes. Dinner tonight. I'm going to go with you to the San Gervasio ruins to see the shrine of Ixchel."

Frankie chuckled. "You mean the goddess of love and fertility?"

Nina laughed out loud. "Since it's only about thirty minutes away, I thought I *should* go."

"What's that?" Frankie pointed to a large white envelope Nina had brought to the stateroom with her.

"The treatment for the show."

"From Owen?" Frankie was puzzled.

"Yes. He's very anxious for me to read it. He needs a decision ASAP. He e-mailed it to me, and I asked the concierge to have it printed out. It's only a dozen pages, but it gives me a good idea where it's going."

"What do you think?" Frankie was eager to know.

"I like it." Nina smiled brightly.

"You're going to take the offer?" Frankie asked hopefully.

"I do believe I am." Nina leaned back in the chair and sipped her coffee.

"That's all you have to say?" Frankie nudged her.

"Did you tell Richard?"

"Not yet. I don't want to rush anything. It's only been two days."

"But it could be more once you move back. Philly to New York is a quick trip by train, and less than two hours by car."

"Let's not get ahead of ourselves." Nina reached for a muffin. "I don't want him to think I'm stalking him."

"Amy and I have the stalking thing covered," Frankie joked. "Does he know you'll be moving back?"

"I mentioned it when he finally realized I was the cute and funny one from *Family Blessings*. I told him the show was canceled and I was considering returning to work as a writer for a sitcom."

"Did he seem enthralled? Interested? Excited?"

"It was an early conversation. We'll see how it sits with him when I tell him it's all systems go."

"And when might that be?"

"I'm not sure. I want this to be a little more organic than contrived."

"Well, listen to you." Frankie grinned. "I have a good feeling about this." She got up and poured more coffee.

"From your lips to God's ears." Nina raised her cup in a toast.

"What about New Year's Eve? Can you believe it's tomorrow night?"

"We didn't discuss it."

"There are five parties going on at the same time. Each one has a different theme. Fifties Rock and Roll, Disco, Country Music, Latin, Margaritaville."

"We don't have to go in costume, do we?" Nina asked fretfully.

"No, silly. They'll be decorated that way. But I suppose if you want to dress like a cowgirl, no one will object."

Nina laughed. "I just happen to have a pair of spurs, hat, and whip in my luggage."

"I think I'll check all of them out," Frankie said. "The parties start at nine. A half hour at each one should be plenty of revelry. And finish off with the fireworks."

"Sounds very revelryish." Nina nodded. "The others have the same plan?"

"I haven't discussed it with them yet."

"If I have a date, we'll set a meet-up point and time. We have to drink that champagne you won. And if I don't have a date, I will be joining you anyway."

"Sounds like a plan."

A vehement knocking at the door started. "Must be Rachael or Amy, or both." Frankie got up to answer. It was both of them, determined to squeeze information out of Nina. Nina first explained that she was taking the gig as a writer. Her news met with giggles and cheers. She told them how much she enjoyed Richard's company, but she wasn't going to rush into thinking anything past the current moment.

"Get to the nitty-gritty," Rachael kept pressing. "Did he kiss you?"

Nina blushed. "Yes, and it was sweet, and no, we didn't do anything else. We took a walk after dinner, and he kissed me good night."

Rachael was bouncing on the bed. "When are you going to see him again?"

"Dinner tonight."

Rachael kept bouncing, chanting, "Nina loves Richard," as if she were in grammar school.

"OK, enough out of you." Nina gave her a sideways look.

"Fine." Rachael pouted.

Frankie addressed the group. "What are your plans for the day?"

Amy was going to the Secret River to do a wading tour through caverns. Rachael was taking a chocolate tour. They would all be gone for most of the day.

"What about dinner?" Amy asked. "We know what Nina is doing."

"Let's try the Cuban restaurant." Rachael tossed her idea around.

"Sounds good. I'll make a reservation. Seven?" Frankie offered. "Ship leaves at six. We should be back by four thirty or five. That will give us time to clean up our acts."

"Sounds good," Amy said. "I wonder how my dad and Marilyn are doing."

"I haven't seen either of them," Frankie said.

"Me neither," Nina added.

"Maybe I should give him a call. Just to see if he's having a good time," Amy said thoughtfully.

"That would be nice. Just in case he's not, he can hang out with us."

"As if," Amy barked. "May I use your phone?"

Frankie handed her the receiver, and Amy asked for his stateroom.

"Hey, Dad. How's it going? Are you having a good time?"

"Amy, sweetheart. I am having a delightful time." He sounded genuinely happy.

"Glad to hear it. I figured if you were bored, you could have dinner with us."

He cleared his throat. "Thank you, dear, but I have dinner plans."

"With?" Amy thought she knew the answer.

"With Marilyn."

"Great." Amy was truly pleased. "Let us know where you're going, so we won't be hovering in the distance."

"Right. I don't want to go through that again." He laughed.

"We're going to the Cuban restaurant, El Libre."

"Good. We're going to the Thai restaurant, Kunya Siam."

"Fantastic. What are you doing today?"

"I haven't quite decided. I think Marilyn is going to the San Gervasio ruins."

"She mentioned she wanted to do that," Amy replied. "Nina and Frankie are going." She paused. "Hey, Dad, why don't we do something together today? Just the two of us. I mean, there can be other people, but this will give us a chance to catch up."

"What do you have in mind?" William Blanchard cringed, waiting for an answer.

"I signed up for an excursion on Rio Secreto. It's a secret river, hence the name. And it flows through connected underground caverns. But if you'd rather do something less adventurous . . ."

William interrupted her. "Sweetheart, that sounds very interesting. Do you think it's too late for me to sign up?"

"Hang on, let me check." Amy looked over at Frankie. "Can you call and see if there is room for one more on the cave-tubing trip?"

Frankie dug out her cell phone and hit the speed-dial key for the ship's main number. She figured it was a good idea to have it handy. Just in case there were any issues when they were onshore. Frankie spoke quickly and gave Amy a thumbs-up.

"OK, Dad, they have room. Let's meet in front of the gangway in a half hour."

Amy was elated. "I don't think I've spent more than a couple of hours with my father in a while. I can't believe he's going to get into a wet suit, a hard hat, and swimming shoes and go into a cave!"

"I didn't hear you mention anything about the attire," Nina joked. "But, seriously, I think it's a great idea. And you were feeling guilty about not spending time with him during the holidays," Nina reminded her.

"Crazy, eh?" Amy said. "Now I'm going to have to see

what my mother has been up to. She's been very close-mouthed about what's going on in her life." Amy twitched her nose.

"Didn't you say she had dinner with Lloyd Luttrell?" Nina asked.

"Yes, and she said she had a lovely time. She also said he gave her 'something to think about.' Twice."

"Did she ever mention why she broke it off with Rusty?" Frankie asked.

"She said they did not have a meeting of the minds." Amy shrugged. "I can only guess it was about the prenup, but I never brought it up. And she and I never discussed it. I didn't want her to think it was some kind of conspiracy."

The others laughed. "But it kinda was." Rachael gave her a wry smile.

"I'm going to give her a call tomorrow to wish her a Happy New Year. Maybe she'll divulge her plans to ring in the New Year."

"Do you think she might be seeing Lloyd? You know, as in a date kind of thing?" Rachael speculated.

"It certainly wouldn't be the worse thing that ever happened." Amy chuckled.

Frankie checked her phone for the time. "We better get a move on if we plan on leaving by nine thirty."

The women dispersed to their staterooms to prepare for the day. Some would get a boxed lunch when they exited the ship, while others would purchase local food.

As they walked to the gangway, it was as if they were moving in slow motion. Four confident women floating on air in brightly colored fabrics. Straw hats and totes completed their vacation attire. As they glided down the gangway, heads turned in their direction. They were a force to be reckoned with. In a good way.

Nina and Frankie saw the sign for the San Gervasio tour. Marilyn was already in the queue. Amy noticed the Rio Secreto poster, and Rachael headed for Chocolat.

Nine people piled into several jeeps, which drove quite a few miles on a long dirt road. It was no wonder it was called the Secret River. It was well hidden in the jungle. When they arrived at the staging area, an indigenous shaman performed a short ritual, blessing the participants as they entered what is considered by some a sacred place. After the brief benediction, the members were outfitted in wet suits, hard hats equipped with halo lights, swimming shoes, and life-preserver belts. Then several guides took them on a wading tour through incredible and dramatic crystal caves covered in thousands of stalactites and stalagmites. Amy and her father were awestruck by the geological formations that revealed some of the history of the planet.

When they returned to the staging area, a sampling of local dishes awaited. Beans, soft tortillas, and plantains.

It was a wholly immersive experience. Amy was enjoying watching her father's expressions of amazement throughout the day. He seemed genuinely happy. It reminded her of the time he had brought her to the boardwalk at the Jersey Shore. He was the guide that day, choosing rides they could both enjoy. She was over the moon sharing this new adventure with him. She said a secret prayer of thanks. It was the best Christmas present she could have asked for. Amy made up her mind to make more of an effort to spend time with him. And her mother. She added a PS to her prayer that she was chosen for the position at MIT.

Nina and Frankie sat together on the small bus taking them to the ruins. Marilyn sat behind them. Conversation was pleasant, but Marilyn was not providing them with any information they did not already have. In fact, she didn't even mention the plans to have dinner with William. Nina and Frankie resisted the urge to eyeball each other. Mind reading would have to do for the duration. They both chuckled, knowing that was what the other was thinking. They always had that ability. A little telepathy.

After the bumpy thirty-minute ride, they arrived at the site of the ruins. The whitewashed stone structures had been built with stucco, honey, crushed shells, and gum. There was an eeriness to the place. An entire culture had ultimately disappeared. There were still questions as to what had caused the collapse of Mayan civilization. Speculation ranged from overpopulation to deforestation to drought.

Nina and Frankie noticed that there were over a dozen groups of ten to fifteen people watching a reenactment of a two-thousand-year-old ritual to the moon goddess Ixchen. In addition to being the goddess of love and fertility, she was also responsible for providing water for the crops.

The performers of the ritual included both children and adults. Approximately twenty-five players moved among the ancient rocks, dancing and swaying to the sounds of flutes and handmade native percussion instruments.

According to legend, even with all her beauty, Ixchen could not get the attention of the one she loved, Kinich Ahau, the sun god. Refusing to be ignored, she took charge and weaved a cloth of vibrant colors, something he could not overlook. Indeed, he did take notice, and they married and produced four children. But Ixchen's grandfather did not approve and had Ixchen struck by lightning. She lay dead for 183 days while hundreds of dragonflies sung to her until she reawakened, returning to her place with the sun god.

The performance was moving. Frankie rubbed her arms from the goose bumps. Nina stood silently, staring at the ruined temple. Marilyn moved closer and put her arms around both of them. She whispered, "Let's hope Ixchen's determination and blessings rub off on us."

Nina and Frankie returned the hug. "Amen to that."

"I also wanted to tell you that as much as your skulking was a bit of a surprise, I see how much you look after each other, and I appreciate your looking after me, too." Marilyn's sincerity was clear and heartening.

They spent the next couple of hours on a walking tour of the rest of San Gervasio, followed by the bumpy thirty-minute ride back to the port.

By five thirty, everyone was on board, back from their excursions and tours. Rachael had boxes of chocolates for each of the women. "It's authentic cacao. I must have eaten a pound already."

"I'm sure you'll dance it off," Amy proclaimed, as the women huddled in Frankie's stateroom, gabbing about their adventure. Amy was animated, talking about her day with her father. Nina and Frankie were in subdued moods. Rachael was bouncing on the bed, the chocolate and sugar high still affecting her.

Nina was planning to have dinner with Richard. Amy, Frankie, and Rachael opted for the Cuban restaurant, El Libre. They planned to make it an early night after finishing dinner. They agreed they were worn out from the day trip, and another was to follow the next day. At six o'clock, the long blast of the horn sounded, and the ship left the dock, leaving Cozumel behind.

Chapter Twenty

Day 5
New Year's Eve
Belize City

The tranquil blue water of Belize glistened in the morning sunlight. Since the water off the port is too shallow for cruise ships, they anchored a few miles offshore. A tender would transport the passengers to the Fort Street Tourist Village, where they would have a dockside view of the colorful open-air shops. The ride usually took about fifteen minutes, giving the passengers ample time to admire the sight of the crystal-clear Caribbean.

Nina was the first to knock on Frankie's door. "Good morning." Nina was beaming.

"Well, look at you, all glowing and smiling." Frankie stepped aside to let Nina in.

"Does it show that much?" Nina was bright and chipper.

"It does. *So?*" Frankie emphasized the "so."

Mimicking her friend, Nina answered. "*So* we had a wonderful dinner. We shared our experiences of the day."

"*And?*" Frankie peered at her.

"*And*, we took a stroll on the deck and found a quiet place to watch the stars."

"Sounds romantic."

"It was. It felt like a real date."

"Did you tell him you were definitely taking the writing gig?"

"Not yet. I'm still a little leery about sounding too aggressive. I don't want him to freak out."

"Freak out about what?"

"Oh, I don't know. Guys. They can be so unpredictable." Frankie chuckled. "And they think *we're* unpredictable."

"What else did you guys talk about?"

"Movies, books. Climate change. I usually press him for details about his work. He was involved in the Flint, Michigan, water crisis, going after several sugarcane growers in Florida, and cleaning up a chemical plant in Pennsylvania."

"Sounds interesting and complicated." Frankie was picking out an outfit for the day trip into Belize City.

Rather than visit more ruins or do any water sports, Rachael, Frankie, and Nina had decided to save their energy for the evening's festivities. They were going on a historical ride through the original parts of the city, a food-tasting tour of Belizean delights, some leisurely shopping. Rachael was looking forward to listening to some of the street musicians playing Garifuna-style music.

Rachael and Henry's crew planned on a few flash mob dances at the five parties, but she didn't tell her friends. Surprise.

All had agreed to have dinner together, then decide where to steer themselves as the evening unfolded. Nina and Richard promised to catch up with each other at one of the parties, but they hadn't decided on a time or place.

"So it looks like you'll have someone to kiss at midnight." Frankie peeked around the closet door.

"I guess so." Nina was absorbing the significance of that kiss.

"Uh-huh." Frankie smiled. "It's kinda nice to have a beau."

"I wouldn't call him that, but yes, it's been nice to spend time with an interesting man who doesn't make me want to punch him in the face. Or puke," Nina said, with a guffaw.

"I would call that progress, my friend." Frankie laughed with her.

Nina flopped down on the bed. "I must confess, I feel like I'm back in high school."

"Just don't get caught making out behind a stack of deck chairs. Or get a hickey." The two women roared out loud. A loud knock rattled the door.

"Open up! I hear you guys making a rumpus in there." It was Rachael, coming to fetch her friends. She had Amy in tow.

"You must be thrilled about your helicopter ride to the Great Blue Hole," Nina commented.

"I am elated." Amy's enthusiasm was written all over her face and in her body language. If Frankie had let her, Amy would have used the bed as a trampoline.

Frankie took one last look in the mirror. "Shall we?"

"We shall," Rachael responded.

Once again, the colorful outfits and their buoyant mood gave the impression that they were walking on air. And once again, heads turned as they passed.

After the tender docked, Amy waved and walked in the direction of the van that had a sign CISCO BASE HELIPORT.

The others found the advertised air-conditioned van for the historic tour.

Vendors standing inside and outside their huts were selling everything from beer to conch-shell jewelry to handwoven baskets in the Mayan tradition. It was a cacophony of voices beckoning tourists to buy their wares, several types of music, and the clanging of boats against the dock. Truly a festival in and of itself.

The women sauntered through the crowd, each feeling confident in her own skin. They boarded the air-conditioned van for the one-hour tour of the former British colonial capital. Sights included the old swing bridge still operated by hand, and St. John's Cathedral, the oldest Anglican church in Central America. It was a pleasant way to see the city.

After their jaunt around town, they met a guide whose mission it was to take them to several local cafés, where they would sample *salbutes*, tiny corn tortillas topped with cabbage, chicken, avocado, and hot sauce. Then on to red beans and rice, followed by stewed chicken. Ceviche and tamales were also on the list, as well as *cochinita pibil*, soft tortillas stuffed with roasted pork and vegetables. The tour finished with fry jacks, puffed pastries filled with cheese.

After one more round of the Fort Street Village shops, they would head back. By three o'clock, they were ready to return to the ship and take a nap.

When they were on the tender, Nina asked, "Why, oh why, did we sign up for that six-course dinner at Remy tonight?"

Frankie laughed. "We're having a gastronomical kind of day."

Rachael patted her stomach. "Oy. I don't know if I can shove anything else into my mouth."

"I'm sure you'll figure it out. The reservation isn't until seven thirty. Dinner should take about two hours. Then we can hit the parties," Frankie said.

Fifteen minutes later, they were back on the *Medallion of the Seas*. "I am beat," Nina remarked, as she slipped the keycard into her door.

"That makes two of us," Frankie echoed.

"Nap time. See you in a bit." Nina gave Frankie and Rachael a two-finger salute.

"*Ciao* for now," said Frankie, returning the salute. "Sweet dreams."

Amy was still on her helicopter tour and wouldn't be getting back until almost five.

By six, the three women had regrouped and were getting ready for dinner when Amy banged on everyone's door to share the photos she had taken of the spectacular Great Blue Hole. She shared the information she had acquired. The Great Blue Hole was a massive sinkhole, hundreds of feet deep, with small stalactites. Jacques Cousteau thought it could be considered one of the wonders of the world. There was evidence that the Mayans had visited it frequently, but to what extent and why was still a mystery. In 2018, a research group had ventured below to levels no one had gone before and discovered a thick layer of toxic hydrogen sulfide, like a blanket, floating across the entire width of the hole. Amy could not contain her excitement. It had been a once-in-a-lifetime adventure.

"This has been some kind of trip for you, hasn't it?" Rachael said.

"Yeah. Seriously. First my dad, then a day with my dad wading through caves. And tomorrow I'm going to the stingray farm. Whew. I'm going to need a vacation after all this."

"Let's not forget your job interview," Frankie added.

"Right. I got an e-mail from the head of human resources, but I couldn't open the attachment on my phone."

"Don't you think it's kind of important?" Nina asked.

"To be honest, I'm worried they'll cancel the interview." Amy looked distressed.

"I doubt that will happen. Why don't you ask the concierge to arrange for the business office to print it out for you? You can access your e-mail from one of their computers," Frankie suggested.

"Splendid idea." Amy hesitated. "Will you come with me just in case it's bad news?"

"Sure," Frankie answered. "Let's do it now, then I'll come back and finish getting dressed. We're going to have a big night tonight." She raised her eyebrows.

Frankie checked the schematic of the ship and located the business office. She picked up the phone to see if they were still open and if they could accommodate their request. The answer was "yes" to both. They scurried out the door, running into Peter in the hallway. He flattened himself against the wall as if he were avoiding being trampled. Frankie shouted, "We'll catch up with you later."

Amy was visibly shaken by the time they reached the office. Frankie put her hand on her shoulder. "I'm sure it's going to be fine."

The office manager showed Amy to a standing desk, where she could log in to her e-mail. She downloaded it and froze in her seat. She read aloud. "*Dear Ms. Blanchard. Upon reviewing your application, résumé, experience, and the letters of recommendation, we find that an additional interview will not be required.*" Amy's heart sank, and she looked away from the screen, trying to hold back the tears.

"Wait," Frankie called out. "It goes on to say, *Therefore, we would be pleased if you would consider accepting the position of associate professor at our institution beginning with the fall semester. Kindly contact Dean Whittier to schedule a development meeting. We look forward to seeing you. Kind regards, Mildred Crenshaw, Director of Human Resources. P.S. A hard copy of this letter is being sent via FedEx to your home.* Oh my goodness, Amy." Frankie started jumping up and down.

It still hadn't sunk into Amy's head. Frankie hit the PRINT button. In a matter of seconds, the letter flipped into the exit tray. Frankie pulled it out and put it close to Amy's face. "See?"

Amy's hands were trembling. "For real?" She was absolutely incredulous.

"For real, baby girl. Come on. We need to tell the others."

Frankie and Amy stopped long enough to print a second copy for Amy's father and to thank the office manager for staying open a few extra minutes. She yelled, "Congratulations. Happy New Year!" to the back of Amy's and Frankie's heads as they rushed out the door.

They were practically skipping back to their staterooms when Amy spotted her father going into one of the lounges. "Dad!" Several men turned around. "William Blanchard." He stopped short. Amy ran up to him. "Dad, I got the position at MIT! I'm moving back East! I'll only be a three-hour train ride away."

"That's wonderful news, honey." He picked her up and swung her around as he had when she was a little girl. "Have you told your mother?"

"Not yet. I literally found out only five minutes ago." Amy was out of breath. "But I'm going to call her in a little while."

"Sweetheart, I am so proud of you. Come to think of it, I've always been proud of you." He had a great big grin on his face.

Amy and Frankie were cackling all the way back to their staterooms. Nina opened her door, and Rachael followed.

The four women were jumping up and down when Peter walked out of his stateroom. "What's all the commotion about?" he asked, with a smile.

"Amy is moving back East. She's joining the faculty at MIT." Rachael whooped.

"That's wonderful news." Peter was genuinely surprised

and happy. "We'll kinda be neighbors. About-an-hour-away neighbors."

"Excellent. You'll get to meet Blinky and Hop-Along." Amy was elated. She would have friends and family within a few hours' reach. "Are you going to hang out with us for the parties tonight?"

"I thought you'd never ask," Peter said cheerfully. "Where shall we start?"

"Let's meet at Margaritaville first. Nine thirty," Rachael said, knowing that was where the first flash-mob dance was taking place. She was also planning on directing everyone to the various parties so they could watch the fun Henry had planned with his students.

"Got it." Peter was happy to be joining the hilarious bunch of women for the festivities. He couldn't think of a livelier group to ring in the New Year. "What is the dress code for this evening?"

"Good question. There are five themes, but I don't think we need to dress for any of them. Who carries a shotgun and travels with a horse besides Walt Longmire?" Frankie mused.

"Who is Walt Longmire?" Rachael looked perplexed.

"A handsome contemporary sheriff in Wyoming." Frankie folded her arms. "Get with the program. It's a huge hit on Netflix, based on the books by Craig Johnson."

"Of course you would know that." Rachael pouted.

"I would have said Gene Autry, but I didn't think anyone would know who he was." Frankie chuckled.

Peter laughed. "You mean the singing cowboy?" All four women gave him a stare. "Oh come on, you've heard 'Rudolph, the Red-Nosed Reindeer,' right?"

"Of course," Rachael chimed in.

"There you go." Peter winked. "I'll catch up with you gals later." He turned and whistled the familiar tune on his way to his stateroom.

The four women retreated to their staterooms to begin their beauty routines for the evening. They decided they would be dressy but casual. Frankie opted for the black sheath, but this time she added several strands of long pearls. Nina decided to wear a long black pencil skirt with a white halter top, accessorized with black-and-white earrings, her hair wrapped up in a black-and-white double-twisted head-band. Amy chose a black-and-white swing skirt with a tulle hem that matched the sleeves and cuffs of her cropped jacket. Rachael was also in black, as were her coconspirator dancers. Henry had arranged for props for them for the different flash-mob surprises. Rachael was proud of herself for not spilling the beans.

The word "enthusiasm" could not cover Amy's delight over being offered a professorship at MIT. She called her mother immediately.

"Mom?" Amy was practically out of breath.

"Dear, is everything all right? You sound out of breath. And why on earth are you calling me from the ship?"

"Mom, I have fantastic news. I got the position at MIT. I'm moving back East this summer to start the fall semester."

"Oh my goodness. That *is* wonderful news. What a nice way to ring in the New Year. I am very proud of you."

"That's what Dad said." Amy realized her gaffe.

"You spoke to him already?" Dorothy sounded disappointed that Amy hadn't called her first.

"It's a long story, Mom. Let's focus on the good news." Amy immediately changed the subject. "So what are your plans for tonight?"

"Well, darling, I am going to the dinner dance at the club." She hesitated. "With Lloyd."

"Really, Mom? That's terrific." Amy could hardly keep her wits about her. "Lots of good news today."

"I'm glad you feel that way, dear. Lloyd is a very nice, interesting man. We have a lot in common." Dorothy was almost apologetic.

"I am very happy for you, Mom. Truly."

"And I am happy you feel that way. I know you weren't a fan of Rusty's." Dorothy cleared her throat. "I hope you understand why I was attracted to him?"

"Yes, Mom, I do. But you mentioned you had some sort of disagreement?"

"It's not worth discussing, dear."

"And I am happy you moved on." Amy paused. "Do you mind telling me what you meant by Lloyd gave you a lot to think about?"

"That's for a sit-down conversation, dear. Now I must be going. You have a wonderful New Year's Eve."

"You do the same, Moth . . ." Amy caught herself. "Mom!"

Around seven fifteen, the women gathered in the hallway. Amy could barely contain herself, gabbing about her mother's date with Lloyd. The other women were pleasantly surprised. Those who had met Rusty were of the same opinion as Amy. And they all liked Lloyd.

They began their parade down the hallway as if they were on the catwalk of a fashion show. Peter was leaving his stateroom at the same time and whistled the famous catcall. None of them turned around. They simply gave him a backward wave. Henry couldn't have choreographed it any better.

Dinner at Remy was sumptuous. Even though there were six courses, they were not full-size portions. They started with a potato leek soup. Next were two chilled jumbo shrimp in a light chili sauce, followed by a small leafy salad with cranberries and honey-roasted almonds. The single grilled lamb chop was served with four roasted fingerling potatoes. The final dish was bite-size pieces of swordfish in a lemon-and-pepper sauce. For dessert, a small chocolate soufflé was served. Four glasses of champagne were brought to the table, "Compliments of Richard Cooper." Everyone made cooing sounds of appreciation.

The clock was ticking, and Rachael had to make sure she was at her appointed station by nine thirty. She didn't want to seem too obvious or overanxious. So she tried a different approach. "Shall we stroll on over to Margaritaville?" She figured "stroll" was passive enough not to sound noticeable but enough to hurry them along.

They got to the deck hosting Margaritaville. The entire waitstaff was wearing brightly colored Hawaiian shirts, and tiki bars were all around the perimeter of the pool. Rachael caught Henry's eye. He nodded. Another woman walked up to her and handed her a small stuffed parrot attached to a headband. In less than five minutes, the opening notes of Jimmy Buffett's song "Saxophones" blasted over the speakers. Eighteen parrot-headed dancers began their flash-mob dance. The place thundered with laughter, hoots, and applause. The dance troupe was becoming a passenger favorite.

When the song was over, Frankie approached Rachael. "I'm willing to bet you have something planned for all the parties."

"Shhh . . ." Rachael put her finger on her lips. "I've got to get moving to the next one. Don't tell anybody."

"Heck, I'm following you. I don't want to miss any of it." Frankie motioned for Amy to follow. Amy grabbed Peter's arm and dragged him in Frankie's direction, at the same time giving Nina and Richard a wide-eyed "come on" look.

The entourage made their way to the second deck, where the country-music theme was jumping. Just as at the previous party, Henry caught the eyes of his dancers. Each was given a cowboy hat. Minutes later, the sound of an accelerating pickup truck introduced major drumrolls, and the sound of a slide guitar blasted over the speakers. It was a recording of Brooks & Dunn's "Boot Scootin' Boogie," and the dancers hopped and bopped the official Boot Scootin' line dance. Again, the crowd went crazy, and several other passengers joined them. By the time the song was over, there were over two dozen people kicking up their heels. Mission accomplished.

Rachael and her personal fan club marched their way to the Latin party, where piñatas were strung from trees, the waitstaff wore sombreros, and a mariachi band played lively music. The band stopped suddenly, and a hush fell over the crowd. The silence was broken by the opening strains of "Latin Boogie" by 2nd Shift. The official, unofficial dance troupe of the *Medallion of the Seas* shimmied through the crowd and did their surprise performance. Members of the mariachi band accompanied them with their percussion instruments. As the song came to a close, the ensemble formed a conga line and bopped their way to the elevator, with the sound of cheers and applause following them.

The disco scene was their next target. They wasted no time pulling off another flash mob to the tune of "Boogie Oogie Oogie" by A Taste of Honey. When they had finished, Frankie said to Rachael, "Do I sense a theme here?"

Rachael laughed. "Do you know how hard it was to find a song by Jimmy Buffett that had the words 'boogie woogie' in it?"

"I can only imagine."

"Thank goodness for Google." Rachael cackled. "Let's go. We have one more, and this is the hardest."

The troupe and their followers entered the last party area. It was decorated with several soda fountains, some serving alcohol, others milkshakes. A dose of Baileys Irish Cream was also available. The female servers wore poodle skirts and cardigan sweaters with sweater clips, saddle shoes, and bobby socks. The men wore slacks, plaid shirts, and bow ties. As soon as the first measures of "Bandstand Boogie" started, eight couples swung each other around all over the dance floor. It could have been a reenactment of the early days of *American Bandstand*. When the song ended, thunderous applause echoed through the room and out to the deck, where dozens had gathered to get a peek at the impromptu show.

Henry was beaming as he hugged each and every one of his performers. "I cannot express my joy for the work you put into this evening. Once people discovered you were the same group as the other night, I was getting commitments for donations. This has been the most wonderful New Year's Eve I have spent. Thank you all." He put his arm around Rachael and gave her a big squeeze. He addressed his other students. "Shall we go watch the fireworks?"

Frankie, Amy, Peter, Nina, and Richard followed the throng to the main deck, where glasses of champagne were being handed to guests. A large digital clock counting down the minutes and seconds hung on the railing.

The crowd cheered: "Ten. Nine. Eight. Seven. Six. Five. Four. Three. Two. One. Happy New Year!" The ship's horn sounded, and a brilliant display of fireworks exploded in the air, the glimmering reflection bouncing off the calm sea.

Frankie and Amy hugged Peter. Nina and Richard kissed. Rachael and Henry pecked each other's cheek. It felt wonderful to be in an idyllic setting celebrating a new year with good friends. Somewhere else on board, William Blanchard and Marilyn Mitchell held hands as the last of the fireworks died out.

About a half hour later, the crowd began to thin, passengers returning to one of the parties or to their staterooms.

They still had one more full day ahead in Grand Cayman before the journey home.

When Frankie got back to her stateroom, she unlocked the safe and checked her phone for any messages. There was one text message.

Hello Francesca, Bandit and I wish you a Happy New Year. See you soon. Ciao. Giovanni.

She stood motionless. *Sweet, but why? Did his fiancée come back to the States with him?* She shrugged and chalked it up to a nice gesture. *My cat wishing me a Happy New Year.* She quickly typed:

Happy New Year to you and Bandit!

Chapter Twenty-one

Day 6
Grand Cayman Island

The shortest day onshore was at Grand Cayman, with only about six hours available to enjoy the island known for its beaches and colorful coral reefs. Amy was the happy recipient of Frankie's generosity for the trip to Stingray City. Nina, Rachael, and Frankie planned to go horseback riding on the beach. It would take about two hours, giving them time for a light lunch followed by some duty-free shopping. It was the one thing they had promised themselves months before. Richard and Peter were going snorkeling with several others from the ship.

The first tender to the island left at nine and took about a half hour to reach George Town, known for its high-end shops and restaurants. Given the absence of street vendors, one could enjoy leisurely window-shopping or plunk down a lot of coin at luxury, premium boutiques. "Duty-free," Rachael reminded them. "And don't forget it's a British overseas territory. They drive on the left side, so when you cross the street, make sure you don't get confused."

Peter pointed to a shuttle that said EDEN ROCK DIVING CENTER. "That's us." He tapped Richard on the chest.

There was a short awkward moment between Richard and Nina. *Should he kiss her?* Instead, he gave her a long stroke on her arm. "See you later. Have fun." Nina smiled back at him.

Frankie spotted the van that said BARKER'S NATIONAL PARK. "We're over there." She pointed it out to the others.

Amy scoured the area, then saw the sign that read STINGRAY CITY. "And I'm over there." She held on to her floppy hat with one hand and waved with the other. "See you guys later. Enjoy."

"You too!" Nina shouted.

The drive to the park for the horseback riding took less than twenty minutes. Frankie was calculating the amount of time they would have for lunch and shopping. "Should be a pretty full day but we shouldn't have to rush around."

They had a typical tourist conversation with the guide. "First time here? Planning on shopping?" etc.

"The island is beautiful," Frankie said, and he responded with pride. The driver spoke English and explained that the different accents to be found on the island were due to the influx of people in the 1700s, when the Cayman Islands were part of Jamaica, then a British territory. In 1962, Jamaica declared its independence, leaving the Cayman Islands a territory. Grand Cayman, only twenty-two miles long and eight miles wide, had become one of the world's largest financial centers. Which was a good explanation for the opulent shopping.

The women stared out the window of the van, admiring the scenery. When they arrived, they were greeted by an athletic-looking young woman. She had a long blond ponytail and a baseball cap. Her jeans were rolled up to her calves. A white T-shirt was tucked in the front, and a light denim work shirt was tied around her waist. She had everyone fill out the proper paperwork, signing off on requirements and waivers. They discussed the experience level. It had been several years since Frankie was on a horse, although she had ridden frequently before moving into the city. Nina had ridden once within the past year, but Amy hadn't been in a saddle since college. They decided a leisurely walk on the beach with a little canter would be appropriate. Anyone who was having any difficulty could give a yell.

The horses were already saddled. The only adjustments were the stirrups. Once they were comfortably seated, the three women and their guide clicked their tongues and gave the horses a little tap with their heels. The horses knew the routine well and began the peaceful trek to the shoreline. The sound of the waves lapping on the shore and the cries of the gulls engulfed them in a state of euphoria. It was one of those rare moments where the surrounding beauty could bring tears to your eyes. It was the closest thing to paradise that one could imagine.

And it put Frankie in a very introspective mood. Not that it took much for her to soul-search. She was always seeking a higher level of enlightenment. Some days she succeeded, others, not so much. But that day was illuminating. She thought about Rachael. Rachael, the girl who kept looking for validation from men and had finally found it in herself and her own accomplishments. Then there was Amy. Brainiac Amy. She was enthralled with discovering new things and solving puzzles. But the road she had been traveling was taking her further away from the things that brought her joy. So she had made a decision to change that path, and now she was moving in a different direction. It was a risk, but one she was willing to take. Staying where she was wasn't a good option. Then there was Nina, who had been forced to make a change.

At first, she hadn't known what course to follow. When she had finally decided to let go, a new opportunity presented itself. *Trust. That's the key*, Frankie thought. *Faith and trust.* She felt a sense of renewal wash over her. She felt it in her heart. Her time would come.

There was little conversation during the ride. When they had reached the farthest point of the ride, the guide asked them if they wanted to run the horses a bit. They nodded and turned their horses in the direction whence they had come. A few kicks and clicks, and the horses began to canter, a more comfortable pace than trotting.

The guide slowed to give the horses a chance to cool down before they returned. The two hours went by swiftly. They were ready for a leisurely lunch and perhaps sampling the local beer. Caybrew claimed to be "the freshest beer you will ever drink."

The woman from the stable recommended either Di Bess Jerk Stand, which was more of a food truck with a canopy, or the Caribbean Kitchen, also an open-air spot with a sign reading PLEASE DO NOT FEED THE CHICKENS.

That was a deal breaker for Rachael. It was Di Bess Jerk Stand for her. And the rest of them.

After they munched on spicy Jamaican chicken and enjoyed a cold brew, they were ready to take on Kirk Freeport, the Disney World of duty-free jewelry, watches, perfume, and leather goods.

They dispersed when they walked into the massive store, with its row after row of displays filled with items by Cartier, Mikimoto, Dior, Gucci, Dolce & Gabbana, and many, many more. It was a who's who of designer selections.

Frankie was overwhelmed. They were like kids in a candy store. She thought she would simply pick up some perfume, but when she saw the prices on gold bangle bracelets, she knew she had to get one for herself. A memento of the momentous journey. A journey she had suggested. Yep. She deserved a treat, so she picked a 14-karat-gold twisted-rope bangle.

Nina bought a Cartier tote for carting around scripts. She thought the pun was apropos. Rachael purchased a silk scarf by Hermès. They also grabbed several bottles of their favorite perfumes and some Cuban cigars. Shopping bags in tow, they ventured back to the dock to wait for the tender.

Amy wouldn't be back until an hour or so later. She had opted for the three-hour tour. First was Stingray City, where you literally walked around on a sandbar and petted any of fifty-plus stingrays. The charter provided snorkeling gear and food to feed the stingrays in the clear, blue-tinted water. After an hour frolicking with the massive cartilaginous fish, the charter boat took them to Starfish Point, where they could lounge in the shallow waters and look for starfish and shells. People were not allowed to take any of the precious native gems from the island, but they were encouraged to take photos. The return trip included an inside look at the pristine Mangrove Channels and the ecosystem. Amy expressed delight at every turn. Her enthusiasm was almost as entertaining as the guide, who, when their excursion ended, jokingly offered her a job as their public-relations director. Amy wrapped a sarong around her damp bathing suit and thanked the guide one more time.

Plans for dinner had been set before they left the ship. All six, including Peter and Richard, agreed on Takumi, the Japanese restaurant, where they served everything from sushi to hibachi-grilled meats and shrimp. There would be a large enough variety to satisfy everyone.

It was another fun-filled day, but it was also exhausting. Frankie thought Amy was right. They would need a vacation after this one. Dress was casual, which everyone appreciated. It would be too much of an effort to think about any-thing more than a pair of capri pants, a tunic, and sandals. The following night would be the final dinner of the cruise and a much fancier affair. Frankie was tired simply thinking about it.

The return trip from Grand Cayman to Miami would be a full day of cruising. Frankie booked a two-hour massage, fa-cial, manicure, and pedicure, and anything else she could find on the spa menu. Rachael was going poolside, as was Amy. Nina and Richard were going to take in the matinee performance of a new comedian. But tonight they would gather and share their stories and adventures over sake and Japanese cuisine.

The women met in the hallway and knocked on Peter's door. Richard planned to meet them at the restaurant, where he waited at the door. Feeling a little loosey-goosey, Frankie decided to break the ice and give Richard a casual hug. Rachael, Amy, and Nina followed suit. When it came to Peter, he turned to Amy and hugged her instead. "I didn't want my arms to feel left out," he clumsily joked. Amy thought it was sweet.

They were seated in a traditional private tatami room, with mats and a low dining table. Diners sat on low pillows surrounding the table with their legs dangling underneath in a pit that went around the perimeter of the table. Once you folded yourself in, it was quite comfortable. Getting out was also a bit of a challenge to avoid looking like part of a cir-cus act.

Two hours of lively conversation filled the small room, with everyone relating the highlights of the day. By nine thirty, everyone was ready for a good night's sleep.

Nina and Richard took a stroll on the deck to watch the lights of the beautiful Caribbean island grow dimmer on the horizon. She decided now would be a good time to tell him she was moving back East.

She looked toward the waning flickers in the distance. "I guess that's what it's going to look like in my rearview mirror."

Richard turned to her. "What do you mean?" He was genuinely confused.

"I'm leaving LA next month." Nina stared out to the darkening ocean.

"Really? Had enough of Tinseltown?" Richard sounded a bit nervous.

Nina could sense his body get tense. She regretted having opened her mouth. He nudged her with his elbow.

"I think the feeling is mutual." Nina turned to him and smiled. "I'll be happy to get back East. Funny how things happen. Two months ago, I had no idea what I was going to do, and now I'm changing jobs and moving. It's a lot to absorb. I'm going to have to think like a giant barrel sponge." She laughed.

"I think you can handle it." Richard was sincerely pleased for her.

"Thanks. It will be an adjustment, and I will have to find my own place eventually because of Winston, but that shouldn't be too difficult. As far as work, Owen lives in Fort Lee, which is only a half-hour drive with no traffic. But there's always traffic, so let's call it an hour. We can meet almost anywhere while we're working on the script."

"That's fantastic, Nina. Will you have to go into the city often?"

"Not until they start production. We'll write eight episodes, then work with the actors."

"So everything is all set?"

"Not really. The network is giving us the budget for a pilot. It could all begin and end there. Show biz. It's a crapshoot until you become a major player with beaucoup bucks." Nina didn't sound bitter; nor did she sound concerned. "I'm happy to be working *toward* something. You know what they say, 'We plan. God laughs.' I think that's finally sinking in. Finally." She turned to face Richard. "I hope we can stay in touch. It would be nice to see you again."

"I'll just be a short ride away." Richard put his arm around her. She really believed it, too.

They stood in silence for a while. Nina was the first to speak. "I should be getting back. I am whipped."

"Me too." Richard hooked his arm so Nina could place hers through his. They walked slowly to her stateroom, where he gave her a sweet kiss. This one lingered a bit longer than the first.

Chapter Twenty-two

Cruising Home

The final day of the cruise was upon them. Packing and relaxing was on the agenda. Dinner would be semiformal in the main dining room. It was the captain's opportunity to thank the crew and the passengers.

Frankie packed everything except her clothes for the evening and the following day. That would give her ample time to enjoy her spa day and not have to do or think about much afterward. Dressing for dinner would be the only task.

Nina, Amy, and Rachael followed Frankie's lead.

Amy phoned her father and asked if he and Marilyn would join them at dinner. He checked with Marilyn, who thought it would be an ideal way to end her trip—the same way it started—with a group of exuberant, talented, and intelligent women. She was looking forward to it.

After speaking with her dad, Amy knocked on Frankie's door.

"Dinner plans. I invited my father and Marilyn to sit at our table."

"Excellent idea. We should also grab Peter." Frankie folded several items and placed them in the large roller bag.

"I'll go tell him." Amy smiled coyly.

"What?" Frankie gave her a look. "You kinda like him, don't you?"

"In a geeky, accountant kind of way." Amy blushed.

"Well, I'll be darned. Why didn't you say anything before?" Frankie stopped what she was doing.

"Because I wasn't sure if I liked, liked him." Amy took a deep breath. "Plus, I didn't know if I was going to get the job, and I didn't want to start to like someone who lived thirty-five-hundred miles away. Plus he had been hanging around with that photographer."

"Yeah. But that got old really quickly. He mentioned it in passing. Unlike us, stalking passengers for the photographer wasn't his thing." Frankie chuckled. Frankie sat next to Amy and put her arm around her. "So? What are you waiting for?"

"I'm going to take it slow." Amy leaned back on the bed. "I have a lot to do between now and summer. I want to take a month off to move, get settled."

"And I'm willing to bet Peter will help you unpack." Frankie reached down and helped Amy up. "Come on. You have someone to invite to dinner." She gave her a pat on the butt and shoved her out the door. Getting Peter to agree to sit with them at dinner was easy. Frankie phoned the maître d' and requested a table for nine. She was sure Henry would want to join his star pupil and her zany gang. After she made the reservation, she phoned Henry's stateroom and extended the invitation. As predicted, he was very happy to join them.

The day passed quickly, and the women began their ritual of hair and makeup. Then the outfits and accessories.

Nina was the first to start knocking on everyone's door. "Ready?" Amy popped out, wearing a deep purple jumpsuit trimmed in pink. It matched her hair perfectly. Rachael wore a jumpsuit with a large watermelon pattern. Nina said she looked like a walking fruit bowl. Rachael smiled at the joke. Frankie donned a cobalt-blue halter maxi dress, and Nina was dressed in an emerald-green Asian-print kimono over black leggings and a black tank. They were as colorful as the flora and fauna of the places they had visited.

A cocktail party in the grand foyer was first on the agenda. The captain moved halfway up the grand staircase for his opening remarks. "Ladies and gentlemen. It has been our pleasure to have had the opportunity to serve you. I want to thank my committed and exceptional crew." Applause filled the space. In the wink of an eye, the sound of hands clapping to a rhythm, voices, and a guitar starting "Uptown Funk" by Bruno Mars filled the room. The dance troupe carefully made its way down the stairs, with Rachael pulling the last strand of the mistletoe with her. Once the troupe reached the main floor, they finished their moves to deafening applause. When it had quieted down, Captain Sideris continued. He raised his glass of champagne. "Here's to good health, prosperity, and happiness to everyone! *Salute!*" He took a sip. "One more thing, I'm going to miss those dancers!" More hoots came from the passengers, then they slowly made their way to the main dining room.

Frankie took over as the push-planning lady and directed people to their seats. She wanted it to be as balanced as possible. There were four men, five women, and an empty chair. Maybe someone would be brave enough to sit with them.

A man around William's age approached the table. "Is anyone sitting here?" he politely asked.

"You are." Frankie smiled and indicated for him to sit. "You realize you're with a rowdy bunch, correct?"

"Oh yes, I've seen some of you in action. Name is Gregory Maynard. Nice to meet you all."

They all introduced themselves, giving him their first name and where they came from. The waiter walked around the table with a bottle of red in one hand and a bottle of white in the other. Lots of friendly chatter followed. Several courses were served while a dance band played softly. When dessert was served, the band began to pick up the sound and the pace, encouraging people to dance. William and Marilyn were the first on the dance floor.

"Well, lookie there," Nina addressed Amy. "Your father seems to be having a good time."

"I cannot tell you how thrilled I am for him."

"And Marilyn didn't do so badly herself," Nina added.

Peter leaned back in his chair. "I'd like to propose a toast. He raised his glass. "To the kookiest bunch of women I have ever had the pleasure to literally bump into." Echoes of cheers and the clinking of glasses followed.

William and Marilyn returned to the table, both a little out of breath. "I'm a little rusty." William panted. He didn't quite get the joke until Amy burst out laughing.

"You are nothing like Rusty," Frankie exclaimed, bringing more laughs to those who knew the Rusty story. She apologized to the rest of the guests. "Inside joke." With that, Frankie stood and began saying her farewells to everyone except her gal pals. She gave everyone hugs, reminding them that if they wanted their bags taken off the ship by crew members, they would have to be tagged and sitting outside the stateroom door before midnight.

Amy spent a few more minutes with her father, promising to spend time with him before she started her new job.

Henry and Rachael stayed behind for one last dance before the music ended.

Nina and Richard went for their final stroll on the deck, making plans to get together as soon as she moved back to Ridgewood. In the meantime, they would stay in touch via text, e-mail, Zoom.

When Frankie returned to her stateroom, she unlocked the

safe, packed her valuables in her tote, and checked her phone again. She hadn't erased the text from Giovanni. She didn't know why. There was another text from the publisher, asking Frankie to call her ASAP. She checked her watch. It was ten thirty. Why would the publisher want to speak to her on New Year's Day? It would have to wait until the morning. Especially if she was getting fired.

Chapter Twenty·three

Port of Miami

The day of debarkation is often chaotic. Bags are hauled, people are scrambling to finish filling out their customs forms and questioning what they need to do next. The cruise director had sent instructions to all the passengers the day before, but there are always a dozen or so people who remain in a state of confusion. Fortunately for the women, Frankie was on top of it.

Bags with their colored tags waited outside their staterooms. The color of the tags determined what time the passengers could leave the ship and go through customs and immigration.

Several hours later, they were finally off the ship and away from the pier, with all their suitcases and carry-ons in a cluster waiting for a van large enough to haul the baggage to the airport. They had been able to book flights within an hour of each other, so they could keep each other company. When they reached Miami International, they went through the laborious security check and found a restaurant to grab a bite to eat.

When they settled into the booth, Rachael ordered her lunch in Spanish.

"Hey. I just realized you hardly used any Spanish when we were on the cruise. You were too busy flashing, I mean flash-mobbing." Amy chuckled at her slip of the tongue.

"I was busy." Rachael winked. "*And* distracted."

"Henry is a very lovely person," Nina said.

"He is." Rachael had an intriguing expression on her face.

"I know that look." Frankie glanced over at her. "What's up?"

"Henry invited me to have dinner with him at Eleven Madison Park."

"Fancy," Frankie noted. It was a block away from her apartment.

"What's the occasion?" Nina asked innocently.

"He said it was to thank me for making the cruise one of the liveliest he's been on. We're going to meet with the foundation directors in the afternoon," Rachael explained.

"Sounds like a date to me." Nina raised her eyebrows.

"He's twelve years older than I am," Rachael squawked.

"When has that ever stopped you?" Frankie burst out laughing.

"Good point." Rachael took a sip of her soda. "We shall see. And to tell you the truth, while it would be nice to date a sensitive and successful man, I am thrilled just to be working with him."

The women nodded in agreement. Frankie turned to Amy. "And what about Peter?"

"He said he would help me unpack my stuff, but obviously I need to find a place to live first. I hope I can get faculty housing, but if not, I'm sure I'll find something suitable for me, Blinky, and Hop-Along."

"Nina?" Frankie eyed her friend. "Richard?"

"I think I like him. Like, really, *really* like him," Nina confessed, with their old high-school declaration.

"Yay." Amy clapped her hands. "See. Aren't you glad you went over and spoke to him that first night?"

"I am. And it wasn't even because I was interested in pursuing him; I just didn't want him to think we were laughing at his socks. Which, by the way, were very cute." Nina took a bite of her sandwich, hoping to end the interrogation.

"We're not done with you yet," Rachael pried. "You're going to see him again, correct?"

"Correct. As soon as I get settled. Happy?" She took another bite.

"Yep." Amy clapped again. Then she realized Frankie was the only one who didn't have a possible date on the horizon. Frankie, the one who'd planned the entire trip. "Frankie, I don't know if I've said it enough, but thank you so much for suggesting this trip, planning this trip, and being our cheerleader."

Frankie got a bit misty-eyed. "I am beyond thrilled that this turned out to be such an exciting adventure. I had never heard 'Feliz Navidad' played by a real mariachi band before." Everyone chuckled. "Or 'Jingle Bells.' Seriously, Amy, Nina, you guys will be close by Rachael, you'll be cha-cha-ing your way through a charitable effort." She stopped suddenly and took a deep breath. "And I will be visualizing something for myself. It's just a matter of time." She knew she had to believe it in her heart of hearts. At that moment, she felt her phone vibrate in her jacket. She looked at the number and remembered she hadn't called her publisher back. With all the confusion of disembarking, and the logistics of getting off the ship, getting a van, and checking in at the airport, it had slipped her mind. She held up a finger, reached in her pocket, and pulled out the pulsating device. "Hello?" she answered tentatively. She felt she was going to be read the riot act for not responding quickly enough.

"Hello?" Frankie winced.

"Frankie? It's Dana. I sent you an e-mail last night but fig-ured you might not have gotten it. Wi-Fi and all that stuff."

"Hey, Dana. What's up?" Frankie moved on without ad-dressing the e-mail.

"Well, as you know there have been negotiations to merge us with another publishing house. The deal has gone through and will be finalized in the next few weeks. Because of this, they are also merging departments."

Frankie closed her eyes and anticipated the worst. "That doesn't surprise me."

Whispers of concern from her friends were in the back-ground, mixed with calls for flights and gates.

"The good news is that they are also establishing a line of authentic cookbooks. Family recipes. No celebrities."

"That's refreshing. No divas." Frankie tried to act relaxed.

"That's why I'm calling you. They need someone to be in charge of development. I thought of you because of all the great work you've done with that category and how much of a foodie you are."

Frankie knitted her eyebrows as she glanced at her friends' anxious faces.

Dana continued. "Here's the thing, Frankie. If you keep your position as head of marketing, you'll be doing double the work for the same amount of pay. I know that stinks, but that's how these big corporations make money. They elimi-nate jobs and balance the books, no pun intended, on the backs of the people in the trenches."

"Yes, I've been on that bus before." Frankie knew exactly what Dana was talking about.

"So, this is what I am suggesting. Take the job as Editorial Director, Product Development. You'll still get paid the same, but it's a new position, and you can drive *that* bus yourself. Obviously, you'll have a budget, but you'll be able to curate a list of original cookbooks. We don't expect them to sell in huge numbers, but there is a market for authenticity minus the hype. You may remember the series Pinnacle had many years ago? Short volumes that can become part of a collection. Reasonable price points. Think about it, Frankie. I really would like you to lead that team."

"Dana. I am speechless. Imagine that? Me. Speechless." Frankie snickered nervously.

"I need an answer by tomorrow. Someone at the top has been making noises that they want to put one of their lackeys in that spot. I want someone who has a work ethic, experience, and good instincts. That would be you, Frankie."

Without hesitation, Frankie said, "Can I have a minute to think about it? OK. Yes." She could barely contain herself. "Dana, this is an answer to my prayers. At least one of them. Thank you so much."

"You are very welcome. Thank you for taking it. I know it's uncharted waters, but I know you can handle it."

"Thank you for your confidence in me." She gave everyone a thumbs-up. Everyone breathed a sigh of relief.

"My flight leaves in an hour, and I should be home by eight. Can I call you in the morning?" Frankie asked.

"Absolutely. Call my cell, and we'll arrange to have coffee. Oh, by the way, how was your vacation?"

"I would have to label it as fabulous." Frankie had tears running down her cheeks. "Talk tomorrow." She hit the END button.

"What was that all about?"

"What's going on?"

"What prayers?"

All three were talking at the same time.

"I've been offered a new position. Developing a line of small cookbooks that are based on family recipes. Authentic recipes."

"Yippee," Amy gushed. "That is so perfect for you."

Nina wrapped her arm around Frankie's neck and gave her a kiss on the cheek. "Bravo!"

Rachael blinked several times. "We went on this cruise because we didn't have dates, yet we came back with new opportunities in front of us." She nodded at Nina. "And those of us who had no expectation of meeting someone, did. And he's not a jerk. At least not that we know of."

Frankie held up her glass of sparkling water. "Here's to the best gal-pal club ever." They returned the sentiment in kind.

An announcement for United Flight 1153 to Newark indicated that it would begin boarding in fifteen minutes at gate 105.

"That's us," Rachael announced. She fished for her wallet and handed some cash to Amy. "This should cover my empanada."

She gathered her bags and did one last "coochie-coochie" for her friends.

"Thank goodness. For a moment I thought there was going to be another flash-mob dance." Nina howled.

Lots of hugs, kisses, and promises to keep in touch as Frankie and Rachael moved on to their gate.

Nina and Amy still had another hour before their flights to California took off. They decided to order a glass of wine and wait in the restaurant.

Four hours later, Frankie was in a taxi on her way to her apartment. She fished her keys out of her tote and pulled her phone out again. No new messages. But the one from Giovanni was still there. It was time to erase it.

The first thing she saw when she entered her apartment was her big kitty, Bandit, waiting on the desk in the foyer. His meow could have woken the neighborhood. Frankie picked up her furry friend and nuzzled and kissed him all over the top of his head. A few minutes of that, and Bandit was ready to be unhanded. He wanted to know what was in those big things she had carted in. He began sniffing her luggage. Frankie bent over to give him another pet. "No catnip, pal. Sorry." When she stood, she noticed a vase with flowers and a note.

> *Welcome home, Francesca. I hope you had a wonderful vacation.*
> *If you are not busy, would you please have dinner with me Saturday night at Marco's?*

Frankie tapped the note against her thumb. What could this be about? She checked her watch. Marco's was still open. She hit the speed-dial button. "Marco's. *Buonasera!*" Marco sounded jovial.

"Marco. *Come stai?*" Frankie's voice echoed his cheerfulness.

"*Molto bene!* You have a nice vacation? We missed you." Marco sounded sincere.

"I had a wonderful time."

"Very happy for you. What can I get you tonight?"

"I'm not calling for food, actually. I wanted to thank Giovanni for taking such good care of Bandit. I don't think he even missed me."

"Giovanni or Bandit?" Marco teased.

She wished she had the answer to that question, so she chuckled instead.

"You know, since Giovanni returned from Italy, he's been a little, how do you say, melancholia?"

"Melancholy?" Frankie asked.

"Sì. He and his fiancée ended their engagement."

Frankie had to sit down for this information. "Oh? What happened?" She pressed her head firmly into the phone, as if it would help her hear him better.

"You see, he had been engaged to Marcella for many

years. It was something her family wanna, but they didn't
wanna her to live in America. Giovanni doesn't wanna to live
in Italy. They go back and forth for a-long-a time. This-a
time, he said 'no more.' There had never been no *amore* between them, so he say 'enough.' "

"Was it mutual?" Frankie was trying not to pry, but she
just *had* to know.

"Sì. They both-a knew it was for the best. But you know,
the holidays. People get *emotivo*, emotional."

"Yes, they do." Frankie understood exactly what he
meant.

"Is he around, so I can thank him?"

"He's-a no here, but I give him a message."

"Tell him thank you, and that I will be happy to have dinner with him on Saturday." She stopped in her tracks. What
if Marco didn't know about the invitation?

"*Molto bene!*" Marco was genuinely excited. "You will sit
at the best table. As always."

Based on his reaction, Frankie sensed Marco knew something about the invitation. "Do you know what time he had
in mind?"

"Eight o'clock?"

"*Molto bene*," Frankie answered affirmatively in Italian.
See you then. *Ciao*, Marco!"

Frankie was glad she had brought back a box of Cuban
cigars. She didn't know if Giovanni smoked them, but most
men seem to like having them around. Must be a guy thing.
She had also bought a smaller box of cigars for Marco and a
bottle of perfume for Anita. Too often people think about the
baby, and not how hard the mother has to work from incep-
tion to age whatever.

She hung up with a light heart. One thing was certain, she
knew who was going to be the subject of the first authentic
cookbook on her list.

*   *   *

Two days later, she met with Dana, and they discussed the five cuisines to focus on. Italian, Indian, Korean, Greek, Cuban. Frankie would be starting her new role in February, so there was a lot of work to be done. She would miss her staff but was promised that her assistant, Matt, could move with her if he wanted to. She'd give him a new title. No extra pay. Corporate America. For the rest of the week, she busied herself with research for the new line of books, googling restaurants and taking notes. The plan was for her to travel in the tristate area to sample many foods at various restaurants and ascertain if there was cookbook potential. Not necessarily an entire cookbook but something worth contributing to the volume on that particular cuisine. The restaurant would get paid by the recipe and also be mentioned in all marketing promotions. It was a win-win for everyone.

As Saturday drew near, Frankie was getting nervous about what to expect. Was it a date? Friends? What? She wished she knew. She shrugged. She'd find out soon enough. The typical question of what to wear lingered. One thing she did know. Whatever she wore had to be cobalt blue.

Frankie was up at the crack of dawn on Saturday. She hoped she wouldn't run out of steam by dinnertime. She decided on decaf that morning. No need to add to her jitters. By five, she was pacing her small living-room area. Bandit watched from the sofa and followed her steps. Back and forth. Back and forth.

After wasting a half hour, she decided to take a shower and begin the process of dolling up. Hair. Blown-out straight. Done. Makeup, a little more than daytime, but not over the top. Next was the decision of accessories. She decided on a pair of diamond earrings and her diamond tennis bracelet. Just enough bling.

She checked herself in the mirror one more time and turned to Bandit. "So, Mr. Kitty Puss, what do you think?" He gave her a big stretch of approval. "Thanks, pal." She gave him a kiss on the top of his head. "Wish me luck." Frankie tucked the cigars and perfume in a black glossy shopping bag and headed for her next adventure. Or so she hoped.

She didn't want to seem too anxious, so she circled the block once, checking her watch every five minutes. It was 7:55. Good enough. As she neared the entrance, she could see inside the windows. Her regular table in the corner was waiting. But she didn't spot Giovanni. Marco greeted her with a kiss on each cheek. "*Bella!* Nice to see you."

"Nice to be here."

"Giovanni will be here shortly. Come. Sit." He pulled out a chair for her and sat down at the table. "You know, we like-a you very much. We happy you have dinner with Giovanni." He winked and patted her arm.

A few minutes later, Giovanni appeared, wearing a white shirt, slacks, and a beautifully tailored Italian-made blazer. He looked incredibly handsome. She tried to look fetching, but she couldn't figure out how to pull that off. Little did she realize that it didn't take much. Giovanni moved toward the table. She put her hand out, and he kissed the back of it. Frankie hoped the goose bumps didn't show through the sleeves of her dress.

"Frankie. I am so happy you said yes to dinner. I think of you as a friend and part of the family. So I invited you to say thank you."

She looked puzzled. "Thank me for what?"

"Trusting your little Bandito and your home to me. That means a lot. Trust is a very important thing."

"It is you I should thank for taking such good care of Bandit and my apartment. The flowers were lovely, too."

She stopped herself from saying, "You shouldn't have." Acknowledge the gift. Period.

Giovanni asked if he could order for both of them. She had absolutely no objection. Their conversation was lively, with both of them sharing stories of their travels. Giovanni never mentioned his broken engagement, which in Frankie's estimation, hadn't broken *him* up too much. They chatted and laughed for a few hours until the staff jokingly told them it was time to leave. Frankie almost forgot the gifts she had brought back. Giovanni was stunned by the gesture. He never expected a gift. Nor did he want to get paid for kittysitting. He insisted "We are like family." Frankie decided to let it go. The cigars were enough of a gesture of appreciation in his eyes.

Giovanni helped Frankie with her coat. She still didn't know if this was leading anywhere, but when he walked her home and kissed her good night, she knew it was going somewhere.

Epilogue

One Year Later
New Year's Eve

As promised, Amy returned to Ridgewood for the holidays. With her boyfriend, Peter.

Richard had arrived a week earlier to spend Christmas with Nina and her folks before her folks left for Florida. Nina's sitcom had been picked up for two seasons, so she had a job for at least another year. Her parents were spending most of their time in Boca Raton, so Nina decided to stay in their house until . . . whenever.

Rachael had been working with the foundation, setting up dance-party fundraisers. Henry was enamored of her, and she had gotten over the age difference. She opened her purse and pulled out a shriveled scrap of mistletoe. "A memento." Everyone burst out laughing.

Frankie had signed up several contributors and had been able to complete the five books she had planned. The list had been met with positive reviews. Now all she had to do was do it again. She and Giovanni had dinner at Marco's, then headed to Ridgewood, where everyone would meet in time for the ball to drop.

The country club was decorated in the standard New Year's Eve glitz and glitter. Both of Amy's parents were there with their significant others, William with Marilyn and Dorothy with her new husband, Lloyd.

Around eleven, ten people stood up and re-created the "Uptown Funk" flash-mob dance. Rachael had secretly recruited people from her dance school. In all the years of the country club's history, nothing like it had *ever* rocked the walls before. The partygoers hooted and cheered.

Just before the stroke of midnight, everyone filled their glasses. A voice from their crowd said, "May the New Year bring as many blessings as this one has!"

"*Cent' anni!*"

"Cheers!"

"*Salute!*"

"Happy New Year!"

The End of One Year!
Cheers to the Next!

Visit our website at
KensingtonBooks.com
to sign up for our newsletters, read
more from your favorite authors, see
books by series, view reading group
guides, and more!

BETWEEN THE CHAPTERS

Become a Part of Our
Between the Chapters Book Club
Community and Join the Conversation

Betweenthechapters.net